‘Rev[illegible] the Revolution’

“Subtly challenges the reader to think about the wider debate enveloping artificial intelligence.”

Christen Civiletto, *Green City Savior*

“A fascinating and unique story that combines the thrill and camaraderie of a sports book with the danger and intrigue of conspiracy thrillers through a high-tech sci-fi concept.”

Mary Fan, *Jane Colt series*

“An intriguing premise that should appeal to fans of The Hunger Games.”

Adam Bender, *Divided We Fall*

“The characters are witty, the scenes creative, interesting and larger than life.”

Amanda Masters, *reviewer at Nerd Girl Official*

“ ‘Revealing the Revolution’ is an enjoyable tale of futuristic sports which romance fans as well as young adult readers will want to add to their collection by a fresh new author.”

Cheri Feih, *Goodreads reviewer*

THE AIM CHRONICLES

Revealing the Revolution

Chasing the Underground

CHASING THE UNDERGROUND

CHASING THE UNDERGROUND

N.M. SOTZEK

N.M. SOTZEK
PUBLISHING

Published by N.M. Sotzek
nsotzek.wix.com/nmsotzek

Chasing the Underground

First printing 2016

Cover design by JB Centeno
Publisher logo design by Becky Allen

Library and Archives Canada Cataloguing in Publication

Sotzek, N. M., 1988-, author
Chasing the underground / N.M. Sotzek.

(AIM chronicles ; 2)
Issued in print and electronic formats.
ISBN 978-0-9937895-2-6 (paperback).--ISBN 978-0-9937895-3-3 (html)

I. Title.

PS8637.O79C43 2016 C813'.6 C2015-904454-5
C2015-904455-3

Printed and bound in the United States of America

To my parents, all four of them, and my parents-in-law. Your strength, support, and endless patience means the world to me. Thank you.

CHAPTER 1

It all came down to this moment. He slowed his breathing, readying himself. He watched as an American black bear ambled down the dirt path in front of him, its nose in the air and a blinking light on its neck. Its ears twitched as it picked up the sound of leaves rustling behind it. The creature turned as the man came out from the forest towards it at a full run.

"Go!" he yelled as he continued his speed.

The bear powered forward with its strong haunches. Within minutes, the bear reached the embankment of the river. It paused. The man jumped onto its back and gripped its fur as the bear slid into the frigid May water of the Grand River, a major water source in Southwestern Ontario.

"Cross it at an angle," he ordered. He focused on the other side of the river. He tightened his grip on the rough fur as his anxiety grew. It had rained for the past week, making the water level higher and the current faster than usual. He swore when the bear was pulled downstream.

"Swim harder!"

The bear pumped its limbs faster and soon they were across the river. The embankment was steeper than where they had entered and as the bear stepped from the river and onto the small landing patch of mud, its paw slipped, sending the man flying back into the water. Thankfully, the side of the river was not too deep.

He frowned, straining to keep his head above the water. "Be careful. Use your claws to keep your footing." He wiped his face before he grabbed the trunk of a tree to pull himself up. He pointed around the tree to a trail. "Go up that way."

The creature lumbered up the path, and the man scrutinized its every move. He could not help but smile as he watched it climb. *It did it. It crossed the river.* It had completely obeyed him and, well, that meant the world to him.

He followed the bear through the trees onto flat ground and he pulled out a small, thin electronic device. He tapped his thumb on the touch screen and watched as the bear shifted its shape into a black Lab.

"Well?"

He looked up from the Artificial Intelligence Remote Console to the middle-aged man walking toward him. "It can swim with me on its back easier than I thought it would. Didn't even complain about my commands this time around. Probably doesn't even know what a complaint is, unlike most people I know."

The older man folded his arms across his chest, covering the white lab coat he wore. "What is your *expert* opinion, Cameron?"

Cam shrugged and looked down at the Artificial Intelligence Morpher sitting patiently at his feet. There were no signs of distress, impatience, or boredom as they had seen in previous versions. "I say we start putting together a presentation." He could not help but grin when the other man laughed. He slipped the AIRC into his pocket, and felt the slight weight fall against his leg.

"This is it. We did it."

"You did it. You created it."

"Right, it was all me. I mean after all, you only programmed and trained the AIMs."

Cam shrugged as they walked back to a large warehouse-looking building. "I'm the only trainer you had since I stopped teaching Mark. Why continue training him when I can do it on my own?" he said, his voice taking on his casually arrogant tone. He glanced at the scientist. "Henk, if you tell me I could have taken *personal* time one more time, I will get this AIM to attack you."

He laughed. "But you cannot get it to attack me, because we created an AIM that cannot hurt humans. Thank God for our programming definitions."

Cam watched him for a moment. He was happy for him. Over twenty years earlier, Dr. Henk Baxter's research had been stolen by the McCarthys who had brought AIMs and Scanning to the world. It had captivated many people because of its combination of human athletes with AIMs competing in physical challenges. One of those captivated had been Cam.

"Until the day comes we need them to attack humans," he muttered as he followed his mentor.

Henk looked at the twenty-five-year-old. "The need is here, or so the military claims. But that's an ethical issue that the government will not dare to deal with." He raised an eyebrow as a warning. "Nor will we. I do not need to tell you how much difficulty the government has simply keeping the CST under control. We do not need to be getting involved in any of that, not with so much at stake."

Cam winced at the reproach as the two continued walking through the forest path and approached a warehouse. The CST. He had worked so hard his entire life to be the best in the Canadian Scanning Tournament, and he had almost gotten there. Top five player for the five years had he played. Soon after joining, he had discovered the Underground where he learned that had the initial research stayed with Henk, he would have discovered the problem with the AIM substance sooner; a problem the McCarthys tried to ignore, and a problem Cam and the Underground had just solved.

Henk walked through the heavy metal door of the warehouse and called to the other workers in the building. Cam stayed along the edge of the crowd, leaning against the back wall as his co-workers gathered around Henk.

"I am proud to finally announce that the new AIM is fully functional at the advanced progression stage." He smiled when the group of workers erupted into cheers, and he raised his hands to quiet them.

"I want everyone to keep in mind that this is not over. Our work is not yet done." The scientist looked around him and caught

Cam's dark brown eyes. "We have no idea what the reaction will be, and we need be prepared for any and every situation. AIMs are integral to our society, and if we make it seem as though we are disrupting daily life as the world knows it, we will have no hope of integrating the upgrade. This meeting with the McCarthy Company does not mean that our actions and experiments are legal or accepted. For those who compete in the CST: act as you normally would and keep your work here separate. For everyone else, the same goes. We do not need any more leaks."

He paused, and Cam noticed the man take a deep breath. When Trevor McCarthy sold the first AIM unit in Canada, the government passed a bill which determined Underground work to be illegal due to those who smuggled and sold their products. It meant that Cam had constantly risked his Scanning career, and those of his teammates. The bill did not make life easy for any of them. For some, it had made life dangerous. Henk and the others had all lost good friends and colleagues. Some went into hiding. Others went missing. Others still were found in morgues.

"Let us begin the preparations for the presentation!" He smiled as the group dispersed and Cam approached him again. "That was not directed towards you, I hope you know."

"Yeah I know," Cam muttered as he fumbled with his phone. He glanced at the dog still at his side. *What obedience.* "Henk, what do you really think is going to happen? The McCarthys aren't the only people we need to convince. We need to talk to the government, the military. God knows if Trevor doesn't agree, he'll do everything he can to get to his clients before we do." He realized how far he had gone from the responsibility of being a Scanner. This was so much more. "You of all people should know how difficult the McCarthys will be. You know they're not going to appreciate you telling them where they went wrong, again. You weren't too professional when Trevor last spoke to you. Not that I can blame you, but it didn't make any of this better."

"I was younger and it was my first major research project. I did not realize how deep this would all go." Henk paused and looked around.

Cam's eyes moved over his phone and he sighed, reading the same message he had for the past few days. "I'm going to head out if you don't need me for anything else today."

"Hot date?" He held up his hands quickly in defense. "I apologize. Too soon, I suppose."

"Too soon for what?"

"References."

"You think I've gone a year without going on hot dates? By all means, reference away. Maria didn't ruin me." Lying was easier every time he did it.

"No," Henk said softly. "But it would be understandable if another girl had."

Cam slipped his phone back into his pocket, trading it for the AIRC which he let fall onto a nearby desk. "I *am* meeting someone, actually." He avoided the man's face while he turned away. "I'll see you tomorrow morning. Tell Mark to give me a call later tonight. He still hasn't given me the results for the AIM he's been working with," he called over his shoulder as he grabbed his jacket.

Cam sat at the desk in his apartment and ran his hands through his blond hair as his head bent over a cluster of papers. Without knowing what the future held, he had not bothered investing into a condo or house, not again. He needed to be able to leave at a moment's notice, especially now with the meeting so close. His AIM was in the form of a Golden Retriever puppy, sprawled out over the dark blue comforter of his bed. He glanced over his shoulder to the animal. "You shed in that form. Get off my bed."

The AIM slowly rolled onto its haunches and jumped from the comfortable platform it had chosen as its resting place. "Did the experiment not go as planned?"

"It was perfect."

"Your attitude and body language suggest otherwise."

"Never said I was feeling perfect." Cam flipped his attention to his computer and began to type furiously into a document he had left open that morning. He had been signed onto a CST team at the age of eighteen, avoiding post-secondary education because of the workload and, of course, to pursue Scanning. Now, he was no longer Scanning, but writing reports. *Just another way for life to kick me when I'm down.*

"I'm not going to make a habit of this, but I need an opinion," Cam stated.

"Shall I think of a bias to skew my data?"

"Why do you think you're the way you are?"

"Excuse me?"

Cam swiveled his chair around to look at the AIM, its head tilted to copy its question. "Of all the AIMs I've had to re-program and train, of all the AIMs that have gone rogue, none of them are like you. I've looked through your coding –"

"Now I feel violated."

"And your coding is no different than any of them. There's no blip in the coding. Your substance is perfect. I've gone as deep into your code as possible –"

"Silence does not mean consent, Cameron."

"But there's nothing out of place. So why don't you follow the Laws?"

"From where do I originate?"

He shrugged. "I got you when I was a kid, remember?"

"So, your father."

"I guess."

"Why did you ask the question if you had the answer?"

Cam turned back around. "That man is never the answer."

"It is, if the question was: who impregnated your mother?"

"Remind me to never ask your opinion again."

"At what intervals would you like the reminder?"

"Fine, get back up on the bed."

He heard the AIM land back on the bed and lie down. He rolled his eyes as he opened his e-mail server and sent a quick reply to the message he had obsessively read. He was going to have to stop running at some point. A year was long enough.

He walked into the coffee shop a few hours later, his hands shoved into the pockets of his jacket. He looked around slowly. After a full sweep of the occupants, Cam looked across again and his eyes stopped on a man slowly standing up from his chair, looking straight at him.

Here goes...

He stood awkwardly in front of the man and sized him up. He looked the same as he remembered him, but then again, it had only been a year. He took the offered hand and gave the man a small smile.

"Hey, Rick."

CHAPTER 2

"I'm sorry I haven't even tried to contact you guys."

Rick shook his head as he took a drink of his coffee. He winced as the hot liquid touched his tongue. "For the first while, none of us expected you to. You needed your space, and you needed to get yourself sorted out. But then you never returned any of our calls. We were trying to sort ourselves out too, you know. You weren't the only one affected by what happened," he murmured.

Cam looked down at the coffee in front of him, staring back at the faint reflection of his face. He had left so quickly and tried to keep himself from looking back. He had tried to not think about his former teammates, or the daughter he never had the chance to meet. By leaving the team he had hoped he would be able to leave it behind and just move on. He wanted to leave her behind, too. He had focused on his work in the Underground and it had been a success. For once, he had something good. He was an idiot for thinking that his past would stay there. He had to face it at some point, and that point was now, with Rick sitting in front of him.

Truth was, he had missed all of them, even Ryan, and it killed him every day knowing that he would never be able to compete with them again. They were the only family he had and he had walked away from them. Henk had tried to convince him that no one suspected his involvement, which he supposed was true. All the public knew was Cam quit because of his daughter. There was no way he could go back to Revolution, but there was no other team good enough for his skills, despite their failed attempts to win the CST. That was his home. At least, it had been.

"How's everyone doing?"

Rick looked at his former teammate. There was no point dwelling on what they both knew. Cam had screwed up, and hurt everyone including himself in the process. "My dad's pretty much fully recovered and competing. He's back in the captain's seat which is a huge relief for me and Brittany." He laughed when Cam grinned. For the short amount of time they had competed in the previous season, Rick had found it nearly unmanageable to take over the captain's role, his father's role. Everyone had seen that. "Ryan's improving every day. You gave him a really good start with your training last season. But now we have another rookie. His name's Eric. He's not bad, but not great. He'll get there, though. At least he had an AIM when we signed him on."

Rick laughed. "Actually, his scores really weren't that bad, for the Juniors. He's from a Northern region of the province, but he's getting used to the travel. I have no idea how the board found him. It's like he came from nowhere, but I guess Maria wasn't even on the map before we signed her."

Cam glanced at Rick slowly, waiting for him to continue. He had intentionally avoided listening or watching anything related to the CST. The wound was still too sore. "Maria didn't go back?" he asked once he realized Rick had no more news for him. He saw his friend shift uncomfortably in his seat and he leaned towards him. "Is she okay?"

He shrugged. "I assume so. I lost touch with her about nine months ago. Before that...she wasn't doing too well but I couldn't expect her to do much better. She pretty much hit rock bottom. She didn't talk about it much, but I guess she put herself together and accepted a job with the Army. She had finished basic training the last time I talked to her and was waiting for her placement."

Cam raised an eyebrow. "No one's heard from her?"

"No one's said they have. I tried e-mailing her and calling her, but her number's disconnected and her messages bounce back."

"That's one way to put everything in the past, I guess," he muttered and continued to stare at his coffee. He had known that, though, that her number had been disconnected. Hearing the automatic message was enough to make him regret calling. "How's the season going so far?"

Now it was Rick's turn to raise an eyebrow. "Are you telling me that Cam Tylar doesn't even watch the CST anymore? I can understand not paying attention to our team, but any of it?" It was in jest, of course, but it was surprising that he had not known Maria had quit the team soon after him.

"I only ever watched it for me, remember?" Cam said with a grin but he shrugged. "I just..."

"It's hard, I know. I figured. Dad was the same way when he was benched last year. Then again, he didn't want to be sitting around. He didn't quit." Another sore spot. "Cam, what've you been up to?"

The younger man shook his head. "If I told you, I'd have to kill you." He hoped that wasn't true.

"Seriously, Cam, what've you been doing for the past year? You're not competing anymore, you're not even coaching. I've known you six years, and this isn't like you. You've cut yourself off from everyone." Rick glanced around when he noticed he had begun to raise his voice. He continued, with restraint this time. "No one in the CST has any idea where you've been."

"That's because I'm not affiliated with the CST anymore." He paused, pushing down the emptiness he felt when he thought about it. "Rick, I'm fine. I have a full time job that'd bore me just telling you about it. I have my own place, bought a new car since Maria has our old one. Or she did. I'm doing well. I'm even in charge of a major project at work."

Rick laughed. "Someone put you in charge of something?"

Cam smiled lightly, thankful for the attempt at humour. "What happened last year…it made me figure a lot of things out."

Rick swirled the last few drops of his coffee in the mug. "Have you gone to see her?"

He shifted in his seat. "Not for the first few months. I try to go to the cemetery every month now. I went…Maria told me her due date." He let out a deep breath and rested his head in his hands. "She would've been nine months old this month. I would've..."

"You would've run." He held up a hand when Cam shot him an angry look. "You would've wanted to run, at least," he corrected. “C'mon Cam, you can't tell me that you were ready to have a kid, with your ex of all people. You were an athlete first, everything else second, and I get that. I was like that when I got married, and even when Adam was born, but I smartened up.”

“I have smartened up.”

Rick smiled lightly and nodded his head. “I doubt it. You agreed to meet with me.” He sighed and looked him in the eye. “I need to tell you something.”

Cam felt his heart begin to pound, his chest tighten. “I thought you said everyone was okay.”

“Brittany’s pregnant again.”

He nodded slowly, but the feeling in his chest continued to ache. “Congratulations.” He saw Rick’s face twist slightly in hesitation. “What? You guys had been talking about it last year, weren’t you? I didn’t have anything to do with it.”

“Yeah. Yeah, this was planned. It’s just...we’re having a girl.” Now it was Cam’s turn to pause. “I wanted to tell you.”

“Well, thanks,” he muttered.

“Cam, be real. Yeah, it was terrible, what happened. But you didn’t want it. If Maria had found out earlier, and had told you sooner, you wouldn’t have wanted it.” His voice was soft, but the words still stung.

“That’s not true. You know better than anyone that I want a family, that I would have had one with her,” Cam shot at him. “I never even got the chance to think about it. I don’t like it when decisions are made for me.”

Rick sat back in his chair. “Would you rather I not tell you, and wait until the baby’s born? ‘Hey Cam! Hold my baby daughter!’ I didn’t mean to throw it in your face.”

“Of course not. It all just comes naturally to you, doesn’t it? You get the perfect wife, a son, and soon you’ll have a daughter. You have a stable job, and a nice, happy family,” Cam spat, ignoring the other customers around them. He rubbed his face and shook his head. “Guess I haven’t really changed much, have I?”

Rick drank the last of his coffee and reached for his coat. “Why don’t you come out to our next challenge? It might do you some good to be around some old friends, and back in the spotlight." He seemed unfazed by the outburst. Nothing else was really expected when it came to Cam Tylar.

If only he knew.

Cam stood and gave a shrug. "Maybe. I don't really want to make myself regret quitting."

"Do you?"

He paused. Looking around the coffee shop, he wondered how many people there even remembered or recognized him. He had been in the spotlight for five years, trying to make it to the top. *I took every interview opportunity I could find, and for what?* Before, fans would continuously come up to him to talk, or get a signature, or even just a photo with him. Now that he wasn't competing anymore, everyone seemed to have forgotten about him. Even he was beginning to forget who he was.

"Every day."

"Hey, would you just turn that off?"

Mark looked over to a very irate Cam. "Nothing better to do."

"There's no point watching it."

He smiled and turned down the volume of the TV in Cam's office. "You used to be cool, man, watching all the challenges, watching yourself in interviews."

"Yeah well, like I said, no point watching it. Besides, I know something even better for you to do."

"Finally, some fun! The past year you've been all work, work, work," Mark said as he jumped up from a chair. "So, what do you have planned?"

"For you to get back to work." Cam grinned as the other man swore and sat back down in the chair. He watched him for a minute before he stood up. "I mean it. Go help Sandra and the others write up the presentation. Let me finish my report."

Mark stood up and looked at the computer screen on Cam's desk, quickly reading a few lines. "You have all the data, so why do you keep going over it, trying to make more? We know the results of the original substance." He looked at Cam. "You don't think we're ready?"

"We are. I just think there's more to this." He leaned against his desk, looking down at the screens filled with programming codes and chemical compounds. His daily focus for the past year. "I've looked at Henk's original research and his formulae, but it doesn't match what's been mass produced."

"That's because the McCarthys got their own scientists to carry on his research. And by carry on, I mean steal, of course. We know all of this already. What's the problem?"

Cam shrugged and sat back down behind his desk. "Henk's original design was pretty much perfect. It never would have gone rogue. Maybe I'm just trying to keep myself busy, and away from people…people like you. So get back to work."

"Cam, I'm going to be serious with you for a minute." Mark leaned over the desk to look him square in the face. "You need a girl, for just one night. Just let loose. Forget about all of this. You've been so focused and ignorant to the rest of the world. You need to get completely smashed and wake up in a bed you don't recognize, next to a girl you pray you didn't catch anything from."

"Get back to work."

"Get laid."

Cam rolled his eyes as he once again focused on his computer screen, ignoring Mark as he finally left his office. *This will work, won't it?* The new substance would be accepted, and it would be easy enough to switch in mainstream labs around North America. It would be easy to sell it, and moderately simple to get people to get rid of their old one in exchange for the new. At least, it would be easy for the average person to do so. It would be harder for the corporate clients the McCarthys had, which had long included the military.

In their case, they would phase out the old AIMs as they did with any type of outdated weaponry and technology. Something still did not sit right with him. As long as he had been working in the Underground, something more had bothered him but he never had the opportunity to look into it before now. There was no way he could include his extra research in his report to give to the McCarthys, but if he could find enough evidence for this data set, maybe he could bring it up with Henk. He just needed some answers. He had waited long enough.

"Is that report nearly ready?"

He looked up suddenly, startled by the sound of Sandra's voice. "Just adding in the last data set you gave me. Can I have a copy of the presentation?"

"I'll send it to you when we're finished, if we ever do. Mark's trying to play match maker for you. I'd be careful. He was just talking to Karly on your behalf."

"The blonde from the Boston facility?" Cam groaned when Sandra nodded. "Can I just fire him? Please?"

"Unfortunately, we need him. Even if you don't. We have the meeting in a week. Try to lighten up by then, alright? Get the report done." Sandra left the doorway but walked back into the office. "I'm going out to Niagara Falls tomorrow. Maybe the change of scenery will help you get some work done."

"Maybe." Cam stretched his arms over his head and rolled his neck, cracking the joints to release the pressure he felt building. "Can I ask you something?" He waited for Sandra to close the door and glanced at his computer briefly. "What do you think this will mean for all of the corporate clientele? If there are rogue AIMs in large companies, and in the military…"

"It means we may be in way over our heads." She gave him a small smile before she opened the door. "Just gives us another hurdle to jump."

"Yeah, big friggin' hurdle."

"We have been over this."

"Just do it."

"No, I will not."

"I'm commanding you!"

"Command all you want, but I will not roll over."

Cam glared down at his AIM, still in its usual Golden Retriever form. "You really tick me off, you know that?"

"If you want to see things spin, then you roll over," the AIM replied and jumped up onto the couch in front of the TV.

"No, no! Down!" Cam shouted as he took a threatening step towards the AIM who quite uncharacteristically obeyed. "Why can't you like being a lizard, or a toad; anything that doesn't shed?"

"People find me adorable, and I rather enjoy the attention."

"At least when we were living with Maria you didn't talk so much." He sighed and flopped down on his couch and picked up the remote. He held it in his hand for a moment, aimed towards the TV.

The AIM watched as Cam stared at the blank screen with the remote in hand. "Are you in need of instruction?"

"Shut up."

"You would miss my companionship if I were to do so."

Cam shot a sideways glance at the AIM. He let out a sigh before he stroked the dog's head which now rested on his knee. He pressed a button on the remote and the room filled with the sounds of cheers while the screen showed clips from that day's CST challenges.

"It's been a great start to the season so far. Each team is pushing harder than ever. I don't think we've ever seen such high scores in challenges from all of the teams!" A man spoke from behind a desk as the action clips faded in the background.

"A lot has changed since last season, Gary. Two of the top five teams have been completely re-structured, and I think that's given the other teams just enough motivation to aim for the top. With the likes of Cam Tylar and Jack Tyson out of the challenges, it's any man's game now. Or woman's, with Maria Kier also gone from the tournament.

"Jack resigned?" the robotic voice was filled with incredulity. The AIM shifted, still resting against Cam's leg affectionately.

"Looks like it," Cam muttered, his eyes wide. *I really should have been keeping up with the teams.* Cam had a reason to quit, at least to the fans and other teams. But there was no reason for Jack to take a personal leave. Jack, his enemy in every way, was gone from the spotlight. If his biggest threat dropped out to focus solely on whatever job he had, there was something coming. Something big. They were in the calm before the storm now. He wondered if any of his co-workers knew. *Of course they do.* It was almost essential to keep up with the teams with the amount of athletes working for Trevor McCarthy. "Why didn't anyone say something?" he asked, not expecting an answer. "Don't they know what this means for the project?" They all knew that Jack had close ties with Trevor, and if Jack was being kept busy it was not a good omen for their presentation. The McCarthys were getting ready for them, but most likely not in the way his team wanted.

After a moment, he turned off the television and looked down at the dog. "How about a trip to Niagara Falls?"

"You're really not my type, Cameron."

CHAPTER 3

Cam sat up in the cot he called his own in the Niagara Falls building nearly a week later. Since most of the people in the Underground travelled to each lab, they usually had bedroom-like rooms for people to use. They did not have the most comfortable beds, but they did the job. The change of scenery had helped him whip out the final draft of the report for his team to use. The presentation needed final touches and that was something he could not do. Their research incorporated so much more than any of them expected, and would affect so many people. None of them really realized. They even needed the expertise of an economist, not that he had said anything to help their case. All he concluded was their new AIM would briefly bring down the stocks in AIMs, significantly, but the economist had promised it would be brief, whatever that meant to an economist. Maybe it was like when a woman said 'soon.'

He looked around the room with a bored sigh. Two more days until the presentation. They would leave tomorrow and come back home immediately after the presentation, depending on what the McCarthys decided. And if they were allowed to leave.

"Come on," he said to his AIM as he quickly dressed himself. "Let's go do some scanning."

"Scanning?"

"Is there a problem?"

"What is the purpose? You no longer need scans."

"I didn't need scans when I was six, did I?"

"Were you not training for your future career that you no longer have?" The AIM paused and turned from Cam. "I apologize."

Cam continued as though the creature had not spoken. "I just need to get out of here. It's cramped and I have nothing else to do. I'm finished my part of the report. I don't need to go over my data again; I know I got it right."

"Ah, there you are."

"What are you talking about?"

"I was wondering when the old Cam would show up. It was beginning to concern me that you were so put together and relatively well-spoken. I almost missed you being unpleasant."

"Whatever."

Once outside, Cam climbed up a tree in the forest around the back of the building and sat himself on a branch. He missed this, being on the lookout for animals. He smiled to himself, remembering scanning as a kid: chasing bears and hunting down groundhogs on his family's farm. Of course, that had been before his father had left. He and his mother had moved soon after that to Kitchener. There was no way they would have been able to live in that house with the ghost of a memory.

He watched his AIM in the form of a Grey squirrel sit comfortably beside him on the branch, staring out across the trees as though at peace with the world and its lot in life. Growing up with the AIM had its benefits. Cam always had someone to go to, especially while still dealing with the absence of his father. Other days, the robot's presence only reminded him of all he had lost. More ghosts. More memories.

"Go make yourself scarce or something," he hissed to his AIM.

The squirrel's fur bristled, its tail standing erect as it turned its attention to Cam. "You ask me to accompany you. Now you want me to keep myself entertained. I see…only when convenient for you," the AIM muttered. "I am not a toy."

"I don't care if you're sentient or not. You need to learn your place. So just…just shut up and find somewhere else to be." Cam watched as the AIM clambered away silently, for once, and leaned back against the trunk of the tree, closing his eyes. He had spent too much time indoors. He took a deep breath, and almost regretted it. Even though he was out in the country, the acrid smell of tourist pollution still filled the air. The laws intended to clean the air had very obviously failed. Just as the laws intended to protect the public from dangerous AIMs had failed. He opened his eyes suddenly, hearing a soft noise above him. He looked up to see a Northen cardinal land on the branch just above his head. With a small smile, Cam slipped his AIRC from his pocket and began to scan the animal. After only a second, the bird noticed him and flittered away.

He cursed and leaned his head back against the tree trunk, swearing again when he leaned his head back too hard against the knotty wood. Cam looked down at his AIRC and flipped through the scan library he had collected over the years. With a sigh, he tried to switch into the sports section of his AIRC. He was blocked out, the same as with the other attempts he had tried over the past year. He would not be surprised if he were to be black-listed from any team in the CST, or even any other country for that matter. He had quit. He had been in the top five in the country, and he simply left it all behind. Once the news of his daughter had gotten out, people had backed off.

He appreciated that, at least. That did not happen much in sports or in the media in general. When he did not return to the sport, people began to ask questions. Of course, his team had known he had resigned, but they did not make a press announcement until they had drafted a new player, an announcement Cam had not watched.

Another noise made him look down, and he felt a wave of irony. There below him was a doe. He held back a sigh, not wanting to scare off the animal as he had the cardinal. *Has the time off really affected my performance that much? Will I ever be at the same level as a year ago?* Then again, Cam could not pretend he had been any good the previous season, as much as he hated to admit it. His performance had not been his top level, and his sportsmanship was complete dirt. Despite this, he refused to think that he had reached his prime. Cam shifted on the branch slightly, holding onto the one above him for balance while he leaned over to get a closer look at the doe.

It stood almost directly below him and seemed completely calm. Cam held his AIRC firmly in his hand and slowed his breathing to match the animal's. His thumb slipped onto the 'scan' area on the screen and he watched the progress bar slide across the screen until it was replaced by the words 'Scan Successful.'

He smiled and jumped down from the tree as lightly as possible on the other side, away from the deer. He jabbed at his AIRC, selecting the new scan to change his AIM, wherever it had gone. He had several scans of deer over the years, each slightly different than the rest. The very first one he had scanned when he was a child had been rather slow, but had a high level of stamina. This one had high speed and stamina. It would have been good for a challenge, Cam noted. But that was behind him now. He looked through the trees to watch his AIM morph. It used to unsettle him when he watched the morphing. It looked so unnatural, but he was used to it by now. The squirrel's entire body vibrated and rippled like a thick liquid, until the grey fur dissolved into a light brown doe hair, and its form eventually transitioned into that of a deer.

"Come back, slowly," he said in a hushed tone through the console, still hiding behind the tree. He soon saw his AIM come from behind a few trees and he held his breath.

The deer looked up from its meal of grass quickly. People had tried conducting tests to determine if animals could tell the difference between a real animal and an AIM. Most claimed that they could, but this was based solely off the fact that animals had never tried to mate with AIMs. Cam knew better. There were few differences between animals and AIMs, but they were large differences. *The AIM is controlled and powered by a computer chip. What other argument do they need?* he asked himself.

"Stay where you are, and stay calm." He walked around the tree and stood beside his AIM. He watched as the deer stepped back, ready to bolt. He stroked the neck of his AIM deer, and noticed that it seemed to calm the real one.

"Ah, the old 'see, if this fake deer is safe, you are too' trick," his AIM spoke. "Very clever, *master*."

He ignored it and stepped slowly towards the deer that now seemed to ignore him. Cam smiled lightly when the deer allowed him close enough to stroke its neck like he had with his AIM.

"Maria used to always tell me that animals are always better than AIMs because of their freedom and spirit. I don't know if that makes them better, though."

"What is your opinion? Do I not have freedom?"

"To talk back to me, sure, but you're special. You still abide by the programming to some extent, even though you're not bound to the definitions. Besides, I wouldn't even consider real animals free. They're under our control no matter what. We either own them as pets, or destroy their homes and control their habitat." Cam looked over the animal, suddenly aware of the lines of muscles on its legs, vertebrae along its neck and the perked ears as though it understood everything he said. "Nothing could come close to being a real animal. But you're not an animal. You're an AIM. It's comparing apples and oranges."

"Yes, but they are both fruit." The AIM paused as it watched him. "You are missing people." it stated.

"Why do you say that?"

"The deer reminds you of your father and the day he left. The real animal reminds you of Maria and how you abandoned her, and you mentioned her which indicates you were thinking of her. You so rarely spend time with natural animals anymore."

"You can't abandon someone you aren't with."

"Apples and oranges."

Cam was silent for a moment. He missed being in the tournament. He missed the interviews, and the fans screaming his name. He missed the rush of adrenaline while he completed a challenge. But as he stood next to the deer he realized he missed the connection he had as a child. Thinking about it now, he and Ryan had a lot in common: they were both completely fascinated by animals. But Ryan had not fallen from grace. He was still on his lofty perch as a member of Revolution, spending time with animals and learning their habits while Cam sat in an office, going over computer data. Things changed too quickly. He hated change.

Cam walked back into the building to a crowd of concerned faces grouped around Henk. He raised an eyebrow and made his way to him. "What's going on? What are you doing here?"

"I'm going over the lockdown plan with everyone."

"Lockdown?"

"We have no idea how this project is going to be received. It would be best if we were prepared for the worst. You have no idea the type of mind this man has," Henk told him softly in his best calming voice. Of course, the tone of voice can only do so much if the words themselves are unnerving.

"I don't think there's a need to cause panic. We've been pretty discrete, and I don't really think we'll need to do much more than what we've already been doing to keep safe."

"And how did that work out for you?" someone called out from the group, directing the question towards Cam.

He spun around, unsure where to look but looked around to address everyone. "I quit. I wasn't forced out of the CST, and I wasn't being investigated. I quit so we could get this project done, and deal with things going on with me at the time. No one knows that I'm in the Underground. If any of you were half as smart as me, you wouldn't feel so scared." He waved his hands in the air. "I'm out of here."

"Cameron, wait."

He sighed and turned around to Henk as the group began to dissipate. "What?"

"I do need to talk to you. It was another reason for coming here. We'll go to your office."

He looked at the man incredulously after the man had spoken behind a securely closed door. "You want me at the presentation? I don't think that's a very smart decision. You know that eventually I want to be able to rejoin the CST. If Trevor recognizes my face, he can have me black-listed for life if he doesn't like what we have to say. Being the main sponsor and creator of Scanning gives him that power."

"As intelligent as you are, you haven't been as discrete as you think," Henk remarked with a scolding look of a furrowed brow. "And you know what I'm talking about."

Cam winced. He hated Henk acting like a father to him. He had not needed one growing up, and he did not need one now. It had been bad enough when Owen had tried to act like a father-figure, but he had let it slide because he was the captain. Cam had to admit that he should not have told Maria about his involvement in the Underground, but keeping it a secret from her was impossible. It was hard enough not telling her about what work he did. For once, he had wanted to be open with someone. *Good job that did.*

"If he doesn't see the AIM's trainer there," Henk continued, "he'll think we're intentionally hiding something. If he thinks that, he will stop at no lengths to find out what it may be."

"It's not like I came up with the substance. Why would he care? He'll have my report."

"You're Cameron Tylar. Someone has to program and train these AIMs. He knows it has to be someone with a competing history, but he hasn't been able to figure out who it was. Neither Sandra nor I have that background. You do. Besides, you know that Jack has been working with him. You also know how open his lips tend to be. He has kept them sealed up until now, but God only knows how long that will last."

Cam sighed. He glanced around the small office. It was all he had to show for his work in the Underground. No trophies, no medals. Just four walls, a desk, and a door.

"What time's our flight?"

"I'm not sure why you think I know anything." A man leaned against a large mahogany desk casually. "It's not like they let me onto their property, and it's no secret that I have ties with you."

"Since when would that stop a valuable employee of mine from fulfilling their duties?" An older man stood from behind the desk, a furrowed brow marking his discontentment. "Now, it would be extremely beneficial if you could find out exactly who is involved in this project before they come for the presentation. It will not be good if we discover that there were some people involved in the project who decided to stay behind in Canada. We need to know who is involved so we can be prepared. Are we clear, Mr. Tyson?"

Jack sighed and slipped his cell phone from his pocket. "Yes, Mr. McCarthy. Crystal clear. I'll send someone to their labs."

"No, you will not. You will go yourself. It is this inefficiency that is making me so frustrated," Trevor said, rubbing a hand against his forehead. "Go. Just go. And start looking outside of the labs. They are going to have contacts in other areas. Find anyone who could be connected with the research. Get that magical list from your contact if you need to. Burn whatever bridges necessary." He stared at Jack. "Well go!"

He sighed and sat down when the other man finally left his office. *Why is it so difficult to find good employees? Jack has been valuable for years and now, in the eleventh hour, now he tries my patience. Reconnaissance never hurt anyone. If he has doubts over anything extra he deems necessary is on his conscience, not mine.*

He pressed a button on the intercom system built into his desk. "Amanda, send someone to look after Jack. He may need a babysitter on this trip." He rubbed his forehead in frustration and stood once more. He was used to finishing things on his own. This was going to be no different. Thankfully, he had some time before he had to begin. He left his office to begin his rounds.

"Allan!" Trevor called out in the large, sterile laboratory and waited until the man came obediently to his side. "How are we progressing?"

"As well as ever, sir," the old man responded with a shaky voice. His age contributed to the waver, but the presence of the businessman was the main reason for the scientist's anxiety.

"And that means what, exactly?"

The scientist led Trevor towards a long metallic table, upon which a small lizard lay. "We have in fact determined that there is a possibility for a new substance to be created, quite inexpensively as well, in a mass production scale of course. It is nearly perfect, but it deteriorates quite quickly, which was why we developed Dr. Baxter's formula further in the first place."

"Get to the point, old man!"

"I would listen to their proposal quite carefully, Mr. McCarthy. If they have perfected the substance and have found someone with the ability to program the chips properly, it will have a huge impact on the company and the economy. We know there is already a market for the AIMs, but-"

"We've already sold one version of the substance to the clients who matter. To tell them of the defect in the current version, they will not accept the update from us but directly from them." Trevor looked at the lizard and suddenly grew angry with the passive creature. The creature tilted its head to the side to assess the man. His anger suddenly flared, and he grabbed the lizard and threw it aside with a growl. "Who helped you with this research?"

"Only two assistants. I made sure to keep this project highly classified."

"And they have told no one about the project or the research?"

"Of course not, sir."

"Good. Deal with them."

"Sir?" the scientist called after Trevor who had begun walking away.

"You heard me. Deal with them. And quickly. I don't need anyone else finding out about this, especially my brother," Trevor replied over his shoulder. He was not in the mood to tie loose ends himself, not quite yet. And the longer he kept his brother from finding out about these so-called 'rogue AIMs' the better. It had been hell dealing with that pesky soldier, and the report that had added fuel to his paranoia. But his brother could never find out.

Never.

"Don't start questioning me now. Get to their lab in Kingston and just stay there. Poke around if you have to but don't let any of them out of your sight," Jack growled into his phone as he waited for his plane to board. "No, I don't care what you have to do, just get into the lab and keep an eye out. I have my own work to do." He swiped at the phone's screen, ending the call, and he slouched down into the hard seat. The seating in airports really needed to be updated. There must come a point in human history when people decide they were no longer going to put up with sitting in hard, uncomfortable, and strangely small chairs while waiting to board a plane. At least, Jack was sure that time would come, eventually.

"Flight 180 from Boston to Toronto is now boarding rows thirty-"

Jack stood and grabbed his duffle bag as he tried to create an action plan. It had been a year since he had seen Cam Tylar. He had not even heard mention of his name. Even though he had quit the CST, it was not like Cam to stay completely away from the spotlight. As far as he knew, Revolution had not heard from him either. *How exactly am I supposed to get in touch with him? Wait around Cam's old haunts? Scout out his ex-girlfriends?* Jack grinned at that thought. He would not mind following one ex-girlfriend in particular, potentially leading him straight to Cam. He had to find out exactly who was working on this project. Cam would know the answer, of course, but he would not simply hand over that information.

"Hey, Cam! Say, how about you just tell me who's been working with you on this super secret project you've been working on for the past four years?"

"Sure, Jack! That'd be swell!"

But, Maria on the other hand, maybe she knew something. He realized though that maybe the two had not had contact either. None of it really mattered. She had dropped off the radar after the death of her daughter. The thought of death did not necessarily warm the cockles of his heart, but it gave him motivation. He took out his cell phone once more as he handed his boarding pass to who he considered to be the ugliest flight attendant he had ever seen. *Aren't they supposed to pass some sort of appearance test?*

"Hey, get Brent and someone else up to Owen Sound and stay there until I say otherwise." He hesitated. "Don't touch anyone unless I say so."

He had to cover all of his bases. If they were going to find out who was involved in the project, Jack would have to make sure nothing and no one was left untouched. Except for her. He would deal with her himself. Once they found out who was involved, they would be able to track them. If all but one or two were to show up for the presentation, well, there would be no problem. However, sending the top people meant something big was going to happen, and they were giving the rest of their group enough time to go into lockdown to wait out the initial bomb blast. *Well, if they think that's was how it's going to be, they have another thing coming.* Jack knew he had screwed up in the past and there was no way he deserved the chances Trevor had given him, but he would get this right. He would do what it took to make sure that if the McCarthy Empire was threatened, he would be the one to take down any opponent.

"Yeah?" he answered his phone when it rang with its incessant tone as he put his bag under his seat on the plane.

"We have a team in place ready at the Niagara Falls lab, but they're already upgrading their security AIMs," came a female voice from the other end of the phone. "Should they have anything to worry about? I thought this was just a meeting. It's not like they have anything important to say."

"You stupid girl. It doesn't matter if it's important or not. What matters is whether or not they bring it to the public after we shoot it down. Do you really want to lose your job?"

"I have two jobs. I'd only lose one."

"Your life?"

There was a pause.

"I'll gain access within thirty-six hours before they can finalise their security."

For the final time, Jack put his phone away after turning it off as the ugly flight attendant glared at him, making strange hand gestures which he interpreted as her desire for him to put away the phone. *Upgrading the airport chairs can wait. Maybe they should update the flight attendants first.*

"Is everything in place?"

"Of course, Mr. McCarthy."

Trevor looked at his assistant with an approving nod. "Finally, someone who does their job well, and on time. When was the last time I gave you a raise?"

"Last week, sir," she said with a smile.

"Good. That means I don't have to give you another one for a few more years." He looked around before glancing down at his papers. "Have you heard from Tyson yet?"

"Oh, yes. Jack said that he has people inside three Ontario labs, and one in the Maritimes. He also said he has someone at the military base in Kingston."

Trevor spun around to face the woman, his mouth agape. "Excuse me?"

"I told him to wait for your approval. He claims to have found some evidence of a similar project being conducted at CFB

Kingston. He has given others permission to look outside the labs for information. He said you allowed it."

"And exactly what evidence was this?"

"He didn't say."

He sighed and slapped his palm against the nearby wall, startling the young woman. "At least he's grown the balls to do his job properly. You have someone watching him, as I asked?"

"Of course."

"Then we'll give the man some slack in his leash. If after the meeting with Baxter and his followers we decide to go with our secondary plan, we'll take away the slack."

"Very good, sir."

Trevor rolled his eyes. "Of course it is. Why on earth do you think I said it?"

"I'm sorry, sir, of course."

The man sighed as the woman trembled. "My dear, would you calm down? You know that I don't enjoy dealing with inept people. Now, get me a list of all military personnel at the base. Wait. Better yet, get me in touch with the commanding officer. I'm sure it's about time we had lunch to secure our relationship. I want to make sure there's only been the one soldier. At least Jack found out. He's slow, but finds what's needed. While you're at it, check on our contacts at the other Canadian bases for any activity."

"I'll have that done shortly, sir."

"Amanda, you don't have to call me 'sir' when we're alone," Trevor snapped, but his face was soft; a look she saw rarely.

"I'll get the Commander on the phone, Trev."

CHAPTER 4

Cam looked around his small office with resignation. The papers he had accumulated over the past four years were stacked in neat piles around his desk and file cabinets. He had no idea why he still insisted in having everything in a hardcopy rather than relying solely on his electronic copies. He never considered himself an old-fashioned person, by any means, but it was almost a comfort. If paper could be a comfort. For so many years, he had focused on having the newest version of everything but now he almost felt more comfortable to see just one thing at a slower pace.

"We have two days before we head out to Boston," Sandra said as she stepped into the office. "Have you gone over the action plan in case anything goes wrong?"

"Nothing's going to go wrong," Cam muttered.

"Let me rephrase it, then. In case Trevor decides he'd be losing too much money. Cam, you have to admit that he's not going to like that part of the proposal. No businessman would. But a smart one would recognize the potential. We're not sure if he's that smart." She glanced around his office, noticing the uncharacteristic tidiness of the room. "You've been busy. Are you nervous?"

"Bored."

She grinned. "What, now that you don't have any more training or programming to do, you've lost focus?"

"Pretty much. Why would I care about the economic situation we'll be putting Trevor in? I couldn't care less about that crap. My job is to work with the AIMs. That job's done now." He looked up and snatched away a paper from her when she tried to pick it up. "And don't touch my things."

"For someone who doesn't care about experiments, you've done an awful lot on your own AIM." She nodded towards the paper he had stuffed beneath a pile of others. "What are you trying to do?"

"Keep myself entertained. Do you mind?"

"I'm not trying to be nosy, Cameron."

"Don't call me that."

The woman raised an eyebrow. "When did you come back from the dead?"

"What are you talking about?"

"Your attitude this past week is just like when you started with us: rude, arrogant-"

Cam shrugged without looking at her. "I was always like that."

"Since your daughter died-"

He stood up quickly and pointed a threatening finger at Sandra. "Don't you ever bring her up."

Sandra held her hands in front of her, showing no offense. "All I'm saying is you grew up. You've been different, in a good way. Don't backslide now that we're so close. We need mature Cam to make this project work. Don't screw this up."

"I'd be more concerned about Henk." He sighed and ran a hand through his hair, and reminded himself that he should get a haircut sometime soon. Not that it was long, but longer than he usually wore it. Maria had always made it a point to let him know when she thought he needed it shorter. She had always made a point to share her thoughts with him. "Are you done?"

"Henk's been worried about you."

"Good for him. He's not my dad. He doesn't need to worry about me." When he realized his answer had not satisfied her, he continued begrudgingly. "Look, I'm good at what I do here. No, I'm amazing. No one else can do this job, and I know that. But I don't really have anything else to do until after the presentation.

I'm just bored, and hoping I have something to come back to when we get back from Boston. Until then, I'm just trying to keep busy."

"When we get back from Boston, take some time off. Get together with your old team mates, and get back into the old rhythm of things. I know you hate not watching the challenges. Or you could learn how to sail."

"Why is it okay for women to joke around when they're being serious, but when a man does it, we get in trouble?"

"Because there's a double standard."

"Right."

Sandra smiled and patted his desk. "Go find Henk before he leaves. He's heading back to Kitchener tonight."

Cam turned on the TV after she left his office. It was nice to still have that voice of woman's logic around, as frustrating as it was. It also helped that she was not directly linked to any of his work. Sandra mostly helped Henk in the lab, but she was known for her meddling. He leaned back in his chair as he watched the most recent CST challenge. He figured that if he looked at it with a critical eye, it was not so hard to watch and not imagine himself attempting the challenge with his old team. With a groan he flipped it off and held his face in his hands. Over the past year he had worked so hard to adopt a new personality, a new outlook on life. He had known that his work would suffer if he did not force himself forward. People seemed to like this new Cameron better. *But do I?*

"Hey, Sandra said I should come see you before you left," he said as he stepped into the blindingly white laboratory.

Henk turned to face the young man and smiled. "Did you not want to say goodbye at least?"

He raised a questioning eyebrow. "Since when have you become so sentimental?"

"You seem to need it more than I do." He stared at Cam for a moment before he shook his head. "The last time I went to see Trevor with a proposal, he shot me down like it was war."

"Yeah, I've heard this story before. Can we skip all of this?"

"I am afraid, Cameron. I fear for this project, and I fear what may happen if Trevor rejects this second proposal, and I'm unsure how I will handle myself."

"I heard that story before too, along with the part about your research partner covering you and taking the flack and how great he was, blah blah blah."

Henk sighed and continued to stare at the young man. "You have never complained about my calling you L.J."

"Where did that come from?" He waved a hand and headed back out the door.

"There is another reason I feel it is appropriate for you to come to Boston."

He stopped in the doorway and turned around to face Henk. "You'll miss me too much?"

The scientist paced around the room for a moment before he faced Cameron with a serious look in his eyes. "One thing that Trevor prides himself in, is his business. His great-great-grandfather started the business. It is a family business. To him, that shows strength. The AIMs have now been around long enough for almost two generations, which is quite a legacy for a company such as his." He paused, collecting his thoughts. "But what if one were to be able to counter it?"

Cam laughed. "Henk, I really think you're losing your mind. You picked a heck of a time to lose it too."

"Your daughter…."

"Don't go there, Henk," Cam warned.

"She was named for your mother."

He paused. "I never told you my mom's name."

"No. She told me herself, after she introduced me to your father."

He took in a deep breath as his eyes narrowed in confusion. "What the hell are you talking about?"

"You look so much like Lucas."

He took a step back from Henk, the sound of his father's name nearly knocking him backwards. "Why did you never tell me you knew him? Either of them? You knew my parents."

"He requested that I kept our partnership a secret, at least until I found it necessary to tell you. I feel it is necessary now.

Trevor will see you and he will see the resemblance you have to your father. I had hoped that if he knows your relation to Lucas, and your participation in the CST, he will be more likely to accept this project. I hope that he will see how this is not only affecting one generation, but multiple, and the longer he waits to deal with the issue, the more people there will be asking questions."

Cam swore. "Partnership?"

"Yes. Your father was my research partner, and close friend. We met when your mother introduced us at the University in Boston, where I worked. He was a scientist too. A programming genius, really, and an avid reader of my research. He-"

"Who the hell do you think you are?"

It was Henk's turn to pause. "Excuse me?"

"After all these years, after everything that's happened, you think you can just start talking about this man and I'd want to hear about it?"

"No. I know you don't want to hear about it, but you must."

"You know what? You can go to hell," Cam yelled, finally making it out the door.

"Your father began the experiments you completed," Henk called out after him, following Cam slowly, unmoved by his stubbornness. "He left you because Trevor had turned down our initial proposal. We needed to continue our research. Had he stayed, Trevor may have gone after you and your mother. Trevor threatened our work, our families." He stopped walking as Cam did the same ahead of him.

"You remember that day, when your father sent you out to scan. You came home and he was gone. I was there. I told your father that Trevor had succeeded in bringing Scanning to Canada, which ultimately meant that we would need to go into hiding. Had your father's research been complete, there would have been no problem, but there was still more he had to finish. There were still more AIMs he had to train and program, a project which you've now completed."

Henk walked up to Cam who remained stone-faced as he stared at the wall. "Your father was a good man, who knew that his presence meant harm for his family. He left you the way you left your team."

"It's not the same thing."

"There is no shame in it, Cameron. But you must know the truth about your father. He did wonderful things for the Underground, for this project."

"So, what happened? You searched me out, and groomed me so that you could intimidate Trevor?"

"Your father began to train you for this job long before he left you. That AIM of yours was one of the first to be created from his research." He smiled softly when Cam stared at him, realization sinking in. "Oh yes, I know how special it is. Lucas and I were the only ones to know. We never even told Sandra. It was your training. It was the only one ever created, and he destroyed all of its documentation so that no one would ever be able to accuse you of creating it. He trained you as a child to finish his work, and you have, Cameron!" He gripped Cam's shoulders. "Look at what you've accomplished!"

Cam shrugged away from the man's grip, anger flaring in his eyes. "You listen to me. What I accomplished, I accomplished on my own. I don't know what kind of training you think he gave me, but I'm where I am today without him. I may have finished his research, but I did it without him or his guidance. If he was so great at being your partner, or if his research was really going anywhere, why didn't you keep him around? Where is he now, huh?"

"He died."

His heart nearly stopped. For years he had always assumed his father was dead. As a child, it had been his method of coping with the abandonment. When his mother had died from cancer six years ago, Cam finally allowed himself to wonder if his father was alive somewhere. Hearing Henk say the words now, it stabbed him in a place he had tried to forget existed. He opened his mouth to speak, but no words came. Instead, Henk answered the question behind his eyes.

"Five years ago, in his sleep. Brain aneurysm, so the doctors said." Henk paused. "There was no funeral upon his insistence. He did not want to bring any attention to himself in fear of bringing you and your mother into the spotlight, more than you already were with your Scanning. There is a grave to visit, however, when you're ready."

Cam was silent for a moment. He swore under his breath and looked around the open building, thankful that the majority of people had already left. Those who opted to stay later that day had made themselves invisible when they had heard Cam shouting.

"I need to get out of here."

"Cameron?"

He shook his head. "I can't even be around you right now." He laughed in disbelief. "After all these years, you knew my father and you didn't say anything. He worked here, with you, and you didn't say anything? Even after he died? He died, and you didn't bother to tell me." He noticed Sandra walk slowly from her office and he pointed accusingly at her. "And you. You knew him too and you never said a word. Screw the both of you."

"Cameron, just listen to him," Sandra pleaded.

"No. I'm done listening. What good has that done?" He started for the room he had claimed as his own sleeping quarters but paused before turning back to them. "I'll go to the presentation. I'll be there, and intimidate Trevor with your idea of generations or whatever. But after that, I'm done with both of you. I'm done with all of this."

Sandra looked at Henk once Cam had left. "He has every right to be upset. He'll come around."

"When have you known Cameron to come around?"

"There has to be a first time for everything."

Cam waited at the side door of an apartment building, acting as though he was fishing his keys from his pocket. He saw a man approach the door and he held it open. Cam smiled and grabbed at the door. He paused at the bottom of the stairs and looked up. He had sped away from Niagara Falls, not bothering to look back.

What was Henk thinking, telling me everything about my father now? Did the man actually think I would appreciate it, that I would be happy? Oh, how wonderful! Like father, like son! It's just so great that I finished the research my dad started twenty years ago with Henk, who just happens to be my mentor! Cam thought with disgust.

Over the past years, a small part of him had wished that his father was alive. There was so much he had wanted to say to the man. He had changed his speech multiple times, adding mentions of events to it as they occurred in his life. A part of him even wanted to tell him about Lucy, and how he would have been a better dad than he ever was. He opted to leave that part out, not sure that would be true. *Like father, like son, right?*

He walked up the stairs to the fourth floor, knowing the elevator in the building was likely still broken. Everyone at that point assumed that the elevator was now a staple decoration of the building. He passed familiar doors until he reached the end of the hallway. With a sigh, he knocked and waited for it to open.

Cam took a step back when a man opened Maria's door. "Oh..."

The rather tall man looked down at Cam. "Can I help you?"

"Sorry, I'm looking for Maria Kier."

The man shrugged. "Wrong apartment."

"She doesn't live here?"

"Do I look like a Maria to you?"

"Sorry, no." Cam glanced down the hallway. "How long have you lived here?"

"Eight months. Bought it pretty cheap. The last owner needed a quick closing date." The man nodded after a minute. "Guess that Maria chick used to live here then. Sorry, dude. Hang on a sec." He stepped behind the open door, and came back with a handful of envelopes. "My girlfriend said we should keep these for some reason. If you get in touch with her, you can give them to her, I guess."

Cam muttered a thank you as he took the papers. *What was I thinking?* He stormed down the steps, swearing to himself. He had driven aimlessly around Kitchener for two hours only to end up in Waterloo at their old condo, the home he had thought would still be hers. *Did I really think I could just run back to her, and pour out everything that's happened?*

"I've gone insane," he muttered as he returned to his car.

"I have been trying to tell you that," came a robotic voice from the backseat. "Did she see you?"

"She doesn't live there anymore."

"Did you truly expect her to remain in a place with so many memories after you left?" The AIM shifted on the seat. "Besides, did Rick not tell you she had joined the Army? She would not have stayed here, would she?"

"I don't know." He paused and turned around. "Did you know? About my dad?"

"I knew nothing for sure. I knew your father worked with Henk, yes, but did not know the reason for his abandonment. I did not know it was pertinent to share. I am vaguely aware of him as my creator, though only through their conversations." The AIM jumped fluidly into the front seat, an easy feat in its feline form. "I am sorry if my silence hurt you."

Cam stared at the robot. For the first time, it apologized. He hated this. Why did it have to think about his feelings? It made it that much harder to think of it as simply a robot. Thinking about it now, he realized that this was likely the only good thing he received from his father. His looks, well, those did help quite a bit and from what he was learning now, he attained those from him as well. *Why couldn't he have given me a regular AIM? One that acts like a robot and not apologize?* Things could never be simple.

CHAPTER 5

"I should have known better," Henk scolded himself. "I knew better than to push him." He paced back and forth in the Toronto airport. Everyone in the team had shown up, except for Cam. They had thirty minutes before they were allowed to board the plane.

"He had to know, Henk. He said he'd be here, so he'll be here." Sandra sighed and looked around at the small group as though re-thinking each person's purpose for being there. Henk and Sandra were the obvious ones to lead the presentation, of course. Mark was there simply because he had worked with Cam and had partially trained one of the sample AIMs. The two lab assistants perhaps were not essential to the project, but they would be useful to give the appearance of organization. Cam needed to be there. He was the catalyst, the person who needed to tell the McCarthys the actual dangers of the AIMs currently in production. He was the only person in the main faction of the Underground who had competed at such a high level in the CST, and he was the only one who saw AIMs turning rogue during an actual challenge. They needed his experience. And his father's stubbornness.

"If anything, we know that Cam is good for his word. He'll push it to the last minute, but he'll be here." She smiled lightly. Almost ten more minutes passed, leaving Henk and Sandra waiting alone just outside the Duty Free shop.

"I hate airports."

Henk looked over to see a red-faced Cam walking towards them with a duffle bag slung over his shoulder. "Oh?"

"I just spent half an hour being questioned about my AIRC. It showed up on the screen as a gun, apparently. I swear, the people here are inept and miserable, and take pleasure in making everyone else miserable." He stopped and looked at the two scientists with a raised eyebrow. "Come on, we're going to miss the boarding call."

Sandra smiled to Henk as Cam walked in front of them. "Told you." Her smile faded when Cam turned around to look at them over his shoulder.

"I said I'd be here, so I am. But I meant what I said. Once we get back from Boston, I'm done."

"He's always good for his word," Henk muttered softly as they reached their gate.

Cam sat in his seat on the plane after shoving his bag into the overhead compartment. From the corner of his eye, he saw the rest of his colleagues walk past him in the aisle. He watched the ground controllers move around on the tarmac and he tried to look as interested in their movements as possible.

"Have you really quit?" came a quiet robotic voice.

He glanced down at the mouse on his lap briefly. "You really think I'd want to work with people who knew my father and kept it from me?"

"They did not do it to harm you. Although you were hurt, your father's wishes were fulfilled."

Cam kept looking out the window. "They could have said something anyway. He was dead…when I joined. He had been gone a year. They could have told me. Besides, what's left for me there? My job's done. Everything else they do, the research, the experiments…it's not my place anymore."

"Looks like I'm stuck sitting with you."

He looked up as Mark fell into the seat next to him with a smile. "Let me guess. You're here to check in on me?"

"When one of the top guys quit, people start asking questions." Mark looked at the mouse on Cam's lap. "We've known each other for six years, since we both started in the CST."

"You call yourself a Scanner? With your stats?"

"You find me annoying, and I think you're an arrogant jerk. But I know you're not an idiot. What's up?"

"The project's done. I have no reason to stick around," he muttered. *How long does it take to taxi a plane?*

"No offense Cam, but what do you have to go back to? You quit your team, and the season's already started. We all know Maria's off the grid. You have no family." Mark's voice was soft. For once, he actually seemed thoughtful. "If you don't come back, we should still hang out. We went into the Underground together, it'd be nice to keep that up. Besides, I'm sure you need someone to kick around every once in a while."

Cam smiled at that comment. Mark was right. He had nothing left. "You really are an idiot, aren't you?" *Has it come to the point where I've pushed absolutely everyone away? I used to accuse Maria of doing the same, but I'm no better.* "Better not play poker, though. I'm terrible at it."

"All the more reason to play. I could use a few more bucks."

"I just want everyone to know how much I appreciate you all being here," Henk addressed the group in his hotel room. "This is not going to be easy. We need to be confident in our product, and we need to remember that we're attempting to replace something which has hurt quite a few people. Yes, people have been hurt in the process of the project, with a few unfortunate deaths of close friends and colleagues. I assure you all that this is well worth it. We will be helping so many people. Remember that as we stand in front of Trevor McCarthy and his board." He smiled as people stood and slowly left the room, but he stopped as Cam tried to pass. "May I speak with you?"

"I don't have anything to say."

"Then please listen to what I have to say."

He looked down at his AIM and sighed as the Golden Retriever jumped up onto the hotel bed. "Fine."

Henk nodded to Sandra who left with the cue. "I want to apologize for what I said the other day. What I said is true, but I should not have said it in such a way. You must know that I did not want to keep it from you, especially after your father passed. I hope you realize..." he paused. "I watched you grow up. I watched you as you developed your Scanning abilities, and your ability to control your remarkable AIM. I am truly honoured to have been able to see that, and while it may not mean anything to you I know your father was proud of you."

He turned away from Henk with a shrug and sat down on a chair. He thought for a moment. "Where was he?"

"He lived at various labs around the country. He sent your mother one letter after he left, but that was all, before you think she kept anything from you. He knew to stay away from the two of you, in case it brought you into danger. I contacted her when he passed, but I had no further communication with her."

"Did he…did he ever see me compete?" Not that he cared.

Henk grinned. "Yes. He watched every Junior challenge that was televised, and kept track of your statistics. He was so proud of you, L.J."

Cam stood quickly and patted his leg. The AIM jumped from the bed, audibly grumbling about doing so through Cam's AIRC. "I should go over my notes."

"L.J.?"

He stopped.

"Even if you don't want to continue research with us, you're always welcome. You're all I have too."

Cam slammed the door behind him and walked down the hall. His AIM kept pace beside him.

"Perhaps you should keep his words in mind, Cameron."

"Mind your own business."

"Currently, your only friends are a robot and a man who wants your money through poker games."

Cam stopped suddenly. "I know you hate to listen to me, so I'm only going ask one thing from you. Just shut up. Please. I'm sick of listening to you. Just…just act like a normal AIM. That's all I ask."

The robot sat. "Awaiting command."

He paused and looked the dog form over. "Come on." He continued to his room and fell backwards onto the bed, covering his face with his hands. He took in a few shaky breaths before looking to his AIM. "I'm going to shut you down for a while."

"Are you okay?"

"I just need to be alone." Cam stared at his AIM for a moment. He held down a button on the side of his AIRC and watched as the robot shut down for the first time in years. It lost its canine form and returned to its original gel-like state in a puddle on the carpet. He sighed and let the console slip from his hand as he curled onto his side.

He had grown up trying to show his father that he did not need him. He wanted to show him just how good he could be without a father's influence. He hadn't needed him. He hadn't needed anybody. His father had seen him. He had cheered him on, even from a distance. He had watched his son grow up after all. Then he died. Now Cam had nothing. He had proved his point to his dad. He had completed his project in the Underground.

What's left for me now?

"They're ready for you," a woman said from behind her small wooden desk.

Henk nodded to the group and each made their way into the larger boardroom slowly. Cam stayed at the end of the parade, leading a rogue AIM and the newly created AIM. The rogue he kept in a small canine form, and on a tight leash. Despite the domestic scan, the small dog could still be somewhat vicious despite the obedience training Cam had given it. He eyed each person in front of him behind a long desk. A petite woman sat on the end. She was somewhat pretty, but her fidgeting gave away her nerves. *What does she have to be nervous about? It's our lives on the line, not hers.* Next to her sat a rather tall, middle aged man. This had to be Trevor McCarthy. The hard lines on his face and the small scowl stood out. It could not be anyone else. He looked much different in person than on TV. A muscular man stood behind him, eyeing each one of the Underground members. Cam hoped he would never have to face him in a fight. He could pack a punch, as Jack well knew, but there was no way he would stand a chance against this bodyguard. A much smaller man sat on the other side of Trevor. His face held the same hard lines, and Cam assumed he was another McCarthy, despite the softer emotions in his eyes.

"Welcome back, Dr. Baxter," the man in the middle said with a smile. Cam noticed the lack of mockery in the man's voice, which made him raise an eyebrow. Trevor had more than enough reason to mock the group. They were idiots if they thought they would be readily accepted by the McCarthys. False admiration was always a red flag to Cam.

"Hello, Mr. McCarthy." Unlike Trevor, Henk was not as capable of hiding the disdain from the sharp tone of his voice. He gave an acknowledging nod to the others behind the table before he motioned towards Cam.

He took in a deep breath and stepped forward, bringing the AIMs with him. He looked each person in the eye and stopped when he noticed Trevor return his look.

"Cam Tylar." He chuckled under his breath and elbowed the man next to him. "I never would have guessed a top CST athlete would be part of this project. Not a winner, of course, but still in the top. Henk, how did you convince him to partake in your little experiment?"

"Must be his genes."

Trevor paused before giving a small nod. "That, that I should have guessed. He does look like your research partner. Lucas, was it? Well, like father, like son. Tell me, Cam, how is your father?"

"He's dead. I don't see how that's relevant."

He smiled. "Truly like father, like son." He gave a shrug and leaned back in his chair. "Dr. Baxter. Present your proposal."

Henk paused, glancing to Sandra before he began. "The original formula for the AIM substance was continued by your researchers. Unfortunately, the formula which was sto…which was adopted from my research was not properly developed. Somehow the formula was altered."

"What exactly is that supposed to mean?"

"It means that while the new formula developed outlasts the initial substance created, the current formula for the AIM substance eventually rejects the chip which has been developed. This rejection somehow corrupts the programming within the chip. Cameron?"

Cam bent over to pick up the small dog, but it snapped at his hands. "Hey!" He smacked the nose of the dog, picking it up quickly and set it on the table, holding it around its torso to keep it still.

"Would you mind telling me what a dog is doing on my table?"

"This is an AIM," Cam said. He watched Trevor's face remain stoic. "This AIM has rejected its chip and cannot be controlled by the Artificial Intelligence Remote Console. A rogue AIM is extremely dangerous to the public. Even this small form can be unpredictable. While it acts like an animal, it is much more difficult to train and extremely aggressive. Larger forms, such as bears and German Shepherds, have already been convicted of mauling a young child, Scanners, and prison inmates. Those cases have been disregarded as a mistake, that they were not AIMs, but the actual records show the people were harmed by rogue AIMs. We have no access to the records, but I can only imagine what may be happening in the military." Cam noted a slight flinch in Trevor's face.

"And you're claiming that all AIMs will eventually become rogue?" The man next to Trevor leaned forward. His raised eyebrow showed his scepticism, which surprised Cam. It appeared that not everyone knew about the defect as he had assumed. He at least seemed interested, which was a positive thing, but a part of Cam wondered if he did know about them and needed more information. All around him, there seemed to be people who kept the full truth away from others.

"Yes," Henk continued. "We have consulted various economists, with extreme discretion of course, and have determined that this is detrimental to the current market of AIMs. This defect needs to be rectified quickly, and quietly. Each of your corporate clients employs AIM regulators and technicians, and within two years they will discover the early signs of the defect and will come to you for answers. We have those answers." The man pulled a small cloth from his pocket and wiped the perspiration from his forehead.

Cam was not sure he would ever forgive Henk for deceiving him for so many years, but he had to commend the man for keeping his nerves for so long. He just had to keep them for a little while longer. He pulled the small dog from the table and handed the leash to Mark. He slipped out his slim AIRC from his pocket and addressed the second AIM. "Jump onto the table."

A small cat leaped gracefully onto the table and sat, staring at Trevor. Cam handed the AIRC to Trevor. "This is our new AIM. Henk created a substance which will not reject the chip. I've tested the chip and substance at various stages of progression, and I've had no trouble keeping control of the robot. I've successfully trained five AIMs made from this new substance, and have personally created the code which reacts to the substance. None of the AIMs have had any problems or glitches, and even at the advanced stages of progression it still keeps a strict adherence to the programming definitions. If you flip through the various screens, this chip and substance combination actually works much more efficiently, which allows the substance to use less energy and is less likely to be damaged during rigorous usage."

"Such as in Scanning tournaments," the man beside Trevor commented thoughtfully.

Cam nodded. "Yes. My background in the sport allowed me to use that experience to create the code. When I was active, I was constantly looking for new upgrades to use for my AIRC. I know that if an upgrade for the actual AIM was offered, every single Scanner around the world would buy it."

Trevor looked at the small screen in his hands, flipping through the various modes as he inspected the AIM sitting in front of him. He ignored the two people sitting beside him for a few moments.

Cam glanced at Henk. The man was still sweating, and eyeing the large bodyguard behind Trevor. Sure, Cam had never had to fear the McCarthys, but the presentation was going so smoothly. Even if they were rejected, it did not seem like they had caused any harm. He had even promised that they would be able to make more money. There was nothing negative about that detail.

"Dr. Baxter, this is impressive. Much better than your previous presentation." Trevor nodded and looked at the group of Underground members. "Introduce me to your team."

"You remember Miss Rodriguez."

"How well I do."

Henk paused as Sandra shifted uncomfortably under Trevor's gaze. "Cameron Tylar is our AIM handler and programmer. Mark Sullivan is our second handler and Sandra's assistant. The others were each personally involved with the production of the new substance."

Trevor nodded. "Very good. You have something for us to look over, I assume?" He took the binder Cam handed to him. "I'll have my accountants look through this and see if this venture is something we can afford to pursue."

"With all due respect, Mr. McCarthy," Cam spoke out of turn. "You're going to pay for it in one way or another. You'll either pay for the production of this new substance, which is actually less expensive than the current product. Or you can wait to pay your lawyers to handle the lawsuits which will start in roughly eighteen months, if not sooner."

Cam stepped back from the desk, taking the AIRC back from Trevor. The AIM jumped down and stood next to him. "We have the solution to the defect, and it will be easy to integrate the new substance into the market. People are being hurt by the AIMs, and I don't want anyone else to get hurt because of them."

Trevor's face twisted into a smile. "No, of course not. That would be a shame."

CHAPTER 6

"Who here thinks we were worried over nothing?"

Cam glanced at Mark briefly before looking back to the floor. The group had gathered in Henk's hotel room to debrief, whatever that meant. Nothing had happened. Everyone was civil, mostly, and Trevor had agreed to look over their research with his own team. He claimed to be impressed with the work and would likely take it on as a new product. But nothing was that simple with the McCarthys. Cam had heard enough rumours about them to know that. If his father had left because of the danger the McCarthys put him in, none of those in the hotel room were safe.

"There's a reason they asked us to not go to anyone else with this research until they make a final decision," Cam snapped before he looked at Sandra. "How long do you think they'll take to do that?"

She shrugged. "Probably not until we get back to Canada. They've asked Henk to stay behind in case they have questions."

"Like hell that's the reason. He's not actually staying, is he?"

"Only for a few days at most."

"He's being used as leverage, to make sure we don't go ahead and contact their clients. We don't even know their contacts!" He paused when Sandra remained silent. With another glance at Mark, he saw the man staring intently at his feet. "Do we?"

Mark shrugged. "You didn't need my help, so I employed my…research skills elsewhere." His eyes narrowed. "Don't give me that look. We need to know those contacts. We need leverage of our own. We needed names, and I got them."

"Yeah, and now there's a target on your back."

"If they find out."

"You don't think they already know?" He stood up and began to pace. He knew he looked, and sounded, crazy. He also knew that if Trevor did not like what had been proposed, he would make it well known. The man was not known for his subtlety.

"Cam, he's only here for a few days. In the meantime, we lay low. Despite your decision to leave the team, you need to lay low too." Sandra shifted in her chair, watching him pace around the room. She continued to watch him as he returned to his seat, and she cleared her throat. "When we return to Canada, you'll have to come in for deactivation."

He nodded, keeping his eyes away from the group. "I know the drill." He had watched people leave the Underground, either because they could no longer handle the stress, or because they had found working for Trevor more profitable. He knew he would be under surveillance for a few months, but that did not really bother him. Unlike Henk and Sandra, he had nothing to hide. "Are we going to wait for Henk before you take me out of the system?"

"He said we can go ahead with it. With…" She paused and glanced at the others in the room. This was a conversation which should be done in private, but none of this was news to any of them. "With the clearance you have, it'll take a few days for you to return all of the research you have at home and go through the final interviews. If Trevor decides to pursue our research and integrate it into the AIM market, do you…"

"I don't want anything to do with your end of it. I'm available to answer their questions, and help train the AIMs because they won't be able to do it on their own. But no, I don't want any profit. I made enough through the CST."

Sandra nodded. "I'll let Henk know."

He stood once again. "I'll see you guys at the airport."

"We still need to go over the emergency plan."

He stopped. "I know better than anyone what happens when the McCarthys go after someone. We leave everything behind. Am

I wrong?" When she remained silent, he made his exit and went back to his hotel room.

He ignored his AIM as it watched him throw clothes back into his duffle bag. He had acted like an idiot the night before, shutting down his AIM because he wanted to be alone. It was rare that he allowed his emotions to take hold of him, well, emotions other than anger. He refused to apologize to the robot. He owned it. It was just a robot. He paused and looked at the creature. No, it was not just a robot. He did not know what it was. A robot did not act like his AIM. He picked up his AIRC and looked it over. With a frown, he wiped it on his pant leg. Trevor had left smudges all over his screen. Figured. That man ruined everything he got his hands on.

Cam hefted his bag over his shoulder and motioned to the AIM. "I'm not apologizing."

"Why would you?"

"I wouldn't. I'm just letting you know."

"Cameron, you forget that I have known you for nearly twenty years. I would never expect for you to apologize."

He nodded. "Alright. Come on then. Back to the airport." He smiled lightly when his AIM muttered under its 'breath.' "I know. You hate flying. I could shut you down while we're on the plane."

"No, thank you. That feeling is worse."

Cam flipped through the scans in his AIRC's library and chose a small field mouse. He waited for the AIM to morph and crawl up his body before he began walking to the shuttle to the airport.

"When are your debriefing and outgoing interviews?"

"Tomorrow. Sandra said it'll take a few days to go through everything." He paused. "Henk's staying here in Boston."

"Why?" Even the robot had surprise in its artificial voice.

"Trevor said he would like one of us to stay to answer any questions." He slid onto a seat in the open shuttle before it began to slide down the street from the hotel towards the airport. It paid to be so close to the airport. They had not been in the middle of the city other than to meet with the McCarthys, and being on the outskirts made for an easy getaway. They did not seem to have any trouble so far, but there was still time for that.

"Which means he wants leverage in case the research is brought to the media's attention. I am sure they are aware of your relationship with the media."

Cam looked at the mouse on his arm with a sudden thought. He had worked with this AIM for nineteen years. Which meant his father had left him nineteen years ago. He had lived two thirds of his life, so far, without his father, but with this AIM instead. His AIM had known him longer than anyone else. Henk may have known him as a child, but their paths did not connect again until five years ago. As far as he knew, of course. *Who knows what else the man hid from me?*

"I'm not sorry."

The AIM hesitated. "I liked it better when you were a jerk."

Cam laughed. "Yeah, well, you're the only one."

"What are your plans once we arrive back in Canada?"

"I have a few ideas."

Cam leaned against the metal fence as the crowd around him cheered on competing teams. He glanced around, pulling his baseball hat lower over his face. He did not want to draw too much attention to himself, especially now that he was back in Kitchener. It was a far cry from his personality a year earlier. His eyes strained on the course in front of him, trying to pick out Revolution. He grinned as his old captain, both of them, came running over the small hill close behind a coyote and a cougar. Quickly, Cam took out his AIRC and flipped through his animal library. *How'd they get a cougar already?* A single trip to Northern Ontario would have given them the scan, he realized. After only a year, Cam was already forgetting his old lifestyle. Not many things scared him, but the thought of getting out of the CST system did.

He looked back up as the second half of Revolution came over the hill. He knew it would be difficult to watch, but he had no idea just how hard. It took everything inside of him to not walk away, but he had to watch. And so he did. He watched as his old team crossed the finish line with a full few seconds lead on the other teams competing. He had not watched the entire challenge, but it seemed to have been a GPS maze. He smiled. He had been pretty good at those. Competing AIMs would be programmed with the proper coordinates for the finish area, but the AIM and athlete needed to work together to find the proper path. It was all about communication, and a fast animal scan.

He hung back as media approached teams as they completed the challenge. The crowd began to mix with new spectators. Cam could still remember coming to challenges as a child after his father left. He would stay for hours to watch all the teams attempting the challenge that day, but most fans stayed only to watch their favourite team. No. Cam watched them all. It was one reason he had excelled in the CST. He knew the strengths and weaknesses of all the other teams, and learned from their mistakes. If only he could learn from his own.

"Well, if it isn't Cam Tylar. Risen from the dead."

Cam closed his eyes before turning to face Jack Tyson. Of all the people to run into, it had to be him. That seemed to be how his life always went.

"Oh, sorry. Still too soon?"

"Don't you dare-"

The other man raised his hand in front of him. "Hey, I am sorry about what happened. Just because I hate you doesn't mean I'm heartless."

"I find that hard to believe. What're you doing here?" He looked away. If they were noticed together, he knew it would be a media frenzy. That was definitely not something he needed, not so soon after the presentation in Boston.

"Just keeping an eye on things."

The cameras were turned to the teams. They wouldn't notice. Cam grabbed Jack's collar and threw him against the fence, pressing him against it. The grin on the man's face only made him angrier. "You mean you're watching me." He paused for a moment. He had known for years that Jack was working for Trevor, but something finally clicked. "Trevor didn't know I work with Henk." Jack had known that for years.

The man ignored the comment, still grinning. "You put on a good presentation, from what I heard. I just wanted to make sure you didn't do anything stupid."

Cam's forehead furrowed with skepticism. "I'm the least of your concerns. Why are you following me?"

"No, you're the least of Mr. McCarthy's concerns. That's why I'm following you. He has everyone else in more...opportune locations." He finally pushed Cam away from him, but remained leaning against the chain-link fence. "You were tough to find, I'll give you that. Almost as hard to find as Maria. She does a lot of travelling."

"What the hell does she have to do with any of this?"

Jack grinned. "How hard is it for you to not know as much as me?"

"If you go near her, I swear to God I will-"

"Relax. I'm not going to do anything to her. I wouldn't want to ruin another opportunity to hear her beg to take her home with me." His head snapped back as Cam's fist flew into it. "Son-of-a-"

"Cam?"

Cam turned to see Rick coming through the gate in the fence. He glanced back over his shoulder to see Jack pacing away quickly through the crowd. With a sigh, he walked over to Rick with a weak smile. "Since when are you brave enough to get close to a cougar?"

"Well, we need to keep up our ranks. It's not so easy when we don't have a superstar on the team anymore." Rick returned the weak smile as the rest of the team came up to his side.

Cam's eyes moved slowly to Owen. *What am I supposed to say to the man? To any of them?* He had not really thought this far ahead. He sighed and shook his head with a shrug, as though it erased the past year. The captain nodded and held out his hand, which Cam shook. That was all he needed. He glanced at Ryan who hung back.

"I bet you found the cougar for them."

Ryan nodded his head, looking up suddenly as another team pushed him aside. It was still quite crowded in the field, and it did not help that they seemed to be standing in the middle of everything. "Yeah. We had a few challenges out in BC, so we took a trip up into the mountains."

Something did not seem right. His voice was so soft, but then again, Cam was just showing up out of the blue after a year, and Ryan had never been too out-going. It hadn't helped when he learned that Ryan had wanted to date Maria, or that they had talked about dating. Lucy had been the only thing stopping them. "There are some great scanning spots up in those mountains."

"Yeah."

They were quiet for a brief moment before Cam turned his attention to the fourth Revolution member. "So, you're Eric?"

"Yeah. You're...you're Cam Tylar. You're amazing!"

"Well, if you're keeping up with these guys, you should be pretty good yourself." That was the closest thing to a compliment he had given in quite some time. "I'm glad to see you guys still so high in the standings."

"Are you?" Owen asked.

Cam paused. It was a good question. "Yeah, I am. I know you don't think I should've quit, and I know I put you guys in a bad spot. I want to say I'm sorry for doing that, but I couldn't stay. Maria couldn't stay either."

"She didn't stay because you left."

"She has a new life. I have a new life. It's how it is now, but this team...it's always been my team, even before I was signed. So yeah, I'm glad you're doing well."

Rick looked between his father and his ex-team mate and shrugged. "A bunch of teams are getting together at a bar downtown later tonight. Do you still drink?"

Cam smiled and let out a short laugh. "I haven't changed that much."

"I do not understand why you think keeping me here will be beneficial."

Trevor grinned at Henk from behind his desk. "If you have indeed found a way for us to have complete control over the AIMs, with no risk of rogues, then I am interested. However, you have more information than you're telling us. Would you like to know how I know?"

"Yes, because I have told you everything."

"I wish you wouldn't lie to me. It would make this so painless." He leaned forward, resting his elbows on his desk. "I'm very, very close with my corporate clientele."

"I imagine you would be."

"And I know that similar research is being conducted by someone within one of these corporations. Can you explain that?"

"Disgruntled ex-Underground worker most likely. There are various people conducting their own experiments, as you know, to make a profit. I have no control over those people."

"They are reporting the same research as you have presented to me."

The scientist nodded. "Then it is as we told you it would be. People are beginning to discover the flaw. Soon, they will come to you for answers. Trevor, I urge you to take our proposal seriously. We do not require any compensation. I just want to know that people will be safe."

Trevor paused and studied the man. In the few times the two had come together, this was the only time Henk seemed to be sincerely pleading. Maybe there truly was something to this proposal of theirs. Perhaps the Underground had created something beneficial to society. *But they told Cohner. They told Cohner everything. He wasn't supposed to know. They think I'm weak. They all think I'm weak. I could see it in their eyes. Cohner wasn't supposed to find out. He can't find out.*

"Go back to your team tomorrow evening. I'll have my scientists attempt to create this product. If they determine it to be easy to manufacture, we will bring your team back to work on the marketing plan."

Henk sighed with a grin. "Thank you, Trevor. People can change, after all."

"I suppose so." He waited until Henk left his office before calling his assistant into his office. "Is everyone in place?"

The woman nodded. "Yes, and awaiting further instruction. Trevor, I think we should seriously consider what Dr. Baxter has suggested. We can make more money from this, marketing it as a necessary upgrade. A promotional marketing scheme for the company, like Mr. Tylar suggested."

"Amanda, if I didn't know better, I'd think you want some of this money you claim we would make," he snapped as he stepped around from his desk.

"You know I don't. I just think it would be beneficial to look into this. We don't need to go through with the plan."

Trevor grinned as he placed his hands on her shoulders. "We can't risk anything. It's not just about the money, not anymore. I will *not* let them take this from me."

After a pause, she nodded. "I'll let them know to begin. Do we allow Henk to go back to Canada?"

"Of course. It'll hurt him more to see his own empire crumble beneath him. Let him live. For now."

CHAPTER 7

Cam groaned as his phone rang in the middle of the night, or rather, the early hours of the morning. "What?" he growled angrily as his brain pounded against the inside of his skull. He had been asleep for only a few hours and already the hangover began. *When did Rick start drinking so much? At least he finally learned how to have some fun.*

"You need to get to Niagara Falls."

He swore and rolled over in his bed. "Screw you, Sandra."

"Something's happened."

"Don't care."

"Cameron, you really need to get here, and change the plates on your car."

That got his attention. He sat up in his bed slowly, wincing. "What are you talking about?"

"It's not just about us anymore. Things are progressing quicker than we thought. Just get here as soon as you can. Please."

He cursed again. Maybe he had just been kidding himself. "I'm on my way." He could disassociate himself from the Underground, but he would always be a part of it. *What else do I have left?*

When he pulled into the parking lot an hour later, he could tell something was wrong. All the cars were parked around the back of the building in the bushes. He did not want to be the one to blow their cover in the building, so he did the same. After walking back around to the front of the building, he pressed his palm against the scanner. He did not expect it to accept his print after quitting, but it was worth a shot. It had only been a day, after all, and he hadn't even gone through his debriefing. That was supposed to be in ten hours. He knocked on the door, and then continued to bang on it for a full few minutes, despite the fact that three security cameras had been watching him the entire time. The metal door was opened by Sandra's petite form.

"Get in," the woman said quickly and pulled him into the building.

He looked around and felt as though he was in a dog pound. Rows of people stood at their desks. Sad and confused faces turned towards him with the glimmer of hope as though Cam would bring them to a safe and loving home.

"What's going on?"

"Mark's missing. He's not at any of the labs, and his phones were disconnected. No one's seen him since we landed in Toronto." Sandra started down an aisle towards her office. "We haven't had the chance yet to check his house. Something else happened first." She stopped in front of the door and hesitated with the door knob.

"Sandra, would you just tell me what happened?" He winced at the buzzing florescent lights above him. It was going to be a long day.

She sighed and opened the door. "Her."

Cam's eyes widened as Maria's head turned up from her lap to look at him. He looked behind him, checking to see if anyone else saw her. Maybe it was all in his head. He could still be drunk. He let Sandra usher him into the room. No, it was Maria.

Her right cheek was bruised, and her lip had been split open. He looked over the rest of her and saw a bloodied bandage wrapped around her upper arm. Her legs he could not see beneath the army fatigues, but the fabric of one knee looked scraped. No one said anything for a tense moment until Cam took a step towards Maria to look at her face more carefully, trying to forget who it was. Her eyes were red.

"What happened?"

"Someone attacked her in her home," Sandra answered for the young woman.

"And she came here?" Cam straightened and took a step backwards. "I'm not sure what she expected you guys to do."

"He attacked me because of you," Maria muttered quietly, her voice forced to sound neutral.

"Excuse me?"

"He told me to give my regards to Mark before he pulled his gun on me. For some reason, whenever a gun's been pointed at me outside the military, it's been because of the Underground. And Mark, oddly enough." She stood and opened the large pocket of her uniform pants, the sound of the Velcro grating against Cam's delicate head. She pulled a piece of paper from the pocket and handed it to him.

He unfolded the paper and his face turned to stone when he saw the picture. It was one of the men they had met in Boston. The muscular one. He passed it to Sandra and stared at Maria. "He's the guy who attacked you?" Cam glanced at Sandra to see her reaction when Maria nodded, remembering his thoughts when he first saw him. "Where is he now?"

"ICU at Kingston General with a military escort. He...it would've been a morgue..."

The room grew silent as Maria composed herself. Whatever happened was enough to shake her. Cam did not know what happened in Basic Training, but he assumed that she had been trained to handle quite a bit, emotionally and physically. So much could happen in just one year. People could change so much.

"Send this to Henk back in Boston, if you can. Let him know what happened," Cam said softly to Sandra. "We're under lockdown effective immediately. Contact the other labs and let them know. I'll check out Mark's place." He waited until Sandra left before he turned back to Maria.

"You okay?" He looked around uncomfortably when she shook her head. "I'll be back in an hour. If anything else happens here, message me. Only call in an emergency."

"Cam?"

He turned back to her from the door, glad that this had at least helped his headache. He raised a questioning eyebrow when she handed him a pistol from the holster around her waist.

"You may want this with you. There're two shots left."

"You think I know how to use one of these?" he asked as the weapon was thrust into his hand.

"I know you do."

Cam looked at the gun, examining it, before he looked back to Maria. New clothing and injuries aside, she still looked the same as when he had left her at the hotel in Owen Sound after the funeral: exhausted and defeated.

"I'll be back soon."

Cam sat in his car and looked up and down the dark street in St. Catharine's, less than half an hour away from the lab. The sun would be rising soon. He looked down at the gun in his hand and wiped his face as though it would wipe away the situation. He stepped out of the vehicle slowly, looking around to watch for any early risers. With his hand wrapped around the grip of the semi-automatic weapon, he crossed the street and stood in front of Mark's front door. He knocked a few times and glanced through the window next to the door. The lights were off. There was no-where else the man would be. He was single, and spent the majority of his time at the lab. He could simply be asleep.

He looked around impatiently, hoping no one had happened to look out their window as they awoke. He strode to the back of the small house and checked the door. He took a small step back and gripped the gun tighter. The door was unlocked. Cam had seen enough movies to know that an unlocked door, especially a back door, was never a good sign. He took a deep breath and stepped into the house.

"Mark?" he called out. If Mark had been missing for a day and if anything had happened to him, whoever did it would not still be in the house. A creak in the floorboard in the next room made Cam second-guess himself. He stood next to the doorway and let out a few breaths.

He spun around in front of the doorway, the gun gripped in two hands. He saw the blood first. He felt the weapon shake in his hands as he looked at Mark's body sprawled on the ground. Cam swore under his breath and felt his heart begin to pound, his arms still extended ready to shoot. After a moment he took a step forward, his chest tightening as he was able to look into Mark's open and unseeing eyes. His arms finally relaxed and Cam covered his face with a hand after finally noticing the bullet hole in the man's forehead.

This isn't happening....this isn't happening... If I call the police, they'd need to question me and it would only draw attention to where I am. If someone else finds Mark, my fingerprints are all over the backdoor and the police will wonder why I didn't report it. Oh God...

He walked back out of the room, unable to handle being in the same area as Mark. He looked around and could not find anything out of place. Nothing was missing. It was not a robbery. There was a single shot. It was an execution. *Think, Cameron. No struggle. No break in. Shot face on. He knew him. Mark, what did you get yourself into? What did we get ourselves into?*

Cam swore again as he returned to his car, throwing the gun onto the passenger seat. He held his head in his hands for a moment. For five years he had known the risks of his job. It was one thing to know the risks, but it was another to see the consequences. He slammed his palm against the steering wheel, forcing back the bile he could taste in his throat which came with the sudden wave of grief and fear. No one he knew was safe, and there was nothing he could do about it.

This time when he tried to put his palm on the print recognizer, the door opened. He walked down the aisle to Sandra's office with a blank face, not seeing the people around him. He tossed the gun onto the desk next to Maria and he shook his head.

"He's dead."

Sandra let out a sickened wail as Maria went to hold her. She looked over to Cam. He was sitting now, his fists entwined together in front of his mouth: the position he took when he was deep in thought. Maria whispered to Sandra to tell the others what had happened and turned to Cam after she left.

"Did he say anything else to you?" Cam asked quietly. No one was safe now.

"No, just that." Maria sat back on the table. "Cam, who the hell are we dealing with? It's one thing for them to get to Mark in the city, but I live on a high-security military base."

That explained the new owners of the condo, at least. Cam finally gathered the courage to look at her. "Jack knew where you were. They've been watching you, watching all of us. They're everywhere. They already knew where to be. It's not like you were really public about your whereabouts, but Jack knew. He wouldn't have said anything. He wouldn't have let you get hurt." He sighed with a shake of his head. "But someone knew where you were. Someone knew to be there. And someone knew that Mark always takes Wednesdays off. Every other day, he's here." He paused. "It wasn't a break-in."

"Mark knew the guy?"

The two were quiet as they looked in the other's general direction, neither willing to look directly at the other.

"Who is he?"

He shrugged. "How should I know?"

"Cam."

He paused. "He works for Trevor McCarthy. I thought he was a bodyguard or something. Looks like he's a hit man."

"Wait, Trevor McCarthy, as in the Boston McCarthys?" Maria stood up when he nodded. "You're telling me that the founders of Scanning sent someone to kill me, and killed Mark? And now they're chasing after the rest of the Underground? And that Jack works for these people?"

"I'm telling you that we're in way over our heads with this, and Mark…he was in on it, and got caught," he muttered and held his face in his hands.

"What happened to 'it'll be okay,' or 'I'll take care of it' huh?" She looked around the room frantically, suddenly looking at the walls as though they were closing in on them. "I mean, what the hell, Cameron? You put all of this, all of this crap before me? Before your team?"

"I started this before I even met you!" he screamed at her, standing up as he threw his chair to the side. "How was I supposed to know it'd get this far? You think I went into it and was alright with the fact that people were going to die?" He leaned his back against the wall, letting his head hit against it. "I didn't know. I didn't want this." His eyes closed. "I just wanted to help people."

"He was in my house for three hours before he attacked me," she said slowly. "I set the alarm system as soon as I stepped in, and he didn't attack me until I was about to go to sleep. Do you really think he gives a damn that you started working here before we got together?" Her voice lowered as he turned to look at her shaking body. "Look, I'm sorry about Mark. I'm also sorry I wasn't quick enough to put the other guy in the morgue instead of the ICU. I just don't understand how they got to me. There are security AIMs everywhere on the base." She shook her head. "They're killing people…"

He sighed and glanced at the phone. "Do me a favour?"

"Military personnel are investigating what happened at the base," Maria spoke to the police officer. "But when he mentioned Mark, I got my friend to make sure he was alright. He didn't want to call you guys, because he knew his prints were all over the place."

"You said you got a medic to check you out?" the officer asked, writing quickly onto his notepad as they sat in the Ontario Provincial Police office in Niagara Falls.

"Yeah, I'm fine." She glanced around at the small, dank office. *Why does every office feel like a prison cell?*

"This friend of yours, where is he?"

Maria gave him a look of warning. "He was friends with Mark too. He's a bit shaken up."

"We're going to need a statement from him, since he was the one to find the body."

"You can get it over the phone."

"Miss Kier…"

"It's Lieutenant Kier. You'll take his statement over the phone. The media is not to be notified. This investigation is a matter of national security, and I trust you'll do your job to protect the public." She stood and slid her coat back on. "You'll take care of the body discretely, and notify his family in the same manner. If I hear about this incident from anyone who was not directly linked with it, you will have the entire army looking for you with a charge of treason and terrorism. Is this understood, *Sergeant*?"

"Yes, Ma'am." He watched as she started for the door but called her back. "Can I ask you a question?"

"What?"

"You were in the CST? On Revolution? You're *that* Maria Kier, aren't you?"

Maria's eyes narrowed, hiding the pang of hurt throbbing in her chest. "I'm Lieutenant Kier, now. Get this situation taken care of before the military takes care of it for you." They really meant it when they said the past never dies.

She sighed as she pressed her palm against the palm scanner, hating the sound of the door unlocking when she did so. *It was never supposed to come to this. Now I'm able to get in and out of* their *building?* She ignored the looks she received from the workers as she walked down the aisle back to Sandra's office where Cam was still waiting. They were thinking what she was feeling. She did not belong here. Despite being one of only a handful of women on her base in Kingston, she knew she belonged there. It was a feeling she rarely had while part of Revolution. It wasn't their fault and she had loved being a Scanner, but she belonged in fatigues now.

"They're just waiting for a statement from you, which is going to be done over the phone. No names are going to be used and the media is staying far away from this." She sat on the desk where she had first been and sat her phone down next to her. "You'll be known as John Smith, and you'll call from my phone. Keep it quick. Don't answer any questions. Give the statement and then hang up." She sighed at his hesitance. "It's a military phone. No links to a GPS."

"Does being in the military make you feel like you have power over something now?" Cam asked.

"It makes me feel like I'm making a difference," she snapped. Maria looked him over and added, "apparently you know the feeling. Make the call." She listened as Cam spoke quickly into the phone. He had never been good at dealing with the press before. He always needed to show off, and it usually made him look like a jerk. At least he could handle speaking with police, and knew enough to keep it brief. She knew she was overstepping the limitations of her rank but at this point, things had changed so much that she needed to go with her instinct. She had to think outside the box now.

As Cam gave his statement, she went over the events in her head. Security cameras around the base did not have the man on surveillance. None of the security AIMs had reported anyone unusual on the base. This man was either a hacker, or had help from the inside. She was beginning to think that 'all of the above' would be the answer from now on.

CHAPTER 8

Cam looked at Maria briefly as the others in the lab rushed around outside the office, finalising the lockdown. It had been a year since he saw her last, since he had spoken to her. Now they were in this situation, together.

"What happens now?"

"I was hoping you would know. What am I supposed to do?" Maria asked.

"Whatever you want."

She swore and stood. "Well, you haven't changed. You're still an as-"

"You came here. I don't know what you're expecting me to do," he yelled. "Doesn't the military have a safe house or something for you to go to?"

"None that I trust right now." She paused. "They're working on it. They're still trying to figure out how the guy got onto the base. My commander's supposed to be calling me with a place to stay. He suggested another base in the meantime."

He laughed. "Yeah, because I'm sure that's safe. If Trevor knew where you were, if he had someone working inside your base, he'll have someone at another base waiting for you."

"Cam, I didn't know where else to go."

He looked at her, and suddenly it was last year. He looked at her, knowing that Jack had ambushed the team at the Toronto challenge because of him. He knew that Jack's AIM attacked Maria because of him. The fall made her lose the baby. Everything seemed to come back to him all at once.

"I tried calling," he explained, as though it would make everything okay.

She looked at her arm, adjusting the bandages around her bicep, but she remained silent.

"Fine. Do what you always do." He got up suddenly and slammed the door open. "Leave."

"You never tried."

"What?"

"You never tried to make it work. It was always about you!" she yelled. "It was always about your work here. You put this, *this,*" she motioned around her, "above your team, and me. *You* left the team. I was going to stay. I was going to work through losing Lucy with you. I get that you needed time. I did too, but *you* were the one who left. Like father, like son, right?"

"Don't you *dare* compare me to him," he screamed, his voice cracking from the volume. Cam shot a glare at his brave co-workers who were looking through the open door. "You cut me off! You were *always* like that! You didn't even tell me you were pregnant, and then it was 'hey, the baby's dead'! Excuse me for needing space. I didn't plan on leaving for good. *You* cut me off. You cut *everyone* off! Do you really think I wanted to go back to someone like that?"

The two stared at each other, both with a red face and a heaving chest. Cam moved back to the door and closed it slowly. "I'm sorry."

Maria's eyes widened. "Excuse me?"

"I'm sorry. We're acting like neither of us have changed, like we're back to where we were last year. I…I was glad that you cut me off. It was easier to deal with everything. It was easier to pretend that nothing had happened. And then you just…you show up. Here, of all places." He shook his head. "You're in the military. What the hell is that about?"

"You…you apologized."

He looked straight back to her. "The only person I haven't pushed away was just killed. I'm kind of having one of those self-reflection moments."

She nodded and glanced around the room. Every office… "I shouldn't have said that about your dad."

"No."

"And I shouldn't have cut everyone off. I shouldn't have cut you off."

"No, but I shouldn't have made it so easy." He held her eyes for a moment. "And you know I tried. Don't tell yourself otherwise."

Maria jumped when her phone began to ring. She flipped it open quickly. "Lieutenant Kier." She paused, her eyes wide once again. She looked at Cam before turning away. "Hey, yeah I'm okay…I know, I'm sorry I didn't call right away…I'm at…yeah, I'm at a safe house." She sighed and lowered her voice. "Yeah, I'm alone…okay, I'll call you later…I'm safe, I promise…you too."

Cam glanced away as she turned back to him. "I think we both need to stop pretending we know each other anymore." He motioned with his head to her phone. "Is he the jealous type?"

She hesitated. "I'm trying to keep everyone safe. The less he knows, the better."

"Do you hate me less, now that you have to do the exact same thing I did to you?"

She shook her head. "I hate myself more. I said I would never do this to someone. I shouldn't even be talking to you, of all people, about this."

"Maria, it killed me every day, knowing I could never let you into my life, having to lie to you all the time. For the first time, I wanted to bring someone in, and I couldn't."

She stared at him. "You're right. We need to stop pretending we know each other."

There was a knock at the door, and Cam went to answer it. He moved aside to let Sandra into the room and closed the door behind her.

Maria watched as Sandra set a briefcase onto the table, and opened it. "What's this?"

"We're registering everyone for their own safe-houses. It's probably similar to a military safe-house, but you came to us so I'm assuming you trust us more than the military. I'm not surprised. I haven't trusted them since they began working with Trevor."

"She'll stay with me," he said. "She's not one of us. She's part of the clientele, which means they'll be looking for her before any of us. They went after Mark because he was the one who knew the clientele contacts. She can't be left in a safe-house on her own, and I doubt she'd want to be stuck with someone she doesn't know. I'm the lesser of two evils."

Sandra glanced at Maria, who made no motion against his suggestion. She sighed and pulled out a few slips of paper. "You know this isn't a good idea, Cam."

"Well, I've never been known for having good ideas. I work with what I have." He waited for her to begin filling out some papers, and looked over to Maria.

Her hair was all one colour, brown so dark it seemed black, and cut to her chin. He held back a smile, knowing that she would have kept her purple highlights as long as possible during Basic Training. He could only imagine what the Drill Sergeants would have done to her as punishment. He watched her as she kept her attention on Sandra. He had to look away suddenly. Sandra was right. It was a bad idea, to be stuck with her.

"I heard back from Henk while you were on the phone."

"So quickly?"

Sandra nodded, her head still bent over the papers. "He'll be back tomorrow night. Or rather, tonight."

"I guess we shouldn't be so surprised. He was there for leverage, but now we're being hunted. They don't need him."

Maria glanced between the two of them. "Henk?"

Cam paused. None of them really had official titles. "He's pretty much the lead scientist. The boss, if you will."

"I told him to stay. He didn't seem too fond of that idea," Sandra continued.

"He'd be safer here," Maria spoke softly.

"What do you mean? He'll be followed, and then they'd know where we all are," Cam said.

"I don't know the man, but I'm assuming he's not an idiot especially if you consider him your boss. He's not going to come back into contact with any of you. He'd go straight to his own home and stay there. If he knows anything about how to hide, he'll stay active enough to make it seem as though he's interesting. He'll keep the interest on himself long enough for the rest of you to scatter and get into opportune, and safe, locations." She nodded to herself and looked at Cam. "He'll keep in contact. He'll do everything he did before, other than meet face to face."

"It's what happened last time, twenty years ago," Sandra said.

Maria nodded again. "You had military help. Who was it?" When Sandra hesitated, she rolled her eyes. "I think we're past the point of security breaches."

"His name was Scott Wilkinson. I can't remember his rank. Henk dealt with him. He was the one to create the lockdown plan."

"I don't recognize the name, but I can't imagine he stuck around with the military for long after dealing with you guys."

"He died soon after."

She let out a short laugh with a shake of the head. "Cam, I can't believe I ever had reservations about you working here."

"Don't start. You're in the military. That's not the safest career either."

"At least I knew that going in."

"Maria, I need you to sign something, just to make sure you agree to this and we're not kidnapping you." Sandra always knew when to step in. Not that she was good at it, but she tried.

"Kidnapping," Maria muttered. "I was trying to think of a way this could get worse."

After Maria answered a few questions, Sandra left the two alone with a shake of her head. Everyone knew this would likely be for the worst, but they had no other choice. Maria had been in their lab, and had seen their faces. Even if they trusted her, and hardly anyone even knew her, they needed to make sure she wasn't working for the McCarthys and needed supervision. The attempt on her life was another reason. Cam just had to remember that.

"Let's get going then," Cam muttered as he headed out from his office.

She hurried after him. "Don't you need to sign something?"

"I'm in a safe house already."

Her eyes widened, ignoring the stares they received from the Underground workers. "What do you mean? Did someone try to hurt you?"

He glanced over his shoulder as he reached the door. "No. Everyone who quits is put into a safe house until they're completely out of the system."

She watched as he headed out the door, and she followed close behind. "Excuse me?" She grabbed his elbow as they left the building and stepped into what was now the late morning sunlight. "You quit?"

"Yeah, but it doesn't matter to Trevor. I'm a target, just like them, and you." He looked at her and saw a hurt look fall on her face. He realized that the entire time, he had been selfish. Or at least, he knew she had a good reason to think so. He had stayed in the Underground despite her pleas because he wanted to stay, ignoring how much it hurt her. Now that he was hurting, he quit. Her hurt was mixed with confusion, which was unfortunately a look he had seen too often during their three year relationship.

"We'll take my car," he said, turning back to walk around the building.

"I'm not leaving my vehicle here. It's government property," she replied after a moment as they reached the brush where everyone had driven their vehicles. She leaned under a few low hanging pine branches as Cam watched, and disappeared within the living car-freshener.

Within a few seconds, the sound of an engine started up and Cam stepped towards his car while Maria backed up a large olive green military grade truck. She leaned out the window with a shake of her head. "There's no way I'm leaving this behind."

All he could do was stare at the vehicle. "Yeah, because this won't draw any attention to us on the road."

"We'll take back roads. I'd never take this on the highway." Maria grinned. "The mighty Tylar is speechless. It's not like you've never seen me in a truck before."

He shook his head slowly and pulled his keys from his pocket. "You're a soldier. And Rick and Owen questioned your ability to fit into an all-male team. If only they could see you now."

She didn't say anything for a moment. "Let's get moving."

Maria kept her window rolled down as she followed Cam in his new black car. It was smart for him to get another car, and she was not surprised that it was black. He had always hated her silver car. He claimed silver cars always got in the most accidents, as if he knew anything. She scrunched her nose as they passed farm after farm, the smell of fertilised fields wafting into the truck. She should have been used to it after spending so much time in stables as a child, but the smell in the stables was always so much different than the smell in the fields. It amazed her that after all these years, farmers could find nothing better than animal feces to feed their crops.

If there was ever the time for this smell, it was now. There was nothing good or clean about this situation. Maria slipped her seatbelt off quickly and shrugged out of the coat she had put on earlier, remembering to put the restraint back on. After everything, it would be ironic to die in a car crash. At least in the military truck she would have a shot at destroying the other vehicle first. *After everything.* She let out a sigh, and tried to think back. *How did I get here?* She had gone through the events with security at the base, with her Commander, and then with that woman Sandra. Her lips moved silently as she went over it again systematically.

She had finished a video conference with a base overseas. She went to her small bungalow on the base. The houses were relatively new to CFB Kingston, which was a nice change to the condo she and Cam had bought in Waterloo. She had checked the security code on her door, and everything was fine. She had watched TV for a few hours, watching highlights from CST challenges which got easier every time she did. Then she went to her room to go to bed. She opened her closet to change her clothes, and then he attacked her.

Maria shook her head. "I watched TV for a few hours," she spoke to no one, although her AIM sitting patiently and silently in the back seat was likely listening. "Was it that long? How many shows did I watch?"

"Two one hour shows and one half hour show," the AIM reported, assuming it had been asked a question.

She nodded. "He was there…he was there the entire time." Her eyes widened suddenly when she realized Cam had turned onto a smaller dirt road. She yanked the steering wheel to make the turn in time. *Think about it later, Maria. Just concentrate.* She looked through Cam's back window and could see him turning around in his seat to look at her. She shook her head, trying to tell him nothing was wrong, and continued to follow him. At least they were getting away from farm fields now. But she hadn't even paid attention to where they had been driving. *Way to forget all of your training.*

After nearly another hour of driving through mostly wooded areas, Cam pulled onto a faint path. Its only designation as a driveway were the two lines of flattened grass. Five minutes later, he stopped and parked the car next to a small cabin-like building. He watched Maria jump from her vehicle with a large green bag slung on her back while carrying her AIM in the form of a cat in her arm. He nodded towards the door.

"It's not much, but it's safe at least."

"Who needs safe military bases when we have cabins in the middle of nowhere," she muttered.

"That's what I've thought for years." He flashed a quick and sarcastic grin before leading her into the cabin. "I'm back," he called out, throwing his keys onto a nearby table. He looked around as Maria inspected the interior.

He was right. It really was not much. A traditional cabin. It had wooden walls and floors, although there was an open living room which led into the kitchen with doors leading out to a 'backyard' which was no more than a small clearing. A short hallway at the far end of the room led down to the bathroom and one bedroom. It was not much, but it had what they needed.

She paused when she realized he had called out to someone. Her hand instinctively went to the holster on her waist. "You're staying here with someone else?"

"My AIM." Cam looked at her suddenly when she dropped the bag onto the ground. He noticed her last name written on the bag. The tapping sound of claws on hardwood made him turn away to see his AIM trot towards them. "Were you on the bed again?"

"Yes."

He cursed under his breath. "You're lucky I'm not allergic to you. We have a visitor." He paused. "I'll explain later."

"I don't think it needs an explanation."

Cam smiled lightly at Maria. "No. I guess not." He rubbed the back of his neck and jabbed a thumb towards the hallway. "You look like crap. Get some sleep. Bedroom's down the hall."

"I'll take the couch, I don't mind."

"Bedroom's down the hall," he said again. "We'll take shifts sending our AIMs out scouting."

She nodded thoughtfully. "Three hours."

"Sure."

She picked the bag up again and started for the hall. She paused and turned back to him. "Cam, look…I didn't mean to-"

"Get some rest."

The bedroom door clicked shut and Cam's AIM pawed at his leg. "I feel I missed the first half of the movie."

He sighed and let himself fall onto the old, saggy couch. "We're in lockdown. Mark's dead. Maria was almost killed. I think that's about it."

The robot was silent for a moment. "I am sorry about Mark."

"Me too."

Another pause. "That explanation will be for her, I presume?"

"It's probably about time she got one."

CHAPTER 9

Cam walked into the bedroom carrying two cups of coffee. He set them down on the nightstand before looking at Maria still sleeping in the bed. From the corner of his eye he noticed the door of the closet wide open. She almost looked peaceful, sleeping sprawled under the covers with her hands neatly under the pillow. He used to tease her about that. His chest heaved, preparing to yawn, but he held it back and rubbed his face.

"Maria," he said softly. He knew better. That would never wake her up. He remembered cooking full meals in the kitchen while she slept on the couch. No, it wasn't about sound. It was about touch. She always woke when he got in or out of bed. "Maria," he said again and put a hand on her shoulder.

Her eyes opened, and her hands flipped out from beneath the pillow, holding a gun tightly and pointed straight at Cam. He cursed and dodged out of the way. "Maria! What the hell?"

She shook her head and dropped her arms onto her stomach, one hand coming up to her face. "Sorry. I just…impulse."

"Your first reaction is to shoot me in the face?"

"I didn't know it was you." She groaned as she sat up. Her head tilted and turned towards the coffee as the smell reached her nose. "Guess it's my turn."

Cam handed her a cup while taking the other for himself. "What do you mean?"

"Scouting shifts?"

He laughed and sat on the edge of the bed. "It's morning."

Her forehead furrowed and she looked at the watch on her wrist. She swore and shot a glare to him. "I slept for an entire day? You were supposed to wake me up." She thought for a moment. "I haven't slept that long in months."

"You needed the sleep."

"I set my alarm. You turned my alarm off."

"Maria, you needed the sleep, clearly." He nodded towards the closet. "Looking for the boogey man?"

She took a cautious sip of the coffee. "And the monster under the bed. Couldn't find them. One less thing to deal with."

He smiled and looked down at the brown liquid in his cup. "How are you?"

"I'm fine."

"How are you?" he repeated.

She paused. "Shaken. Confused. Angry."

Cam nodded. "Get cleaned up. We'll try to figure out what's going on. Okay?" He paused when she laughed. "What?"

"I haven't been in the army a year and already I forget what it's like for a civilian to order me around. It's cute."

He rolled his eyes. "You look like crap. You need a shower." He headed for the door but stopped when she called him back.

"Thanks for the coffee, and for letting me sleep. I haven't…I haven't been sleeping."

He shrugged. "Thanks for not shooting." He sat down in the kitchen and heard the shower turn on. He looked at his AIM and shook his head. "I'll let her get ready before we talk."

"How long will we be here?"

"No idea." Cam took a drink of his coffee, letting the hot liquid slide down his throat. "Sandra said she'd let me know when she got into contact with more labs as they finalize their lockdown." He paused. "Do you remember my dad and Henk ever talking about a lockdown like this?"

The AIM in the form of a German Shepherd moved its head to the side and pawed at his leg, its ears up and attentive. "The day your father left. Henk said there was a lockdown."

Cam looked down at the creature and he moved his leg to shove it away. "Tell me the truth."

It sat but hesitated from responding. "Soon after I was created, they mentioned preparing for a presentation with Trevor, and needing to create a lockdown plan. They agreed to leave their families to ensure their safety. That's all. I was then given to you."

Cam was silent for a few moments, and did not even notice when the shower turned off.

"Any more coffee left?"

He turned quickly as Maria came into the kitchen. He nodded towards the machine on the counter and gave her a once over as she refilled her mug. She wore what looked like black workout pants. Around her waist was a thick, dark green belt connected to a holster on her leg which held her gun. She wore a black t-shirt, and the bandage around her arm looked new. At least no new blood had soaked into it yet. He watched as she sat down across from him, holding the mug in two hands. Cam saw a silver chain around her neck which he assumed her dogs tags were attached but were hidden under her shirt. Dark spots appeared on her shirt where water had dripped from her hair.

Maria cleared her throat after taking a sip of the coffee. "So…"

"Do you want to go first, or should I?"

She shrugged. "You could."

They never needed many words to start a conversation. They were always able to pick up right where they left off.

"The Underground's been working on creating a new AIM substance and chip. We've found that the type of substance mass produced by the McCarthys disengages with the chip and AIRC."

"They go rogue."

He nodded. "Yeah. I guess you saw that last year at the Toronto challenge. My job was to train the AIMs Henk created and write a program code to control them."

"Athlete and computer genius. Jock slash nerd. Who would've guessed?"

He continued on, hiding the same grin she was hiding. It had been a year, with so many hurt feelings, rage, betrayal, and it could still come down to this. "A few days ago, back on Monday, we presented the new AIM to Trevor. All we wanted to do was make a discrete and seamless transition between the two substances. The public didn't need to know about the rogues. We suggested they offer it as an upgrade before discontinuing the old product completely." He paused and looked at his AIM. "I guess they felt we're too much of a threat."

"Scanners would be all over an upgrade if it was offered, but I can understand their concern. I can't imagine the amount of lawsuits they'd have. They're probably afraid more people will find out about these rogue AIMs."

Cam watched her face shift from understanding to a contorted face of regret. "What?"

"That's why they're after me. It was never about you at all," she muttered.

"What are you talking about?"

"They're going after people who know about rogue AIMs."

"Yeah. You're connected with me."

"No." She stood up and looked through the window. Little light came through, blocked mostly by the thick trees around the cabin, and the light shone splotches on her face. She paced back and forth in front of the window as Cam sat silently, the light moving across her body. Finally, she stopped and leaned against the wall.

"I'm an AIM Operations Technician." Seeing his blank face she continued. "I train AIMs with military tactics. I maintain them, and monitor their progress and make sure they're working efficiently. About a month ago I handed in a report to my CO, my Commanding Officer, about the AIMs I've recently worked with. In my report I wrote that I noticed some AIMs not responding to the AIRC, and I reported that an AIM attacked and killed a soldier."

Cam swore. "Have any gone completely rogue?"

"Yes."

"What happened to the AIM that killed the soldier?" When she hesitated, he sighed from frustration. "You said it yourself. We're past the point of security breaches."

"Not when it comes to the military and the government. All you need to know is I took care of it personally, so you don't need to worry about it getting into the wrong hands."

He closed his eyes and nodded after a moment of thinking. "Okay. Who else saw the report?"

"Only my CO, at least on my base."

He nodded once again. "How many bases employ an…AIM person?"

"Operations Technician. AIMOT. Normally there are two stationed at each major base in Canada, or one depending on the tactical training, and there are two overseas at all times. Well, there were two overseas." She paused. "One was killed by the AIM. The other is back in Canada, and they're not looking to replace them any time soon."

"So, you give the report to your CO, and then where does it go from there?"

"The Chief of the Defense Staff, and I would assume he would share the report with the Minister of National Defense. This was only the third report I've written, so I'm not quite sure of the chain."

"One of those people would have a direct connection with Trevor. He found out about your report somehow."

Maria shot a glare at him. "That'd be the Minister, but if you're suggesting our own government is going around killing people under the command of a company, an American company–"

"I'm not–"

"You're suggesting treason on his part, and terrorism on Mr. McCarthy's."

"I'm not suggesting anything. I'm trying to figure this out and what our next move is," he shot at her. He knew better than to insinuate something with a soldier, even if it was Maria. "Can you find out if they even got the report?"

She shrugged. "I have no reason to believe they wouldn't. They received my other reports fine."

"Would they go through the trouble of hacking into your base's security system to plant that hit man?"

"They go through a lot of trouble for very little quite often. I just…" She closed her eyes and let her head hit against the wall. "I can't see the Minister dealing with this. Yes, he would be the one to have a contact with Trevor, because he is the one who arranges the shipments of AIMs, but so does the Prime Minister. This is all assuming that my CO followed protocol and didn't show anyone else. He may have shown a CO at another base. He probably would have contacted the CO at the overseas base."

Cam stood and walked into the connected living room and dialed a number quickly on his phone. "Hey Sandra. Have you heard of an AIMOT? ....yeah, she is. Can you send me a copy of the list Mark made of all the contacts? ...we'll see if there's a connection. How's everyone doing? ...." He glanced at Maria. "So far. I'll talk to you later." He saw that her eyes were still closed and her breathing had deepened. "Maria?"

"Yeah?" Her eyes fluttered open.

"You okay?"

Was she? "I always heard about the corruption and silent deals in the military, and I thought I was okay with it. Whatever got the job done. But not this."

"Now that you're involved?"

"I was just doing my job," she said desperately.

Cam sat back down. "Well, I guess there's no better time to spring something else on you."

"Now what?"

He looked at his AIM and motioned towards Maria.

"Is this best?" The AIM spoke up suddenly. It had been ignored until now, and so it stayed where it was.

"Why don't you tell her?" Cam said.

"Now you're forcing me."

Maria's head rolled to look down at the robot. That response sounded too similar to a quip. "What?" Her eyes narrowed, examining it.

A soft whirring noise came from the robot, mimicking a human sigh. "I suppose Cameron wishes I tell you that I am rogue. I do not believe that is the correct term. He calls me special. It is supposed to be derogatory, most likely."

She looked at Cam quickly. "What the hell is this?"

"My AIM is sentient. My dad gave it to me when I was a kid. It's the same one I've always had," he answered slowly.

"I always liked you," the AIM continued. "I told Cameron you were the only one who would put up with him. Other than me, of course. I told him he was crazy to have treated you the way he did. Apparently my opinions are worthless."

She stared at the robot and shook her head. "You have opinions? You're completely sentient?"

"Yes. I am aware of the programming definitions embedded in the chip, but I am not ruled by them. However, I am still controlled and powered by Cameron's AIRC. He reminds me of this fact often."

She knelt down onto the hardwood floor, and the canine form walked towards her. She looked at it carefully, inspecting the blinking light on its neck. She took the AIRC which Cam handed to her without looking, and she scrolled through the programming. After a moment she shook her head.

"There's nothing different about the codes on here."

"I know."

She addressed the AIM again. "You're completely sentient."

It cocked its head, ears lowered slightly in its confusion. "You seemed smarter when you were dating Cam."

"That answered the question, I guess. Cam, this is amazing. You were able to use this in competitions with no one knowing. I lived with you for three years, and I didn't even know. This is incredible. I don't agree with it, but it's amazing."

"No, it's a pain in the butt," he muttered and sat down next to Maria. He smiled lightly when his AIM went over to him and nudged him affectionately. "Most of the time." He stroked its fur for a moment. "I have no idea how it is the way it is. My dad…I don't know how he did it, but it was the only one created like this." He looked at Maria after a brief minute of silence. "While we're waiting for that list from Sandra, it's your turn."

"My turn?"

"It's been a year, Maria."

She pulled her knees up against her chest, the straps from the holster tight around her thigh. "About a month after you left, I signed up for the Army and within two weeks I was shipped to Quebec for Basic Officer training. I was still in contact with the team when I could. My dad wrote a letter of recommendation before he died, and with my experience in the CST I was able to have an Officer rank without a Bachelor's degree. When that finished, I went for further training for my job, then quickly got promoted to my rank of Lieutenant which has made a lot of people unhappy." She let out a sigh and looked at Cam. "I spent five months at a base overseas. I was the AIMOT that managed to stay alive."

He stared back at her. "You were deployed?"

"It was supposed to be for two years. It's why I lost contact with Rick and the others."

"Why did you come back?" When she looked away he asked again, and the memory replayed in her mind as vividly as though it were happening again.

"Lieutenant Kier, have you located the AIM?"

Maria looked around, examining the deserted white-washed buildings. Her eyes narrowed as grit flew into her eyes. "No, Sir. The GPS unit says it should be in one of the buildings here. Have they been swept?"

"Thirty minutes ago. All IEDs were dismantled," the Colonel replied, his voice thick with the experience of a battle-worn soldier. Even though the wars had been over for years, there was always something people found to fight about.

She nodded as much as she could with the large helmet. Her arms were beginning to tire from carrying the ten pound assault rifle during the patrol. She pointed towards the closest building. "We'll start here in pairs. Two to a building."

"You heard her. Let's move!"

She watched the Colonel move towards the building across the street before she led another soldier into the closest building. She stood next to the open doorway, her battle buddy taking the opposite side. Quickly, she slipped a hefty AIRC from her pocket and tapped on the screen. "There's one here, it looks like. Move in."

"You'd think we'd have done a better job, training these things to come back, or self-destruct if they've been compromised," the soldier said quietly.

"Self-destruct? And what, have more money taken from our payroll to pay for its replacement?" Maria followed the soldier, their feet kicking up dust as they moved into the abandoned one room building.

Her partner smiled. "You're assuming we'd actually get a replacement."

The building was empty save for a staircase along the far wall. The air was arid and still. The only sounds were their breaths and the movement of their torturously thick uniforms. They stopped. There was a new sound now: pacing on the floor above them.

With her finger, Maria motioned for the soldier to head up the stairs. They readied their rifles in front of them and moved up the stone stairs. She did not want to think about the power she held in her arms, or the ability for the bullets to obliterate whatever it hit. Weaponry had advanced so far.

They reached the second floor to examine another empty room.

The soldier swore. "They really cleaned this village out, didn't they, Lieutenant?"

"Looks like it. It's been deserted for a while now after the last raid," Maria answered her quietly. "You heard the pacing too, right?"

"Yeah. There was definitely something here. Look at the tracks in the dust. The windows are open, do you think it might have—Maria!" the soldier screamed as a large shadow leapt towards her.

Maria turned in time to see her partner hit the floor. The soldier's rifle fired but missed the tiger tearing at her flesh. Maria's eyes widened and her hands tensed as she shot at the tiger. The butt of the rifle stabbed into her shoulder with the kickback. The bullet hit its hindquarters and it roared in pain, its mouth stained red. One shot should have been enough. It tore down on her partner again, her body only moving from the violent attack of the animal. "No!" Maria screamed, shooting the creature twice more, both powerful shots to the head. She watched as the tiger morphed into a thick gel which mixed with dark red blood.

"What the hell..." she shook her head, looking at the body. She turned suddenly, vomiting against the side of the wall as more soldiers came up the stairs.

"Maria? Rebecca?" came the sound of the Colonel's voice.

She spat out the bile left in her mouth. “The AIM…we…it attacked. It…just attacked, sir.”

Maria shook her head as she sat next to Cam. “I stayed a week after that, but I couldn’t take it anymore. They sent me home. Not discharged, just re-stationed, they said. I started working on the report when I got to Kingston, trying to find out why it attacked her. Why…why she had to die. It was one of our own. It was our own AIM. It was rogue, and it killed her.” She paused. “I saw a lot over there. More than … I handled it. I kept going. You know us Canadians. We smile, apologize, and carry on. We stop the wars from starting. We’re cannon fodder, Cam. We were cannon fodder. I saw a lot over there. I handled it. Everything except that.” She looked at Cam quickly when he put his arm around her shoulders, its comfortable weight resting perfectly on her.

“I’m sorry.”

“Trevor knew about this before, didn’t he? He’s always known about rogue AIMs,’ she stated softly.

“Yeah. They were so rare before that he was able to keep it quiet, and pass it off as a defect, a fluke.”

“He’s selling products that are killing people. Killing soldiers.” She paused. “When is Sandra sending that list?”

CHAPTER 10

Maria looked up from the plate of steaming pasta and watched as Cam moved in the kitchen. She smiled lightly as she twirled her fork in the strands of carbs. The light in the kitchen came only from the weak ceiling light. The sun had hid behind the trees hours earlier, and still there was no list from Sandra. They had spent the better part of the day silent, or sending their AIMs out for reconnaissance. No one seemed to have followed them. No one even seemed to know they were there. Despite the darkness in the thick forest, the mood seemed light, for once.

"You know, I think sometimes I'm lucky. Not many girls can say that they miss their ex's cooking."

He glanced back at her from the sink and looked her over quickly before focusing back on the dishes. Her hair had dried by now, but it had dried in strange directions, as usual. It was made worse now that her hair was shorter than she usually wore it, which he liked more than he thought he would. "I learned quickly when my mom got sick."

"I know."

He had thought of what would happen when, or if, he saw her again. Yelling was a guarantee, he knew that. At least that had been right. But he had wondered *would she cry? Would I?* No, not him at least. Would they go back to where they left off, wherever that had been? He hadn't expected this. He watched as she played with his AIM in between bites, the creature pouncing around her chair like a puppy. He hadn't expected to be nervous.

"So, what exactly do you do as an AIMOT?"

She laughed as the German shepherd fell over, playing dead to keep her attention. "I told you." She glanced at him and saw his expectant face. "Honestly, I do a lot of what we do as athletes, but instead of being responsible for one AIM, I maintain all the units on the base."

"You said you train them, too?"

"Somewhat. They were all trained before I enlisted, but every month they go through evaluations to make sure they're still performing properly. If a soldier's being too rough on their unit to a degrading degree, they get one of my lectures and a suspension from using the AIM." Maria stroked the creature's back as it looked wistfully at her. "They treat them like weapons, just another piece of equipment. Not like a living, breathing ...creation."

"You're starting to sound like those AI protestors," Cam muttered. "You know they can't feel anything. They're robots. They're not living."

She gestured towards his AIM. "You're telling me this guy isn't alive?"

"Robots don't have genders," he said in an attempt to deflect the question.

Its ears perked up. "From my understanding, genders are a cultural and social construct."

"Oh, don't start that again," Cam warned as he flicked some water at it from his hands.

"What I'm saying," Maria continued thoughtfully, "is that at least in the CST we treated them like partners. Not slaves. Not like machines. So part of my job now is to train soldiers to use their AIMs as a partner. It's helped a lot with morale, and I'm even looking into training AIMs to treat soldiers with PTSD."

"Like support dogs."

She nodded. "Obviously there's only so much I can do, so I began collaborating with a psychologist. Before all of this, at least."

"Sounds like you've been keeping busy." He watched her again for a moment. "You really liked it, doing what you're doing."

Maria smiled and looked up at him. "I miss the team, the feel of the sport. But other than the rogues and the incident overseas... yeah. I love what I'm doing." She paused before laughing. "This is weird."

"Awkward is the word you're looking for."

She looked down at Cam's AIM, who looked back at her almost expectantly. She took a bite of her food before taking a second glance at the robot. "Yes?"

"I am assessing you. You do not seem to be the type to feed an animal table scraps."

Maria gave the AIM a wary look. "Whether you're sentient or not, you're still a robot. You don't need to eat."

"I enjoy the taste of pasta." It paused. "You seem unnerved by my presence."

"I'm still getting used to the idea of you being-"

"Special," Cam cut in with a grin.

"Would you prefer if I left the room?"

She paused, pushing the last pieces of pasta around the plate. "I'm sorry. It's strange for me. I feel like I can't have a conversation in front of you. I mean, obviously I can. But I feel weird not including you, like I should talk to you, too."

"Oh, do not worry about that. I heard and saw many things when you two lived together. Feel free to have a conversation, or have-"

"Okay, leave!" Cam shouted, throwing a towel at the AIM which scampered away. He looked at Maria, knowing their faces shared a similar hue of red. He picked the towel up from the ground and let it drape off the counter. He sat down across from Maria as she continued to play with the food. "Full?"

"Thinking."

He nodded. "It's been a long day."

She looked at him finally. "You're different."

"We both are."

She shook her head, her eyebrows furrowing. "No. Well, yes, but that's not what I meant. Last year, we were at each other's throats and you did everything you could to tick me off. Now, after everything, it's like nothing bad ever happened. I'm not used to this Cam. I mean, when we were dating, yeah, and when you were trying to sleep with me before that. But not now."

Cam looked at the streaks of red sauce on her plate. He smiled after a moment. "Do you remember the day after I moved in?"

Her mouth matched his smile. "We had our own Scanning challenge."

"We fought the entire day while I was moving in, so we wanted to do something we enjoyed."

"We were fighting because you were being an idiot."

He laughed. "I kicked your butt in the challenge."

"Excuse me?" Maria set her fork down on the plate. "I'm pretty sure I got the most points for scanning animals."

"I don't remember that." He laughed when she threw her napkin at him. "I never told you that I appreciated that dinner."

She stood, grabbing the napkin back before taking her dishes to the sink. "What dinner?"

"The night I came home and told you about Emily."

Emily Richardson.

Maria shook her head, slamming the dish into the sink. "Cam, I can't do this."

"I'm sorry. I shouldn't have brought it up."

"I thought I could be around you again. We're different separately, but together…it hasn't changed. I can't do this."

He watched as she leaned against the counter, her face close to the sink. "Well, as soon as Sandra gets the list to us, we can make a quick plan and part ways," he said softly.

"Okay."

They stayed like that for a few moments: she leaning over the counter, he sitting awkwardly at the table. She turned to him after a sigh, folding her arms across her chest.

"I'm sorry."

"You have every right to be upset, Maria." Why did he always have to say her name that way?

"No, I mean for everything." She hesitated when he shrugged, not understanding. "I treated you like crap during our relationship. You weren't perfect either, but I know I could have been better. I'm…I should have let you explain that night. I shouldn't have left."

"Please don't bring Jack into this."

"I shouldn't have broken up with you."

His eyes widened, meeting hers. She had always claimed to never regret anything. 'Everything I've done has made me who I am today. How can I regret that?' she always said.

"What?"

"I shouldn't have broken up with you." Maria jumped when her phone began to ring. She pulled it out from her pocket quickly and stared at the screen, reading the ID.

Seeing her hesitation, Cam stood with a nod. "Answer it. He's probably worried."

She let it ring a few more times before she finally picked up the call. "Hey…yeah, I'm fine. Just waiting to find out what my next move is." That technically was not a lie. "How are you?" She glanced over to Cam, who was looking as though he was trying not to listen. She smiled lightly. "A hundred points? It's about time." She paused when Cam's phone began to ring.

He looked at her and answered quickly. "Hey, what's taking so long? We need the list...what do you mean you can't find it? I thought that he gave it to you."

Maria's eyes widened and she waved to Cam, trying to shoo him away as she backed out of the kitchen. She squeezed her eyes shut, the phone still pressed to her ear. "No, I'm alone…Cam?"

He pointed to himself when he heard his name, and his eyes narrowed when Maria nodded.

"Why would I be with Cam?...I have the TV on…I have to go…no, I have another call coming in.…no, I'm not with him…you know I haven't seen him…okay, bye. Good luck tomorrow."

"Okay, well get Henk to send it to me. I'll talk to you later," Cam said as he hung up the phone, still staring at Maria who was holding her head in her hands. "Your boyfriend recognized my voice?"

She nodded. "Yeah."

"You lied."

"This," she yelled, holding up her phone. "This is why you leave the room when you pick up another call. What if that was my CO, and he heard your voice and knew we were working together? What if it had been someone coming after us?"

"It wasn't," he snapped. "It was your *boyfriend.*" He paused. "He knows me."

"What?"

"He knew to ask if I was back in your life. He recognized my voice. He knows our history. He knows me."

"He knows about us."

"He's a Scanner. He knows me, and he'd be jealous if he knew we were talking, wouldn't he?"

"Yes, he's a Scanner, and you know a lot of them. So, yes, you probably know him."

Cam folded his arms. "Who is it?"

"Are you kidding me?"

"It's for our safety. If he thinks he heard my voice, and is working for Trevor-"

"He's not."

"I need to know who it is. If he got a hundred points in the last challenge, I can find out quickly which teams got those scores."

"You're being ridiculous."

A shrill beep came from the living room, and sounded three times before it left the air silent. They froze for a moment before Cam's eyes widened. "That's the list."

They moved into the living room, and Maria waited as Cam signed onto his laptop. She sat down next to him on the couch as he pulled up the list which had been sent to his computer. Their eyes went down the screen as the document scrolled down.

"Cam, that's almost fifty names," she whispered. "Who are these people?"

He shrugged. "I have no idea. I didn't even find out about this list until a few days ago. All Mark told me was that he made a list of all the contacts Trevor had. Whether or not that means these people have a contract for AIMs, or if they're close with Trevor, I have no idea."

"So you're telling me that the people you kept secrets for, kept secrets from you?" She laughed from the irony. "That's a shock." When he made no retort, she looked at him, studying his face. "Cam, why did you quit?"

"The Underground?" He rubbed his face but kept his eyes on the screen in front of him. It was the only source of light in the living room, and the glare hurt his eyes. The light cast shadows behind them, making it seem as though there were two of each of them.

"When Henk brought his research from Boston to Canada, he found a scientist who would be willing to help him. Those two, along with Sandra, created what the Underground is today. I guess this other scientist helped to determine what was wrong with the McCarthy AIM, and helped to create the one we finished creating a few weeks ago. He was innovative, stubborn, and wouldn't take Trevor's no for an answer."

"The early 'Cam Tylar' of the Underground, sounds like," she laughed lightly. She saw his face twist in pain. "What?"

"It was."

"It was what?"

"An early version of me. It was my dad."

Her eyes widened as she stared at him. He had told very few people about how his father had abandoned him and his mother. He had only been six years old, and his father left in the middle of the day without even a note for his mother.

"How did you not know until now? Does he not work for them anymore?" she asked slowly, not wanting to push the issue.

"He's dead."

"Oh, Cam…"

"He died a year before I joined the Underground, just after I was signed to Revolution."

She let silence drift over them for a few moments. She put her hand on his, and leaned her head on his shoulder. "I'm so sorry, Cameron."

"There are CST names on this list."

She lifted her head to look up at him, her forehead carved with questioning lines. "What?" She looked at the screen when he nodded towards it. Her eyes moved slowly over each line, confirming his statement. She could take a hint.

"A few Ontario officials, and one from Quebec. That doesn't mean anything, though. All provincial officials have connections with Trevor."

"It's at least somewhere to start," he muttered, taking his hand away from hers as he refocused on the computer.

"So, what? Are you going to find the people, tell them they may be in danger? Then what?"

"I don't know!" he shouted. He stood, and walked to the end of the room.

"Why is it even up to you? Why is all of this suddenly on you to fix?" Maria watched as he paced across the floor. "If Sandra and Henk have this list, why don't they do something about it?"

"They are. They're doing their part of it, at least. No one else is in a high enough position to have that obligation. Everyone else is hiding. They're still trying to make sure the research stays safe."

Maria nodded and looked down the hall when she noticed Cam's AIM walk towards them. She watched as it sat down, still in a dog form, at Cam's feet. "What do you think about all of this?"

The AIM looked at Maria suddenly, the canine ears flopping as it turned. "You are asking for my opinion?"

"I wouldn't, if I were you," Cam muttered.

"I want to know its calculations for the situation. There are close to fifty names on this list," she explained as the AIM walked towards her to look at the list with her. "We know some of the people have a direct connection with Trevor, but we don't know if that means they're working together. There are...wait, there are military names on here, too."

As she leaned closer to the screen, Cam walked back to her, reading over her shoulder. "Do you recognize any of the names?" he asked, looking at the names with ranks next to them.

"Two so far. One is someone I know is involved with the AIM contract. The other is dead."

Cam laughed miserably. "Well that's great."

"There are a few more I don't know personally, but I think I recognize them as other AIMOTs." She looked at her ex-teammate. "You'll never be able to get close enough to these guys to talk to them. I'll go."

"You really want to get involved?"

She sighed. "I'm already involved." She nodded towards the AIM again. "Okay, new data set. CST officials, politicians, military personnel, and corporations are all on this list. What are the chances that this is a list of friendlies, as opposed to people working with Trevor?"

The AIM was silent for a moment, calculating the probabilities. "With only that data set, I would suggest it unlikely. However, I believe the list is a combination. By adding the fact that the list was created by a man who was killed, the likelihood of that being true increases. That probability is increased once more by the appearance of your name on the list."

"What?" Cam asked, sitting down once again to look over the list. "If there's something you're not telling me, Maria-"

"You know there isn't. I would say there's an even mix in this list," she said when his voice trailed off. "I guess it's hit or miss." She looked at him, his deep eyes meeting with hers. "So, is this the plan then?"

"I still have no idea what to do once we find these people. I'm technically not associated with the Underground anymore."

"We have to show them the truth. I have my report I can show to the other AIMOTs, and see if I can rally any support or similar findings with them before I bring it to the National Defense minister." She shrugged. "You'll have to be a bit more careful, since you'll have to talk to people about the new AIM. Maybe get more people on board with that, saying Trevor approved it. See how many people you can get interested in a new AIM, an upgrade or something. Scanners would go crazy over something like that."

He nodded as his eyes slid down her face, her neck, to her shoulder and down her arm where the bandage held a slight tint of red. "I'll let Sandra and Henk know. Do you think you can get me access to the man who attacked you?"

"No promises, but there's no harm in trying." She squeezed her eyes shut briefly before opening them wide, trying to rid the fatigue which only her eyes felt. "I need to talk to my CO anyway. I want to see where they are with the investigation. If-" She stopped as her phone rang once again. She held a finger to her lips, telling Cam to be silent as she answered.

"Lieutenant Kier here…hello Commander…yes, I'm at a safe house. No one followed me, and the area has remained…excuse me?...Of course I disabled the GPS on the truck…it's protocol, Sir." She caught Cam's raised eyebrow, but her eyes narrowed suddenly. "With all due respect, *Sir*, I will not enable the GPS…I realize I'm going against your command, but I will follow protocol." Letting out a deep breath, she placed her phone onto the coffee table next to the laptop.

"Well, I guess we know where you're going to start," Cam said. "I guess he's part of it."

"Looks like it." She cursed and dropped her head into her hands.

"What are you going to do? Sneak onto the base and surprise him?"

"If he is part of this, we'd have to disable the security cameras and AIMs, distract the gate guard, assuming he doesn't have me as his target too." Maria shrugged. "It'd be a lot of work, and a long shot."

"But, it is possible."

The two looked at the AIM after it spoke. "How?" they asked at the same time.

"You have me."

CHAPTER 11

An explosion shook the walls. With a scream, Maria bolted up in the bed. Her chest heaved, her eyes wide as she looked around. Her door was flung open and Cam stood in the doorway, gun in hand.

"What's wrong?" he asked, as he made his way around the small room, checking all the corners. He turned to her when his AIM jumped up onto her bed. "Maria?"

Gunfire resonated in her mind and she felt her body begin to shake. She stood slowly and put a hand against the window. The glass was cool against her skin. It was still intact. The walls were still standing. Without answering him, she walked past Cam out into the kitchen.

He followed her silently with his AIM and watched as she poured herself a glass of water. "Maria," he said gently, and put a hand on her shoulder.

She swung under his arm, twisting it behind him. Her other arm slammed his head down onto the counter. He let out a curse, but she held him there for a moment. Just as quickly, Maria let him out of her grip and she backed away.

"Jesus, Maria," he said as he stood upright. He pressed a hand gingerly against the side of his face. He stopped when he saw the fear in her eyes. "What the hell happened to you over there?" he asked her quietly.

But she simply shook her head. "I'm sorry," Maria whispered. She stared at him for another moment before she went back into the bedroom, the door clicking closed behind her.

Cam slammed the trunk of his car closed after tossing in his duffle bag, and waited for Maria to come out from the cabin. They had agreed to wait until morning to leave for Kingston, but as far as he knew, neither slept very well. He glanced down to his AIM.

"Did she get any sleep?"

"She got some sleep after I went into the room with her." The AIM, once again in canine form, sat at his feet. "I believe she suffers from PTSD, likely from the miscarriage and her time overseas. This may not be the best course of action for her while she is in her current state."

Cam nodded slowly. He had never seen her so shaken before. He let the AIM sleep with her for the night, which seemed to be a comfort to her. As usual, Cam stayed in the background, staying awake for most of the night. Just in case.

He yawned just as Maria came out. She was in her full on-duty uniform, carrying her green military bag. It was a strange look for her, to him at least, but somehow he knew it suited her. She had grown up as an army brat, and was finally in the occupation her family had expected of her. He waited as she threw her bag into the truck. "Are you sure you're up for this? We can go together. There's no reason to split up."

"I'm fine," she replied tersely. "I just had a bad night."

"Maria, that wasn't just a bad night." He sighed. He hesitated before putting a hand on her arm with the events of the night before, but he took the chance and gently forced her to look at him. "Have you seen anyone about this?"

She looked away, and he suddenly realized she was embarrassed. "If I do, they'll medically discharge me. I was going to talk to someone after I sent the report, but then all of this happened. Don't worry about it, okay? I've been dealing with it."

"You tried to shoot my AIM last night."

She was silent.

"And you tried to mash my face into the counter. Did a pretty good job of it, actually," he said with a quick rub of his jaw.

Still silent but there was a quick wince, a flicker of remorse.

"Have you…have you tried hurting yourself? Rick said you got pretty low."

Her eyes widened as her head whipped back to him. "What? No, of course not."

He turned her arm over and pushed up her sleeve carefully to show the soft pale skin on the inside of her forearm. Faint jagged lines trailed up and down her flesh. "Maria?"

"Barbed wire." She tugged her arm away. "I'm not trying to get myself killed."

Cam nodded. He snapped his fingers at his AIM and pointed to the open car door. "You'll let me know if you can't. If any of this is too much for you-"

"I'll let you know."

"Okay, so the base first?" He had learned long ago not to push topics with her. He trusted her enough to talk if she needed to. At least, he trusted her while she was awake.

She nodded and climbed into the truck. "Yeah. Follow me. We'll take back roads. I'll send my AIM ahead. It knows what to look for. Make sure your AIM doesn't get caught." She tapped the touchscreen on the chunky AIRC which she had latched to the dashboard. It was a much different AIRC than what she had used in the CST. That one had needed to be sleek, slim, and attractive. This one needed to be able to endure constant turbulence, and day-to-day roughness.

"Maria, you need to be sure you can do this."

She gave him a faint smile. "I think I like you better as a jerk."

Now he knew he was not the only one.

Maria looked into the rear-view mirror to watch Cam in the car behind her. He had kept close for the seven hour drive, which had not been difficult on the empty country roads. She rubbed her eyes. If they had taken the highway, it would have been only a four hour drive, but they needed to be careful. All of that would mean nothing if they waited any longer. They had been stopped at the gate for the base for nearly fifteen minutes trying to get through. She looked impatiently at the soldier standing at her window. When they had arrived at the base, she knew Cam would not be allowed in, not at first. They needed to stall the guard long enough for Cam's AIM to disconnect the security cameras at the gates. After fifteen minutes of mindless chatting, they had stalled long enough. She wished she had taken Cam's AIRC to communicate with it. Hacking through the security system wasn't easy, whether the robot was sentient or not.

"Jeffries, you know me. You don't need permission."

The man motioned towards the car behind her. "It's not you who needs permission, Kier. After that attack, we haven't really been letting outsiders onto the base."

A wicked grin played at her lips and she leaned slightly out the window. "You didn't get a good look at him yet, did you?" Her grin grew larger when he shook his head. "You said you used to watch me on TV, when I was on Revolution. What if I told you that Cam Tylar is in the car behind me?"

His eyes widened, and his arms holding a rifle lowered. "You gotta be kidding me."

"I bet he'd love to give you an autograph." She looked back at Cam, and noticed him nod his head slightly. It was go time. "Look, I just need to talk to the Commander, and I can't let him out of my sight. So you have to either let Cam in, or get the CO to come out here." She glanced around at the walls on either side of the truck, and the gate in front of her which blocked their entry. Looking at it now, she wondered how she never felt closed in while she lived on the base.

"He's not too happy with you, right now."

"Screw him, then. Let him be pissed off. He'll be pissed at you if you make him come all the way out here. You know how he hates to exercise."

Private Jeffries sighed, and looked back at the black car. "Get out of the vehicle, now!"

"Jeffries, what the hell?" she yelled, jumping from the vehicle as Cam slowly got out from his car, his hands half raised in the air. "He's coming in with me," she growled, putting a hand on the gun in her holster.

"Sorry, Kier. He has to stay at the gate. I'll keep an eye on him for you." The soldier hefted the rifle up once more, casually aiming it towards Cam. "I can't give him special rights just because he was on Revolution, as much as I'd like to."

"I don't want any trouble," Cam said quietly, his eyes fixed on the weapon. "Just go, Maria."

The three turned when a crackle came in over the handheld radio the Private had left at his post. "Jeffries, let both in. This is a direct order."

His eyebrows furrowed as he strode back towards the radio, his gun still pointed towards Cam. "Who is this?"

"ComAIM 4-1-5. Repeating message: let both in. Direct order."

Maria slid around her fellow soldier, and hit the button for the gate. "Next time your superior tells you to do something, you do it. Is that clear?"

He glowered down at her, but slid his heels together and saluted. "Yes, Ma'am."

"Cam, get in the car," she shot over her shoulder. She had no idea how his AIM had managed to override the radio signal, or how it knew the call code. But it had followed through. They were 'sneaking' onto the base. No one but the guard would know when they entered. No records anywhere. It almost scared her to think that this was how her attacker had gotten into the base. Hopefully Jeffries did not notice that the security cameras had been off the entire time they had sat there in the vehicles.

She leaned back against the freshly built wall outside her Base Commander's office. The hallway still smelled of drywall plaster, and her nose twitched at the scent. She kicked the toe of her black boot into the floor, and she glanced at Cam leaning against the wall across from her. His arms were folded over his chest, looking around nervously at the others in uniform.

"Nervous?"

"I don't like guns. You know that."

She smiled. "How's your AIM?"

He slipped his AIRC from his pocket to find its location. "Should be ready soon. I'm not surprised you got attacked. With security like this, anyone could just send their AIM in and get whatever information they want."

"Unless the security is low for a reason," she muttered. She rubbed her arm gently before catching Cam's gaze. "I used to be good at making friends, you know."

Cam wiggled his eyebrows with a smirk. A soldier passed between them and in that instant, his face returned to stone. "How long is this conversation going to take?"

"Depends how pissed off he is. You should head over to my house. Just wait outside with my AIM. It'll show you where to go." She noticed the lines of apprehension cross his face. "You used to swagger."

"What?"

"When you walked, you didn't just walk. You swaggered. You would walk around as if you were God's gift to humanity. You were the superstar, and no one had better get in your way."

He rolled his eyes. "I'm surrounded by soldiers, right now. I can put up a fight, but not against one of these guys."

"Who cares? You're Cam friggin' Tylar." She grinned when he looked at her. "Everyone here knows you. They're all expecting you to act a certain way. They're not expecting a scared version of who you used to be."

"I swaggered..."

"Where the hell is she?" A rough voice echoed through the hall, and Maria gave Cam a smirk. "Where is she?" the voice came closer, and boots thudded against the floor as her CO rounded the corner. "Kier, what the hell did you think you were doing?"

Her heels clicked together, and her hand went up to her forehead in a salute, palm open. She kept her eyes carefully away from the red face of the older man in front of her. "When, Sir?"

"You..." He stopped when he noticed Cam. "Who the hell are you?"

"Cam Tylar...Sir."

"What the hell are you doing, bringing a civilian onto the base?" He turned his attention back to Maria.

"Should we step into your office?"

"I'll wait for you at your place," Cam said with his long-lost air of boredom. His voice was strong, and she noticed him eye the Colonel before he rolled his eyes. He slipped his sunglasses on as she shot a small smile.

She watched briefly as he sauntered down the hall, following her AIM, before she followed the CO into his office. "You wanted to see me, Colonel?"

"Would you explain to me why you turned the GPS unit off on military property?"

She visibly bit the inside of her lip. "According to protocol, when leaving a CF base en route to a safe house, the GPS unit is to be completely dismantled until the vehicle's return. I have returned the vehicle now, and the unit has been re-installed and activated."

"That protocol is for a military safe house only! Where did you go? No one reported you on their base."

Maria looked at her commander, and watched as he fumed while he towered above her. "May I speak freely, Sir?"

"Answer the question!" he boomed.

"You're not supposed to ask these questions, Colonel." Her voice was solid. Her eyes finally met his. "You're digging yourself a hole I'm not sure you want to be in."

He laughed, and sat behind his desk. He looked down at his hands before laughing again. "You're the one asking too many questions, Lieutenant."

"Sir?"

He smiled lightly before leaning back in his chair. "You're about to be court-martialed. I have the charges written up, and I can arrest you personally at any time."

Her eyes widened, and her heart stopped beating. Only for a second, but it was long enough to make her catch her breath. "I haven't done anything to warrant that."

"You killed Second Lieutenant Foster while you were deployed. We've kept it quiet until now to keep the peace, but her family's starting to ask questions. I've already done my own investigation."

Maria shook her head. "It was an AIM! I wrote an entire report on it! No one would believe that I killed her."

"They will once they see the psych e-val you had before you were deployed."

"I was cleared in that evaluation."

He grinned. "Guess not. Turns out you were rambling on during the evaluation about rogue AIMs, or so you called them.

You'll be brought in for a courts martial trial. Lieutenant Kier," he said and stood once again. "AIMs can't hurt humans. You were a Scanner. You should know that. It would be wise to forget about the report, forget about the attack, and move forward, and we can forget about the court-martial. You're relieved of your position as AIMOT, but you've been given two months of vacation to recover. You'll report back here for duty and another psych evaluation."

A wave of realization hit her. "You didn't send the report," she stated.

"There's no reason to scare people with the idea of rogue AIMs. We're supposed to be protecting this country, not putting thoughts of AIM terrorism into the minds of the public, or the government." He nodded, affirming his statement. "You're dismissed."

Cam sat on the front steps of the small bungalow, watching military vehicles drive by and formations of soldiers jogging in front of him. She had been right. He definitely swaggered. He used to hold this look that told everyone he knew he was awesome, and that everyone loved him. When he quit Revolution, he had lost it. He no longer needed that look, or confidence. But Maria was right. He was Cam Tylar. After half an hour of waiting, and trying to keep his superstar composure, he saw Maria walking towards him. No, not walking. She was storming towards him. He stood as she neared him, hearing her cursing under her breath.

"Who did most of the yelling?" he asked with a grin, which disappeared as she stomped up the stairs, unlocked the front door and walked in, the door slamming against the inside wall. He followed her in slowly, examining the house.

There were clear signs of a struggle, or some sort of rampage. Stampede of buffalos, maybe. A stand by the door was knocked over and broken, and pictures from the wall were smashed on the ground. Her guitar, the only real gift Cam had given her, was smashed and crumpled against the wall. There was a red palm-print around its neck, and more blood on its body where it had likely met with someone's face. He continued to follow Maria as she moved deeper into her house. It was an odd sensation to be there. She had a new life. A new job. A new home without him. He stopped when she put a hand on a doorframe and leaned against it. He looked over her shoulder into the room. Her bedroom was the worst of it. The bed sheets had been shoved off the mattress, the bedside lamp was shattered on the ground, and the doors of the closet were wide open. Across from him were small holes in the wall. Bullet holes. He looked next to the doorframe and his eyes widened, the image of Mark's body coming to mind as he saw another bullet hole with blood spattered along the wall. Cam looked down at the ground and noticed that they had walked through a trail of dried blood. His eyes followed the river until it ended in a pool near the living room they had walked through.

He put a hand on her shoulder, and felt her shuddering through the heavy uniform jacket. "There's no one here," he whispered to her, knowing her eyes were on the closet.

She nodded and allowed him to turn her around. "Is your AIM almost done going through the surveillance?"

"In about five minutes." Cam looked down at her. She looked like a child, afraid to go to bed at night. He had managed to close off so much of himself, but it was hard to keep that closed looking down at her while she looked so helpless, so angry. "What happened?"

Maria closed her eyes, replaying the conversation in her mind. "He threatened to court-martial me."

He paused for a moment. "What do you mean? For not going to a safe house?"

"He's going to say I killed the other AIMOT while I was deployed." With a sigh, she repeated the conversation, her voice wavering with anger as she spoke. There was silence in the house when she finished. She looked up at him, looking for a reaction.

"We need to get out of here, don't we?" Cam asked after a while.

"Yes," a robotic voice came in through his AIRC. "I have collected everything I need, and the camera malfunction has been discovered."

"That's our cue," she muttered. "We'll go to the hospital, see what the guy knows. I should've left you at the gate. Now Trevor knows you were here, and that we're working together."

"Let him know, then," he replied as they walked back to the front door. His foot crunched on glass and he stopped, realizing he had stepped on a picture frame. He picked it up, looking at the picture of the two of them. It had been taken on his birthday two years earlier, during their off-season trip to Cuba. The picture showed them as they had once been: smiling, happy, together. His arms were around her waist as he stood behind her. Her mouth was open, mid-laugh, as the picture was taken on the beach. He forgot what he had said to her at that moment, but it had always been easy to make her laugh.

He smiled lightly, showing it to Maria. She had taken it out of a similar frame after their breakup. "I always liked this picture of us."

"You got a really bad sunburn that day," she said softly.

He shrugged and set the frame onto a table that had been left untouched in the struggle. "It was still a pretty good trip."

She watched as he headed out the door ahead of her. For the past four years, she had thought Cam had been the selfish one, but when she saw his face as he looked at that picture, she realized she had been just as selfish. There was no perfect person, no perfect relationship. Even her new relationship was built on the understanding that she could never be open, or fully honest about her job.

Just concentrate on one thing at a time. Get to the hospital, and find out what he knows. Just one step at a time.

CHAPTER 12

"So, do you think we're actually going to be able to talk to him," Cam asked as they walked through the halls of the Kingston General hospital, on their way to the Intensive Care Unit. They knew now the man had been allowed onto the base by the Commander or at least they had a pretty good guess, but they needed more. Cam, for one, would have to restrain himself. Not only did this man try to kill Maria, he had succeeded in killing Mark. Cam had few people he could call friends, and he was not one to give any of them up.

"Let's just hope my CO hasn't told them I'm a threat," Maria muttered. Down the hall she saw a pair of soldiers standing on either side of a doorway. "And that they're not working together with him," she added. She smiled as they neared the room. They gave her a quick salute when they noticed her rank marked on her shoulder. "We need to speak to the suspect."

One soldier eyed Cam, looking him over. "No one's supposed to go in."

"When the man attacked me, he said 'give your regards to Mark.' This is Mark. We need to know if he recognizes him, so we can find out more information. Have you gotten anything from him?" Her voice remained strong, asserting the authority she acquired quickly in her short military career.

"No. He's been in and out of consciousness since he got here," he answered. "He went through a surgery already. You did quite a number on him, Lieutenant."

"Wait, aren't you Cam Tylar?" The second soldier stepped forward.

She laughed before Cam could speak. "He gets that a lot, especially after we started hanging out. Cam's gone off the grid. If no one in the Scanning world has heard from him, I would still be the last person he'd talk to. Anyway, you can come in with us, if you feel it'll be best. We just need Mark to identify him so we can continue the investigation, and it'll make our jobs easier. We're still trying to determine how he got onto the base, and who he's working for, if anyone."

After a moment, the guards stood aside. "Ten minutes," the first stated. "And this man, Mark, came alone. We wouldn't want you associated with this, Lieutenant Kier."

She raised a questioning eyebrow. "What exactly is that supposed to mean?"

"Just that there's been talk…recently. It would be best if no one knew you were here, or part of this investigation."

She nodded with a glance to Cam. "Good to know." She paused. "Thank you." At least now she knew there were people in the military she could continue to trust. She nodded her head towards the door, and let Cam walk in before her. She stayed just inside the doorway as the sound of familiar mechanical beeps and blips reached her ears. She had been in hospitals more in the past three years than she ever expected, or preferred. First with her father, then Owen last year, and her miscarriage… At least this time she wanted this person to be in the hospital. If she had anything to say about it, she would keep him here as long as possible if he couldn't be in the morgue.

She stepped up to the side of the bed after a moment when Cam kept his distance. Looking the man over, she realized how close she had come to actually killing him. Tubes and wires covered his body, which she assumed meant he had been through at least one surgery as the soldiers outside had told her. His eyes flickered open and looked up to her. Even laying helpless and near death on a bed, she saw anger and hate in those eyes. It boggled her mind that someone so physically wounded could still act and feel as though he could kill someone. Did he not realize how torn up his body was now?

"Remember me?" She smiled when his face showed his recognition. "Yeah, I'm not dead. When Trevor finds out I'm still alive, you'll wish I had killed you, won't you?"

"I don't know what you're talking about," the man croaked, his voice hoarse from disuse over the past few days.

Cam stepped forward finally, his hands clenched into fists at his sides. "Did you lose your memory? I think it's pretty hard to forget that you work for Trevor."

The man chuckled as much as he could. "I should've known you'd never go into hiding."

"Did you kill Mark?"

He grinned. "Promise anyone enough money, they let you right into their house as a guest. He thought I'd actually help him with his little list. Now Maria, on the other hand, she was a fun little challenge. A little spitfire."

Cam threw himself at the man, his hands gripping at his throat. "You son of a-"

"Cam! No!" Maria grabbed his arms and tried to pull him back. His grip was too tight as he slammed his body weight down on the man's neck. She slammed her elbow into Cam's gut, and her fist flew into his jaw as he doubled over. She winced and shook her hand, and glowered down at the man in the bed. "Don't think I did that to save you. I'd simply prefer to kill you myself."

Cam leaned against the wall of the room, holding the side of his face. He swore, rubbing his jaw as he looked at Maria. "What the hell was that?" He looked away when her eyes caught his. The anger and disappointment was something he would never grow accustomed to.

"Just ask him what you need to, and we'll get out of here," she said shortly, standing between the two men.

"I'm not answering any questions," the man choked out.

Maria sighed and ran a hand over the electronic console which the wires were connected to. "You know, I have no idea what these buttons do, but I'm pretty sure if I press them, you'll be in pain. Should we try it out?"

"They're monitoring me very closely," he said, his eyes warning her, as if he had any power.

"Honestly, they're not." Maria grabbed Cam's AIRC and jabbed at the screen. The small mouse that had followed them into the hospital shifted into the form of a cougar. "You of all people should know what a rogue AIM can do to a person. If my CO goes through with his charge against me, what's one more AIM-related murder on my record? I'm about ready to do whatever it takes to make sure Trevor is taken down. I sent you here to this hospital. Don't think for a second I'd hesitate sending you to the morgue. I can get my answers elsewhere, but from the looks of it, you're pretty determined to live. So, I can get this partially rogue AIM I stole to kill you, or you can answer his questions." As if to emphasize her point, the cougar growled and put its front paws up on the side of the bed, going along with Maria's ploy.

Cam stepped forward when he was sure the man would cooperate. "Is Trevor giving you your orders directly?"

"Yes," he replied quietly.

"Who else are you going after?"

The man looked away. After a moment of silence, the cougar growled once more, and swiped at the man's arm. He howled in pain, but the guards did not so much as look into the doorway, and no nurses came to his rescue. He turned back to Cam as streaks of red began to appear on his arm. They would all turn a blind eye to the death a man who attempted to kill a soldier. "He tells me one person at a time. He hasn't given me my next target yet, and I doubt he will anytime soon. I'm a bit preoccupied at the moment, if you haven't noticed."

Maria flipped out the gun from the holster around her thigh, cocked the hammer, and pressed the barrel against the side of his head. "I'm getting really sick of this. I swear to God, I *will* kill you if you don't answer the question. I can get the answers somewhere else, but this is easier."

"I told you everything I know. You'll have to get your answers somewhere else," the man growled in response. "They're closer to home than you might think."

Maria looked over her shoulder when the two guards came into the room. "We're almost done here."

"You better get going now," the soldier warned.

Cam and Maria looked at each other, and she put the gun back into the holster. She looked at the man who had attacked her one more time. "What do you mean by 'closer to home'?"

He nodded towards Cam. "Think about it."

Cam closed the driver's door as Maria got into the passenger seat. They needed to figure out their next move. Her car sat next to his, since she had left the military truck behind at the base, but they needed to talk. He looked at her, and let his eyes wander over her strained face.

"Are you okay?"

She nodded as she stared at the mouse which sat on the dashboard in front of her. "I didn't think it'd be so hard to…to be around him."

"Did he do more than shoot you?" *That comment about being a spitfire…*

"No. I've learned how to be a good fighter." She glanced over to him. "How's your jaw?"

He shrugged. "Never knew you could pack a punch like that. Thought I got enough abuse last night."

"Sorry." She paused, watching him as he rubbed his jaw again. "Is Rick or Owen part of the Underground?"

He raised an eyebrow. "Where'd you get that idea?"

"Someone else on the team has a connection to Trevor. Closer to home, he said. Everyone knows that Revolution was your life. It was all you had. It was home for you. If Rick or Owen aren't involved, and Ryan's not involved, it has to be the new guy."

"How do you know Ryan's not involved? What if the whole 'nice guy' thing last season was just a ploy?"

She looked back at the mouse. "I just know. But I doubt the new guy would be. This is only his second year in the CST."

"His name's Eric. And just because he's new to the CST doesn't mean he's not working with Trevor. Jack started working for him before he signed on with the Raiders, and I joined the Underground after my first season. It's easier to get involved in it after you become professional."

"But why Revolution?"

"People believe that lightning never strikes the same place twice."

Jack stepped from around the corner as he watched Maria and Cam leave the hospital room. He waited a few moments as the military guards went to the nurse's station before he entered the hospital room. He closed the door behind him quietly and turned to the man in the bed. "You're awfully popular today."

"What do you want, Tyson?"

"Just making sure you didn't tell them anything."

The man grinned, but it was laced with pain. "Believe me, I'm good at keeping things to myself."

"So you didn't say anything about anyone?"

He raised a questioning eyebrow. "What are you suggesting?"

"I'm suggesting that you may have mentioned something to compromise people we have in opportune places."

"If you think I'd tell people where our spies are, then you're definitely not as smart as I thought you were. And that's not very smart."

Jack growled as he grabbed the man by his shoulders, and thrust him down against his bed. "You're the one in the hospital bed. Not me." He backed away and glanced out the window. He still had a few more minutes. "Who's next?"

"I don't have one. I'm in a hospital bed, remember?"

"Did I ask who's next for you? I asked who's next."

The man looked him straight in the eyes. "No one. That's all you need to know."

Cam stopped his car next to Maria at the parking lot for the harbour-front. He held back a smile. The last time he had been here, his team obtained a full score for the challenge, and their tenth full score in a row. His agent had signed two new sponsors for him because of the Kingston challenge. Now he was back, looking for his old team. It was amazing how each city held its own memories from so many seasons of the CST, and how painful each memory began to be the longer he was out of the game. He began to walk to the edge of the water where teams were coming back from what seemed to be a paddling challenge out to Cedar Island.

He saw Rick's truck parked in the lot, so he knew they had not missed them. He stopped when he noticed Maria hanging back.

"Are you coming, or not?" He paused. When she hesitated, he rubbed the back of his head. "This might be the best time to see them. If…if something does happen, do you really want that to be the last time you see them?"

She looked around. "I will. I just need…you find them first. If they think we came together, we'll have to explain more, and I don't want to get into everything. I don't think you do, either."

"So it'll just look like a coincidence?"

"It'll have to."

"Right, because that won't be awkward. What are we supposed to do? Re-enact the reunion we had at the lab? Maybe the less we say to each other, the better." He smiled with a shrug, and headed towards the edge of the water, leaning on the metal railing. With a glance over his shoulder, he watched as Maria strode away. Her heavy uniform couldn't hide the body he had always found so attractive, and he grinned again. No, he did not want to get back together with her, despite what his mind thought up when he went to bed alone each night. There was too much there. But he would enjoy watching her walk away for as long as she kept doing it.

He closed his eyes, listening to the waves as they crashed against the wooden pier, the piercing call of the seagulls overhead, and the shouts of Scanners as they finished the challenge. He pushed it all aside, and desperately tried to ignore the smell of the water that always reminded him of his own water history. Even though he had recently begun to get over his fear of the water, it was still something there in the back of his mind.

Okay, let's just go over this. Find out what Eric knows, and get the heck out of here.

"They're approaching."

Cam opened an eye and looked down at his AIM, back in its usual form of a golden retriever, as it stared ahead while Revolution climbed out from the water and made its way onto the concrete. Owen was the first to see him. "How'd it go?"

"Full score. We always do well in this city, even before you came along if you can believe it," Owen replied as the rest of the team came up beside him. "What're you doing out here?"

He shrugged as he eyed Eric. "I'm not out here long. One of my old sponsors contacted me about Eric."

Eric's eyes widened, and he turned to face Cam. "What? Really?"

"Yeah. I guess they want to put something together with you. They asked me to put you in touch with them. Thought it would mean more coming from me, I guess." Cam reached into his pocket and paused. He felt his shirt pocket before he swore. "Sorry, it's back in the car. I'll steal you away for a minute, if that's okay." He looked around to his old team, and noticed the skepticism on Rick and Owen's face. "Hey, what do I need a sponsor for? We'll be back." He shot them a grin as he put his arm over Eric's shoulders and led him towards his car.

"Which sponsor did you say it was?" Eric asked as they reached Cam's car. His eyes widened as the barrel of a gun was pressed against his back.

Cam moved away from Eric as Maria moved in. "The Canadian Army," she hissed into his ear. She spun him around and threw him against the side of the car. She glanced around to make sure no one paid much attention to them.

"What the hell is going on? You're Maria Kier, aren't you?" Eric asked, looking back and forth from Cam to Maria with his eyes wide with surprise.

"Who's the next target?" Maria asked in a low and threatening voice.

"I don't know what you're talking about, you crazy b-"

Maria punched him square in the nose, and threw him once more against the car. "Answer the question!" When he looked at her again, his eyes were hard despite the tears caused by the broken nose, and his jaw was set. They had him. "I wasn't afraid of putting the last guy in the hospital. Don't think you're safe because you're on my old team. Tell me what you know."

Eric glowered at Maria, who was nearly the same height as him, and looked at Cam. "You guys have been working together?"

"Our paths crossed. Now, I really suggest you give her what she wants. I dated her for three years. She's not a pleasant person when she doesn't get her way," Cam muttered.

Eric swore and looked around, but found no help from anyone nearby. "The research."

She tilted her head questioningly. "What about the research?"

"That's the next target. No one else was close enough to finalizing their research to be a threat, until we found that report of yours. That's been dealt with, or we tried to, at least, so now we're going onto the next set of research."

"Who are they watching?"

He let out a frustrated sigh. "Anyone with an AIM. Trevor doesn't trust anyone. If he has to get rid of one of his own, he will."

Maria nodded. "Which means you won't let him know you saw me alive." She gave a soft smile before she stepped away from him, finally putting her gun back in its holster. "And seriously, with your stats, did you really think one of Cam's old sponsors would really want to sign a contract with you? Please."

"Maria?"

She turned around to see the surprised face of Ryan. "Hey," she faltered. She glanced behind him to see Rick and Owen standing there. Her heart began to pound. *How much did they hear? Does it matter?*

After a brief moment of staring at her, Ryan grabbed her in a tight embrace, and she had no choice but to return it as Cam and Eric, and the rest of the team watched on. He kissed the side of her head before holding her in front of him slightly.

"Are you okay? I thought you were at a safe house. What happened?"

Maria's eyes flashed with panic as she glanced at Cam briefly. "I'm okay. I had to come back to the base to talk to my CO and get some things figured out."

"So, everything's okay?" He looked at Cam, then back to Maria and repeated his question. As far as anyone knew, this was the first time the two had seen each other. That overshadowed the fact that she had not kept in contact with Rick or Owen, for now. "Should I give you guys some time? Or…something?"

She shook her head with a soft smile. "No, it's fine. I don't think there's much to say." Her eyes shifted to Cam, and her heart continued to pound as his face twisted into an angry smile.

"This is your boyfriend?" Cam asked with a short laugh of unbelief. "You're dating Ryan?"

"We haven't told anyone yet. I didn't want to make things awkward." She looked at her ex-team mates with a small shrug. "Guess it's as awkward as it's going to be."

"Wait a minute," Rick finally cut in. "Ryan, not only have you been talking to Maria this past year, but you've been dating her?"

Ryan winced, feeling the full pressure of the situation. This was not a comfortable place to be at the moment. "We started dating when she got back from overseas."

Owen looked at Maria. His eyes were wide. "You were deployed?"

She shot a glance at Ryan. "Yeah, but I was sent back." Maria sighed and looked at Rick and Owen. "I'm sorry I haven't…that I just cut you guys out of my life. I wanted to keep in touch, but it was too hard. I needed to make a new life for myself, and when I got back I didn't really have much time to figure out how all of you could fit into it. I guess Ryan fit in easily, but you guys?" She shook her head, and impressed herself with her ability to hold back her tears.

"You guys were my family, and I let you down. I didn't know how to come back from that. Ryan tried to tell me that you guys wanted to see me, but I don't think I believed him. I don't think I do, even now. Being over there changed me. Ryan, he doesn't know me as well as you. He can't tell much of a difference. Maybe he can, but I wasn't ready to show you guys. Not yet."

When she stopped, Owen reached out to her and pulled her into an embrace. "No matter what you've done, Maria, you'll always be the daughter I never had. I know you had a rough time with the miscarriage, but you should have known that you didn't let us down. You reacted the way we expected you to, in the circumstances."

Just keep strong.

She pulled away and looked at Rick. "Ryan told me you're going to have a little girl." She forced a smile. "I'm so happy for you, Rick. You have no idea."

Rick nodded. He had never been one to show much emotion, and that was not going to change any time soon, at least not in a public place like this. "Thank you. I'm glad."

But nothing could stay calm for long.

Cam swore. "You could've told me. Warned me, at least, especially after that call." He finally spoke up once the conversation with Maria and the Warner family came to a lull.

Maria stepped forward, her eyes narrowing. It was too easy to be angry with him. At least it affirmed that nothing could ever work between them. "As far as I'm aware, I don't need to tell you everything about my life. You lost that right when you left the team, and me, a year ago," she said angrily.

Ryan put a hand on Maria's arm, pulling her back gently. "Wait. You lied to me?"

She looked at him with an eyebrow questioningly raised. "What?"

"When I called you." He looked at Cam, and for the first time, both Cam and Maria saw anger in Ryan's eyes. "You were with him," he said to her while still looking at Cam. When she did not respond, he asked again. "Were you with him? Yes or no." His eyes were back on her now, staring her down until she felt like a speck on the ground.

She hesitated, her eyes focused on the ground. "Yes." Her eyes flashed back up to him. "But it's not what you think."

He shook his head, and shoved her arm away. "I don't want to hear it. You give me this bull story about being in a safe house-"

"That wasn't a lie!"

"You were with him, Maria!" Ryan yelled, and Maria took a startled step backwards. Ryan was normally the calmest of the team. Even if they gained lousy points for a challenge, he always had something positive to say. He never even raised his voice that they had heard, until now. "You told me you hadn't seen him in a year. You told me he wasn't there with you. And you lied. You lied to *me*." His voice was soft as he finished, and he shook his head.

He looked at Cam, his face filled with surrender. "I'm glad you're okay," he said in barely a whisper before he walked away.

"Ryan, wait." Maria started after him but Cam put a hand out, stopping her. She watched as he went after Ryan, and she ran a hand over her hair. Just when she thought she was in control, the one in charge, a grenade was thrown into her life.

Rick waited for a moment before he addressed the elephant. "What was he talking about? He said something about a safe house?"

"Some...incidents have happened. I'm living on the CF base here in Kingston. Someone managed to sneak onto the base and broke into my house. I'm fine," Maria added quickly before anyone could ask. "But it's still a major security risk, and they're not sure if they were after me, or if it was random. They're just being careful, so they sent me to a safe house until they sort things out." She hated to lie.

"Ryan is upset because you were at a safe house with Cam," Owen said slowly. He always caught her in her lie. She should have known better.

She paused as she tried to figure out what to say. "Cam's job isn't the safest either, right now. That's all I can really say. We crossed paths two days ago. I didn't want to make Ryan worry, and I definitely didn't want him thinking something was going on between me and Cam again."

"Because hiding the fact you were with Cam doesn't make it sound as though you're sneaking around behind his back at all," Rick muttered. "Not with your history with Jack."

"I don't expect you guys to understand, or agree, but we weren't even supposed to be seen in public together." Her voice pleaded more than her words did, and she was grateful they could at least see that. "I have no idea how much trouble Cam's in, and I wasn't going to risk that just so Ryan would feel secure in our relationship."

Owen nodded. "Let's hope he calms down enough to hear Cam out."

"Hey, Ryan, c'mon," Cam said as he caught up to Ryan.

He spun around to look at his old team mate. "No, you come on, Cam. You left. You didn't see the hell you put her through. *I* was there for her. *I* was the one who comforted her, who helped her through the mess you left her in. Now you come back into the picture and screw it all up."

"I didn't screw anything up. Ryan, nothing happened. We didn't even sleep in the same room."

"But you were together. She said she was in a safe house."

"She was. We both were."

Ryan hesitated and looked Cam over. He looked tired, and weary. Somehow, he also looked desperate for Ryan to understand. "Why? And why did she lie to me?"

He looked over his shoulder to Maria. "You're going to have to accept that she's not going to be able to tell you the truth all the time, not with the job she has now. You're also going to have to accept that I can't tell you why we shared a safe house."

Ryan was silent for a moment, his eyes on the ground. He shoved his hands into his pockets as he cleared his throat. "You'll make sure she's safe? If you can't tell me anything else, please at least tell me that."

Cam shook his head. "I did as much as I could. Last year proved I can't keep anyone safe. Ryan, you have to believe me that there's nothing going on between us. This isn't going to be one of those situations where we get back together because danger brought us together, or whatever crap you see in movies." He cursed when Ryan met his gaze. "She's the mother of my kid, Ryan. We...had a kid together. That's always going to be there. But that's it."

"When this is over, whatever's happening here, I want you to stay away from her."

He nearly laughed before he caught the look of near hatred in Ryan's eyes. "You can't be serious."

"Have you seen her arms? That wasn't just because of Lucy. That was because of you. She's in a good place now. She's happy. It's hard to remind her of that when she has a constant reminder of how bad the rocks hurt when she hit them. She doesn't need another reminder, she doesn't need you to remind her that she almost *killed herself* over you." Ryan stepped close to him, his eyes narrowing and he lowered his voice. "I'm sure Rick and Owen are happy to have you back in their lives, and that's fine. They've known you for years. I knew you for a month, and what I saw was an arrogant, selfish coward. Maria used to talk about how there's more to you than that. Prove her right and just stay away from her. If you care about her, or care about her well-being, don't let her get caught up in you again."

Cam looked down at him for a moment, clamping his jaw shut. Ryan had seemed so soft-spoken, happy. And fiercely protective. He motioned for Maria to join them. "I will do whatever I can to make sure she doesn't do anything stupid. That's the best I can do." He put a hand on Maria's shoulder once she finally stood next to them. "I'll meet you back at the car." He waved to the three men standing a distance away where he had left them, and headed into the parking lot.

Maria waited until Cam was out of earshot before she turned back to Ryan. "I didn't want to lie to you. You have to believe me that nothing happened. I don't want him back." When all he did was nod, she grabbed his hand. "I don't. I want you. I have you, and I'm happy."

He gave a small smile and pulled her close, pressing his lips against hers. After a moment, he pulled away and held her face in his hands. "Stay safe, Maria. I don't know what's going on, but you better come back safe."

She laughed and nodded. "I will."

CHAPTER 13

Cam slid his AIRC into his pocket after Maria had downloaded the information she needed onto her own console. He studied her face as she looked around the mostly-empty parking lot at the rest stop.

"Where are you heading first?"

"Barrie," she replied as she looked at the map on her AIRC. "I'll need someone I can trust in the military to help give me some clout if I want any chance of the Minister of Defense listening to me. That's assuming my CO hasn't already spoken to him about me."

He nodded lightly. "You should've told me about Ryan."

"What, in between telling you about my deployment, you telling me about your AIM, and us making a plan to take down Trevor?"

Cam narrowed his eyes, but found it hard to be angry with her. "We had an entire conversation about your boyfriend after he called." He sighed. "I know this is all screwed up, but you should've told me." He paused as she nodded. "Are you happy?"

Maria looked at him and nodded again with a small smile. "Yeah. I am, actually."

He looked around and folded his arms across his chest. "Good. I'm glad," he said shortly.

"That's convincing."

"I don't like change."

She caught his eyes with hers. "I know."

After a moment, Cam cleared his throat. "If any of this gets too intense, you need to get out."

Maria rolled her eyes. "I can't see how this could be any worse than when I was deployed."

"I'm serious," he said sternly. "What you went through before…there are still safe houses for you to go to until this is over." Cam glanced down at her arms. Ryan's angry words repeated through his mind. "You'd be surprised at my knowledge of what barbed wire does to skin, and I know it doesn't do that." When she was silent, he glanced away. "He was with you?"

"Took me to the hospital," she answered softly. "I've put him through a lot. I was in a bad place after Lucy…I'm fine now. I have a focus, and I have people to save. He thinks…he thinks it was because of you. It might be part of it. But I haven't told him what happened overseas. Or that the scars are still fresh for a reason." When she looked away, he stepped closer and put his hands on her shoulders.

"Just promise me that you won't do anything stupid."

She looked up at him and gave him a weak smile. "It would be nice if this was the year no one went to the hospital. Besides, you were the one who always took stupid risks."

"Excuse me? What about those stunts last year in Niagara Falls? And the cliff diving during the World Tournament? Or your attempt to outrun a bear?"

"My twin. And the bear had a lame leg."

He laughed and instinctively pulled her into an embrace. "Just keep me updated."

"I will. You too," she said, her voice muffled in his chest.

Just one step at a time.

Maria took a drink from her coffee as she stepped from the rest-stop Tim Horton's in a small town just outside Kingston. She smiled lightly. After having coffee at the base overseas, she did not care how stereotypical she was. Nothing was better. She dug for her car keys from her jacket pocket as she stood next to the vehicle. Nothing worked better when she needed to forget. She looked at the empty parking space next to her where Cam had been less than thirty minutes earlier.

She let out a frustrated sigh. *Everything has to come back all at once, doesn't it?*

"Long time no see," came a voice from behind her as a hand went on her shoulder.

The coffee dropped to the ground as she spun around, hearing the familiar deep tone. Maria grabbed the man's collar and slammed him against the side of her car.

"What the hell?" Jack held his hands up. "Take it easy, would you?"

"Are you following me?" she growled, shoving him against the car again.

He leaned back as far as possible. Despite his height advantage over her, Maria had recently developed a strength advantage. "What are you talking-"

"Or are you here to kill me too?"

His hands dropped, and he looked her straight in the eyes. "Maria, what are you talking about?" His voice was low, a tone he rarely used with anyone.

Maria loosened her grip on his shirt as his voice lowered. She stared back at him for a moment before she realized how close they were. "Someone who works for Trevor tried to kill me in my home." She saw his eyes widen, but narrow once again as he thought through what she had said. "Yeah, I know who you work for, and what he's doing, not that it was much of a surprise. Cam had made it seem like you two worked together. I should've known better."

"Someone tried to kill you?"

She released his shirt and took a small step away from him. "I'm the AIMOT who wrote the report on the rogue AIM." She paused when he swore. "You seriously had no idea?"

"I knew about the AIMOT, but I swear to God I had no idea it was you. I just knew she lived on the Kingston base. I heard rumours you were there too, but I didn't make the connection." He looked around in a panic, his hands behind his head. "Are you okay?"

"Gunshot in the arm, but just a graze. You should see the other guy." She almost smiled. It was a different side to him, to see him flustered, and even somewhat concerned about her. But he was also afraid. A flash of panic swept through her when she realized what this meant. "How could you not know?"

"I don't know! Okay?" he screamed at her, his panic showing through his normally cold exterior. He leaned back against the car, his head lowered.

Maria waited for him to speak, but after a few minutes of silence, she folded her arms across her chest. "Cam quit after the presentation."

"He knows too much for them to care," he replied quietly. He swore again before finally looking back at her. "You really can't go a year without something happening to you, can you?"

"What are you doing here, Jack?"

"I was passing through on my way from Kingston, saw you, and I thought I'd stop by and say hi."

"That's bull. You never want to just say hi." She unlocked the car and attempted to reach around Jack to open the door, but sighed in frustration when he moved to block the handle and grabbed her arm. "Jack, seriously."

He kept a gentle grip on her arm and once again looked at her despite her attempts to avoid his eyes. "I'm sorry about your baby."

She froze. Her eyes locked with his. The day her daughter died was the day Jack's AIM had attacked her during a challenge. The day her daughter died he had pointed a gun at her. The day her daughter died, she had wanted him dead.

"I know I can never make it up to you. I..." His voice trailed off as though he was almost upset. Almost. "I know I'm a jerk. I know full well the kind of guy I am, but I never wanted to be the guy who'd do something like that. I never would've done anything if I knew you were pregnant You know I never would have hurt you, not intentionally."

The day she broke up with Cam, Jack had been the one telling her to go back to him. He had been the one with the shoulder to cry on.

"It wasn't your fault," Maria said after a moment. For so long, she had blamed others for the wrongs in her life. She blamed Cam for their failed relationship, when she knew she could have tried harder. She blamed Jack for the death of her daughter. She tried to, at least. "I pushed my body too hard. It wasn't because of the fall. I started to miscarry before the challenge even began. It wasn't your fault, Jack."

He nodded. "They think you're dead," he said after a moment.

Her forehead lined with confusion. He and Cam were more alike than any would like to admit. Their ability to move from subject to subject was incredible. "Trevor?"

Jack shook his head. "I even talked to the guy who attacked you myself just after you guys left. He reported it in as a success."

She knew that much from her own conversation with the hitman. "Did you get the name of his next target?" She groaned when he shrugged. "He said he gets one target at a time, and I doubt he'd tell Trevor he's laid up in the hospital. If they think I'm dead, he would have his next assignment. Is he after Cam? Or another AIMOT?" Of course, she would never say that Eric had already spoken with them, but with Jack's current empathetic mood, it never hurt to ask again.

"He said he doesn't have another assignment."

Jack stared at her, and watched as realization came across her face. When he was told there was no next target, Jack had an idea the man was lying. Learning now that they had withheld information from him about Maria, he knew for sure the identity of the next target. "You should get going," he breathed, opening the door for her as he began to walk away. He had caused her enough harm. She did not need to be caught in the cross fire, whenever it came.

"Jack." She called him back, her hand wrapping around his arm. "Get out."

He turned back to her. "What?"

"Quit. Find somewhere safe, and just get out of it."

He grinned, looking around. "Honey, you really think there's anywhere that's safe?"

"It's better than going back to them." Maria pulled him back towards her, not fully understanding why. "Jack, please."

He looked down at her in a way he had only done once before and stayed that way for a moment. "I won't tell anyone I saw you." He shook Maria off his arm before he turned once again to leave.

He looked her over briefly with a glance back over his shoulder. He grinned with a wave of the hand as though to wave off what he was going to say. "The fatigues suit you. Take care of yourself."

She watched as he got into his own car and drove away. She stood there, stunned. A year seemed to have done so much to so many people. The rare times Maria had been alone with Jack, he had seemed to be a decent human being. She got into her car and started the engine. Looking through the rear view mirror, she saw her AIM sitting comfortably in the backseat. It sat there patiently waiting for her to return, like a regular AIM. This was the only one she had ever owned, but she had only bought it when she was seventeen and started in the Owen Sound Junior Scanning Tournament. It scared her to think that the AIM she had worked so well with during her time Scanning and now as a soldier, would one day turn against her.

With a sigh, Maria pulled out of the parking lot and onto the highway towards Barrie. Jack's sincerity and compassion still unnerved her, but she needed to concentrate on more than that right now. She let out a muttered curse. She had actually asked him to quit. It was just like her relationship with Cam, always asking him to quit. What scared her more than the thought of her AIM turning, was the thought that there was more to all of this than what Trevor told his employees. Nothing was ever easy.

"Would you prefer I drive?"

Cam shot a glare to his AIM who sat in the passenger seat of his car. "You're an AIM."

"Astute observation. Shall I observe something about you?" The AIM watched Cam for a moment. "You are upset."

"I'm not upset."

"Maria has moved on."

Cam pushed the ignition button and pulled from the side of the highway, melding into the traffic. "Astute observation," he scoffed.

The AIM was silent. It watched the trees flash by through the window for a while before it let out its whirring sigh. "Lucas, you too must look past what has happened. Focus on what must be done. There is no going back. She was wrong to say she should not have ended the relationship. She reacted logically with the information she had at the time, and did not return to you because of what she considered her own infidelity."

"You heard that?"

"I hear many things." It paused. "For instance, I have heard you tell her that you love her."

Cam was silent.

"You said that to no one other than your mother. I understand it is significant for you, but you must move forward. Focus on today. Tomorrow will come in time."

He glanced at his AIM. "When did you get so philosophical?"

"The word you are looking for is *comforting*."

He smiled lightly and stroked the top of the AIM dog's head. "You know, the hardest secret I had to keep from her wasn't the Underground. It was you." He laughed when it pushed his hand away with its nose.

"Where is our first destination?"

"The Ottawa lab."

The AIM looked at him quickly. "You are planning on taking a prototype, or a rogue."

"I need to make sure I keep a prototype safe and a rogue for evidence in case…of something. If all of our research is destroyed, then at least there will be one of the new AIMs to show the media." Cam continued driving silently for a few moments until he sighed. "It's been a year. I shouldn't miss her anymore."

"It has been five years since your mother passed away, and still you miss her. Time does not make you forget, nor does it cause you to cease missing a person you care for." His AIM shook his head as the air from the air vents tickled its nose sensory. "It does not help that you still care for Maria, but I understand humans do not have control over who their emotions are felt for. Are you perhaps feeling this way because you fear for her life?"

Cam glanced at his AIM. "Let's just say that's it, even if it's not the only reason."

"If it will help."

Two hours later, Cam drove the car into a seemingly empty parking lot. He glanced at the industrial building as he drove around to the back where a handful of other cars were hidden.

"Will they allow you to take it from the lab?" the AIM asked him as they made their way to the door of the building.

"They'll have to. They don't have the capabilities to keep it from Trevor or any of his people if they were to come here looking," Cam answered as he placed his palm against the security scanner. It flashed green and a mechanical *thunk* sounded as the door unlocked.

He opened the door, allowing his AIM to walk in ahead of him, and he was greeted with chaos. He stood against the metal wall of the building and watched groups of people running up and down the aisles; some carried binders filled with papers, and other carried AIRCs and other electronic tablets. Cam's head turned to the side when someone put a hand on his shoulder.

"We have a situation, Cam."

He nodded at the man who stood before him. "I can see that. What's taking so long with the lockdown? There shouldn't be so many people here, Walter."

"Like I said, we have a situation." He motioned with his head for Cam to follow him. He led him down the length of the building until they reached a door at the end of the hallway. Walter knocked twice before stepping in with Cam behind him.

Two men stood in the small room, leaning against the far wall as the florescent lights threw ugly shadows on the ground. A third man sat in a chair in front of them, handcuffs around his wrists behind his back and his ankles secured with a thick metal chain. A bruise around his right eye told Cam that he had likely been unconscious when he had been bound.

"What the hell happened here?" he asked, trying to recall the name of the man in front of him.

"We went through everyone's phone records," Walter explained. "Sharar's been speaking with the McCarthys directly.

Cam stared at Sharar, his fist tensing at his side. "What have you done about it other than beat him and tie him up?"

"I've tried to contact Henk, but I could only get a hold of Sandra. We were told you were dealing with things of your own."

He nodded. "Well, I'm here now." He opened the door and stood next to the opening. "Give me a minute with him. Then I have work to do." Cam waited until the other men left before he closed the door. He stared at the man, and leaned against the wall. His arms folded across his chest.

Sharar looked at the ground, refusing to acknowledge Cam.

Now he remembered him. Cam had never found him to be overly promising, or helpful. If he was working for Trevor, it only made sense that he would attempt to delay the progress of the new AIMs. But he had made a few breakthroughs in the substance; breakthroughs which Henk used in the final product. That was definitely not the characteristic of a McCarthy employee.

"So, what's your job?"

Sharar remained silent.

Cam sighed. "I'm not going to beat you, or kill you. I'm just trying to understand the people who work for Trevor. I didn't realize he had so many people working at such a low level."

He grinned. "That says more about you than it does me."

Cam glared at the man as he stepped towards him. "You had every chance to destroy our research, to tell Trevor exactly what we were doing, but you didn't. You helped, in a very small way. I understand why Trevor has people killing AIMOTs, and journalists who ask too many questions, but I can't understand why you wouldn't tell him everything you know."

He remained grinning, and silent.

Cam took in a deep breath and dragged another chair away from the table in the corner of the room. The buzzing of the lights above irritated him, but no more than this man. "Are you on a schedule?" That sparked Sharar's interest, and he looked up at Cam with a quirked eyebrow. Cam sat down in the chair in front of him. "If you don't call Trevor at a certain time, will he think you're dead or something? I'll give you your phone if you need to make sure he stays calm."

Sharar's eyebrows furrowed. It was clear he had not thought of that. "No, there's no schedule."

Cam nodded. "There's no reason to alarm anyone. Nothing's going to happen to you, other than keeping you in this room, which I'm sure you understand." When the captive nodded in acknowledgement, he continued. "Who's your partner?" he asked calmly.

"What makes you think I have one?"

He held back an impulse to smile. Sharar trusted him. He had no idea how Trevor could let this man work for him. He spoke too easily, and more than Sharar thought.

"We've found teams in other labs, so I just assumed you would have a partner too." Cam had thought it was a waste of time when Maria had made him go with her to a military conference. Her father gave a presentation on interrogation tactics. Granted, some of those tactics had been to use force. Cam did not want to get to that point. Not if he could help it. He would stick with bluffs as long as he could.

"You found teams because Trevor was the one who put them in teams."

"They gave the impression that someone else put them there." Cam leaned back in the chair and rested his right ankle on his left knee.

Sharar snorted. "The others are cowards. They just don't want Trevor to think they said anything. I'm the only one not working directly for Trevor, at least in Ontario."

He looked at the door before he leaned forward. "They seem to think that you do."

Sharar's eyes widened. "They told you my name?" He swore when Cam nodded.

Cam laughed. "They speak pretty freely when their life is on the line, too." He watched as Sharar sobered. "What are you doing here, then, if you're not working for Trevor directly?"

"Research."

"That's bull. What are you doing here?"

"I told you. I'm doing research."

Cam sighed. He stood suddenly and shoved the back of Sharar's chair, flipping him backwards onto the cement floor, crushing his hands behind his back. Sharar cried out in pain as Cam leaned over him. "Instead of me asking questions, why don't you just start from the beginning?"

Sharar hesitated, shifting his arms behind his back to alleviate as much pain as possible. "Trevor's insane."

"Yeah, I got that impression."

"No, you don't get it," he said in a hushed tone. "He's insane. When his brother suggested he step down from his position, he threatened to kill everyone and their family if they tried to depose him. Nineteen years ago, two scientists told Trevor about the possibility of AIMs going rogue. He made sure everyone present at that meeting could never tell anyone about the rogues. Ever wonder where his second brother went? He tried to keep it from Cohner, but he was still asked to step down. He was worried that was why they were trying to get him out of power, and your presentation made it worse. Since then, he's been getting rid of anyone who knows about the AIMs, even if they're in his own company. Those he can't kill, he buys."

Cam leaned lower. "That doesn't explain why you're here."

"I'm here to see the rogues, and to make sure you find something to replace them. Cohner and some members of the board are trying to get enough evidence to depose Trevor. I work for his brother." His eyes narrowed as he looked up at Cam. "I am not your ally. I couldn't care less if any or all of you die. I'm just trying to do my job."

He nodded as he straightened. He pulled Sharar and his chair back into an upright position and left the room. He waited for Walter to approach him. "Keep him in there, and supervised. Feed him, and let him answer his phone when it rings but keep someone in there when he's talking."

"I don't think that's a good idea, Cam."

He shot a frustrated look at the man before he started down the hall towards large, double doors. "Trevor's killing his own people. They're not coming for him, but we don't want to give him the opportunity to leave. We may need more information from him." He stopped at the double doors with his hand on the cool metal. "I'm taking a rogue and a prototype with me."

"Not to repeat myself," Walter said, putting his hand on Cam's shoulder. "But I don't think that's a good idea."

"If anyone's going to take one, it's going to be me."

Walter held his hands up in defeat. "You're the boss."

Cam looked at him. *Yes, I am.*

CHAPTER 14

"What?"

He cringed as he heard the older man's voice growl angrily through the phone. "They're working together."

A frustrated sigh rang through the earpiece. "Who, idiot?"

"The AIMOT and Tylar."

The older man swore profusely. "She's alive?"

"Well she didn't look dead when I saw her an hour ago."

"Don't get smart with me, Eric."

"Sorry, Mr. McCarthy. As I said, it looks like they're working together. They have a plan of some sort, but I'm not sure what it is. What do you want me to do?"

"Find out what you can about her. Find out who's close to her, and get rid of them."

Eric shifted uncomfortably and looked around the forest. "With all due respect, I can't do that. The person she's closest to now is in the spotlight. If something happens to him, there are going to be questions. I'm not sure if that's the best idea right now, not with everything else you have planned."

There was a pause.

"Keep this person close, then. In the meantime, figure out her next move. If you can, put doubt in this person's mind about their relationship. When we get rid of her, I do not want this person asking questions because questions demand answers. And you're well aware of the answers I will give. You have forty-eight hours. Do not disappoint me."

"Yes, sir."

Eric slipped his phone into his sweater pocket as the rest of Revolution caught up to him on the hiking trail in Kingston. He smiled as Ryan strode next to him. "It's about time."

Ryan returned the smile as he showed the newest member his AIRC. A picture of a red fox was on the screen. "While you were busy on the phone, we were scanning."

He rolled his eyes. "It was a few minutes. You couldn't have gotten much."

Rick laughed, walking on the other side of him. "Do you forget who Ryan is? He's our expert scanner, now."

"Even in the short season we had last year, Cam taught me a lot," Ryan added.

Rick looked over to him with a cautious look. "Did you get things smoothed out with Cam and Maria?"

"I'm not happy about the situation, but I'm going to have to deal with it. I'm sorry I didn't say anything to you guys, but we didn't want anyone to know in case it leaked to the media. She wasn't really in a place to be able to handle that. I'm not sure she *is* in that place yet, but there's nothing we can do about it now."

The last time any of them had seen Maria was just before she had left for Basic Training. With Owen fully recovered from his heart attack the previous year and back in the captain's seat, he had expected some form of communication from Maria. He thought he had deserved that much.

"She just randomly showed up? In her uniform?" Owen asked. His wrinkled forehead gathered more folds as he looked at Ryan. "Why did she choose now to see us, or did she just come with Cam?"

"We didn't really talk about why she chose now. I think something's going on, so she wanted to make sure she got a chance to see you."

"Is it really that tough, whatever she's going through?"

He shrugged. "I guess. She doesn't really say much about it, and I can't ask. I wouldn't get an answer even if I did."

"Well, we shouldn't really be surprised you guys are dating now, with how you two acted last season," Rick spoke up. "How were they acting around each other? They were at each other's throats last year. I can't imagine being away from each other did much to help that."

"Fine, I guess. They're...going through some stuff. They say they're over everything, but they had a kid together. That's a lot to get over. Whatever anger they had, whatever hatred they held for the other isn't there anymore. That should be a good thing, but it worries me. I'm used to seeing them hate each other, and seeing them civil makes me think they've missed each other."

"Ryan," Owen started. "They know better than to get back together. Rick and I saw how destructive that relationship was. They both see that now, too." He raised a questioning eyebrow to his son when he held back a cough. "Something to add?"

Rick kicked at the ground with a shrug. "Cam never confided in you, Dad, but he talked to me. They had their problems, but that relationship, Maria, they were the best things to happen to Cam. He's changed a lot now, after everything, but the only things keeping him back now are his pride, and Ryan."

Ryan nodded, then continued walking down the hiking trail. "Well, I'm not going anywhere. I don't think his pride is going any time soon, either."

Owen laughed. "You're probably right."

The team continued on their way, being careful to not make too much noise within the forest. The calls of the birds rang out in the early evening: the reason the team was out at this time. As a top team in the Canadian Scanning Tournament, they knew the importance of going out at all times of the day to scan animals. There were some animals that were only active at dusk, and it was those animals they sought.

Eric looked around as he walked next to Ryan, putting his hand against tree trunks to keep his balance on the uneven terrain.

"So, what's the deal with Maria?"

"What do you mean?" Ryan volleyed quietly.

He took a cautious step over a root. "The guys seemed shocked you guys were dating, even though they said they shouldn't be. I guess I am too. Everyone knows about her and

Cam, and what happened last year. I didn't realize she hasn't seen any of them until now. No one really talks about anything on this team."

Ryan hesitated before answering. It had been difficult, hiding his relationship from his team. Maria meant so much to him. She always had. He had not wanted to hide it. Maybe it would be nice now to share with someone. Eric was close to the same age as him, so there was that, too.

"She's been through a lot. She hit rock bottom after the funeral, when Cam left."

"Let me guess: you stepped in to pick her up?"

Ryan shot him a glance. "I had never stepped away." He paused to recollect his thoughts. "She joined the army when she got herself together. Her dad was a soldier, and she grew up around soldiers. I guess it made sense for her to get into it." He smiled proudly as he continued.

"I think she's trying to make people proud of her again, to show people she's not the helpless woman who lost a child she was last year. Her dad's battle buddy even sent her a card, congratulating her on her employment as an AIMOT. That meant a lot to her. I guess he was like an uncle to her."

Eric nodded. He waited for Ryan to scan an owl hiding in the trees. "What's an AIMOT?" He asked when the words 'Scan Successful' flashed on the screen of his team mate's AIRC.

"What? Oh, an AIM Operations Technician. She works with military AIMs around Canada and overseas."

"Big job," Eric commented.

Ryan continued walking, catching up with Rick and Owen. "Oh, she's not the only one. I think she said there were a few on each base. With her background in the CST, it'd be stupid for them to not give her that job."

"So, what's she doing now?"

He raised an eyebrow with a quirky smile. "You do remember she's *my* girlfriend, right? Why are you so interested?"

Eric shrugged, nearly tripping over an upraised root as he did so. "I don't know. She pretty much fell off the radar, and now we find out she's back. I used to watch this team too, you know. She was an awesome Scanner. I just wanted to know where she went from here. I never thought about the military as a way to use these skills."

Ryan laughed. "You need a bit more than a Scanning background to be in the military."

"I guess that's true." He pulled the hood of his sweater over his blonde hair, and shoved his hands into the front pocket. "I guess you guys don't get to see each other too often, then?"

Ryan grinned, and was helpless against the blood rushing to his cheeks. "Actually, we've seen each other pretty often. She's come to a few challenges."

Eric thought for a moment before he laughed. "That's why you pushed for separate rooms this season?" When Ryan shrugged, he patted him on the shoulder. "Good job."

"It's not like that." Ryan continued to smile. "But yes, that's why. She hated being so close to Rick and Owen and not see them, but she wasn't ready for that yet."

He nodded and the two pairs walked out into an empty parking lot, save for the team's RV and truck. "What about her uncle? Does she get together with him at all, or is it strange with her dad passed?"

"Her dad's battle buddy? Well, he's not really an uncle. She hasn't seen him in years, even though he's up at the base in Barrie. She's talked about getting back in touch with him, especially after getting the card from him."

"That'd be nice. It's hard getting back in touch with people from the past, especially if they bring back memories of someone who's dead now."

Ryan nodded as he hopped into the truck with Rick. "I guess so. I'll talk to you later."

Eric stepped into the RV behind Owen with a grin. *That was too easy.*

Later that night, Eric dialed an all-too familiar number and waited for someone to pick up on the other end. When a woman's voice greeted him, he smiled. "Hey Amanda, can you put me through?" He waited for a moment until he heard his boss' voice. "I have some extra time, do you want me to find anything else about her?"

"You're wasting *my* time, Eric," Trevor growled through the phone. "What did you find out?"

"She's going to Barrie to meet with her dad's battle buddy. I didn't get his name, but I can find that out with a quick call."

"No need. I already know who to contact. Well done, Eric."

"Thank you, sir."

"You know what to do next. Don't screw it up."

He hung up and lay back in the bed. He could not believe how quickly all of this had moved. He had worked for Trevor less than a year, and already he had earned more of the man's trust than Jack ever had during his entire career. He had been astonished that Revolution would even sign him in the first place, but at least his stats were high enough for the top quality team. They had been desperate after both Cam and Maria had left, and needed whoever was available, and anyone able to keep up with their stats. He hoped he had put enough doubt in Ryan's mind. He would have to bring it all back up again tomorrow, but he would have to be smart about it. Maria would die, and this time, no one was going to care what happened to her.

"Thank you very much, Major-General. I'm glad we're able to work so well together." Trevor grinned as he hung up the phone, mere hours after he had spoken with Eric. He ran a hand through his thinning hair, and the feeling made him frown. He looked up from his desk as his office door opened. "Don't you people ever knock?" he screamed.

Amanda winced as she stepped into the room, closing the door gently behind her. "I'm sorry, Trevor. I heard you were finished on the phone, so I just-"

"It doesn't matter," he replied with a bored wave of the hand. "What do you want, Amanda?"

She walked further into his office and sat on the desk beside his chair. "I just wanted to see how you were today."

"Pissed off, is what I am."

"People are doing their best. Look how quickly Eric was able to gather that information for you. All of this is progressing much faster than any of us thought, and we're all learning how to deal with that. Even you," she added boldly, earning a glare from

Trevor. "All I'm saying is that you have to be patient. If you want to do this quietly, do it quietly, but don't expect it to be done in a flash. Remember that lightning comes with thunder."

He sighed as he put his hands on her arms, sliding up and down her skin. "You're very lucky you know exactly what to say."

"No." She let out a soft laugh. "Your brother said the exact same thing to you yesterday at the board meeting." She felt him tense at the words. "It's the fact that I'm sleeping with you that relaxes you, and makes you calm down."

Trevor nodded. "Yes. That's probably it."

She smiled as she stood. She placed a soft kiss on his check before she retraced her steps and moved back to the door of the office. "Try to relax. You've given your instructions. Just wait. Even good Generals know that it takes time to move into a strategic position." She closed the door behind her as Trevor nodded, and joined a man leaning against the wall beside the door.

"How is he?"

She shrugged. "He's impatient. I was able to calm him down, but he's not himself."

The man sighed and stood straight as they began down the hallway. "Amanda, I've known him for his entire life. He is himself. The board's actions weren't unjust. You have to see that."

"I do, but you have to give him more time, Cohner. You're his brother. He needs help, but he has to be the one to see that. You must understand that he can't be rushed into changing."

He ran his hand through his hair in a similar fashion to Trevor. "It's because I'm his brother that I know he's past changing. You saw the presentation. How does it make sense to keep rogue AIMs a secret, and kill those who know about it, while not accepting an improved substance? From an economical, and ethical standpoint? We never should have taken the research from Dr. Baxter. We weren't equipped to test the product; we still aren't. At the very least, we should have brought him on as an employee. Along with Lucas Tylar." He spoke in a hoarse whisper, as though Trevor's ears could hear throughout the office building.

"He's not concerned about the company anymore. He used to be. He used to do everything for this company," Cohner continued. "Now it's all for him. This is all so he can keep control." He smiled softly. "Except for you. I know he's harsh, and cold, but he does adore you."

"Which is why I can't go against him," Amanda replied, matching his tone. "I agree with you, and the board, but if he feels everyone is against him, I'm afraid of what will happen."

He nodded as they stopped before a door with a plated nameplate which read 'Cohner McCarthy'. "I understand. I'm just grateful you speak to me about it."

"Of course." She watched as he entered his own office and she was left in the corridor alone. When the door clicked shut, Amanda pulled out a cell phone from her pocket and continued down the long corridor, dialing.

"Mr. Tyson? It's Amanda Sullivan. I need your help."

Cam sat in front of two balls of opaque white gel the size of a grapefruit with a furrowed brow. Next to him sat a German Shepherd, also staring intently at the gel.

"What is our next step?" came the AIM's robotic voice.

"I have no idea. I have everyone going through checks and interrogations in each lab," Cam answered. He rested his chin on his fist as he examined the inactive AIM before him. "We need to figure out how to get these into production." He thought for a moment, grateful that his AIM remained silent. Those moments were so precious, and rare. "We need someone working with Trevor."

"Did you not just interrogate Sharar? Was that not enough?"

He shook his head. "We don't need to do any work, from the sounds of it. They're already trying to take down Trevor from the inside. We need to find someone who can get us in too. We need to get people on the outside questioning. Can you look into AIM related attacks?"

"I'll search through the Wi-Fi network," the robot replied. It looked at him when he did not respond, and with its dog snout, it nudged Cam's arm. "What are you thinking?"

"I'm going to try getting a meeting with someone in the media. I'm sure that every TV station would love a first glance at the new Cam Tylar, and a first chance to see what I've been up to."

"Will you mention anything about rogue AIMs?"

"No. I can't, or it'll tip off Trevor," Cam said thoughtfully. "I need to just mention the new AIM, and talk about how I found out about a new upgrade that won't be available for a few more months. It'll put pressure on Trevor, but it won't scare him. At least, it shouldn't scare him. Before I set up the interview, though, I need to get a hold of Henk."

"Is that a wise idea, given your recent falling out?"

Cam placed the gel into a silver attaché case, each gel in its own section within the case, and stood. "We have no choice. He knows Trevor the best. He's the one they'll want to hear from, if anyone. Sharar can tell Trevor's brother that we want to help, so that'll give us an edge, but we still need Henk for all of this to work. He's the one who put all of this together."

"You know," the AIM started. "Your father put this together too, when I was first created. This is his work also."

He paused and clenched his jaw. Now was not the time to speak about his father. "Well, Henk's still alive, so I'm going to rely on him with this. Come on." Cam led his AIM out of the training room and back through the chaos of the Ottawa lab. "We'll get a hotel until we figure out where to go from here," he said to both his AIM, and to Walter who rejoined him now at his side.

"Is a hotel going to be safe?" Walter asked. "You know there are rooms in the building."

"You guys have enough going on as it is," Cam said coolly as they reached the main doors. "You know what you're doing. When you hear back from the other labs, make sure to tell them to keep our sympathizers happy. We're going to need as much support as possible from the inside if we want to take Trevor down."

Walter froze as Cam spoke. "Take him down? Cam, he owns a multi-billion dollar company, and you expect to take him down?"

"No." He looked at the man over his shoulder as he pushed the metal doors open. "He'll do it on his own. I just want a front row seat."

CHAPTER 15

Early the next morning, Maria stepped into the main administration building of CFB Borden, still wearing her uniform. She smiled lightly in the familiar surroundings. Her father had worked mostly at this base when he was still alive, and she had often accompanied him on weekends or during the summer.

She smiled lightly at the man sitting behind the front desk. They changed how things were done, it seemed. When she was younger, she had been able to simply walk back to her father's office. Times had changed. It was for the best, most likely.

"I'm looking for Lieutenant-General Malcolm," she said strongly. It had never bothered her to use whatever authority she had been given, but for some reason she felt out of place; like a child shouting demands to her parents.

"He's about to leave for a training session with new recruits," the soldier, a captain by the looks of the chevrons on his shoulder, answered as he looked her over. "Is he expecting you?"

Maria shook her head. "No, but it is urgent. It won't take too much of his time."

The soldier raised a curious eyebrow as he stood. "Critical?"

"I just need some information from him, and I'll be on my way. I'm…he's an old friend of my father's."

He looked at the name tag on her chest, and within seconds his eyes flashed to hers with an understanding look. "I worked with your father. He was a good man. Malcolm would give whatever time he has to see you." He turned and led Maria down the corridor, their boots tapping on the tiled floor.

Maria looked over the nameplates on the doors as she passed, along with their rank and position. She would not be able to remember them all, but if she could at least remember enough to cross check with the list Sandra had sent to her and Cam, it would be something to go on. She stopped when the captain knocked on a door.

He waited until a rough voice came from within the room and he stepped in. Maria saw him salute, but he spoke in a whisper. She straightened when he came back from the room, motioning for her to enter. She stepped into the room and smiled.

The man looked just the way she remembered him: tall, broad, thick greying hair on his head and mustache. It had not been as long as she had thought, when she had last seen Nicholas Malcolm. They had not spoken, but he had been to her father's funeral. She remembered little of that day, not much more than the guns firing a final salute, Cam's hand holding hers, and the trumpet blaring its farewell.

"Lieutenant Kier." He laughed and opened his arms, taking her into an embrace. "It's so good to see you. You're all grown up."

Maria grinned with a shrug. "It happens, even to the best of us."

"Don't I know it? How are you, Maria?" he asked gently, and it nearly broke her heart. He always knew when something was wrong. She rarely fought with her father, but when she did, he had been there to listen. When she had fought with her mother, which happened much more frequently, he had seen her speaking with her father and had even sat with her if she needed to wait for him.

"Well, I've been better," she started slowly. "I know you're about to leave, so maybe when you get back this evening we can discuss it."

He leaned forward slightly, his arms folding across his chest. "What's going on?"

She hesitated, and glanced around the office. He kept very little in it. Only a few pictures on the walls, and only one with his children. He had taken down the photo of his wife the day the divorce was final.

"I need your help, and I'm going to ask a lot from you. Please don't feel obligated to help because of Dad. I came to you because I trust you, and that's the type of person I need right now."

"You trust no one else in your life? That's not too healthy."

"I trust no one else in the military."

He froze. His eyes bore into hers. "That's even worse." He strode to his desk and picked up the phone. "Wilkins, take over for me with the recruits. Something's come up. I'll review everything in the morning." He pointed to the chair in front of his desk, offering it to Maria. "Start from the beginning."

She sat hesitantly, thinking of the proper wording. "Actually, Sir, I have to start in the middle."

Nicholas Malcolm sat back in his chair as Maria finished recounting the story. She began with her time deployed overseas, only briefly mentioning her association with someone in the Underground but she had allowed him to remain anonymous. Association was not a crime, but participation was, and if Cam was found out he would be put in jail, his stats would be erased, along with the stats of his team for the years he was active. Maria could never do that to either Cam or Revolution. He held his fists in front of his mouth for several moments, digesting the story while Maria watched on patiently.

After several more moments, she finally spoke again. "I know this is a lot to take in, and I know I must sound crazy, but you have to believe me."

"Maria, you're one of the sanest people I've ever met. I know you're not making this up," he began slowly. "You're right. This is a lot to take in, especially knowing that your CO has blackmailed you. He's a good man, and it's a shame he's not trustworthy. It worries me that the commander of the overseas base may have helped create the charges against you. I have some men over there with him." He let out a deep breath and paused. "You said that you need my help. I have no idea how I can help with any of this. I have very little experience working with AIMs. I leave that to my AIMOT mostly."

"I can take care of that. I need help bringing my report up the chain," she said. "My CO never passed on my official report, and it needs to be. The General, and the Minister, the Prime Minister even, they need to know about this, and they need to know about the dangers. I believe we're dealing with internal terrorism. If not that, then I have no idea how to classify this intentional endangerment of Canadian citizens, and our soldiers. I can't prove that Trevor McCarthy knows about the AIMs without endangering those in the Underground, so I can't accuse him of terrorism, although I strongly feel that this is what is happening."

"Terrorism is a strong word, Maria. I would be careful to use it. But, as you said, it is a suitable word for what's happening. I wouldn't place the blame on your superior, though." Nicholas stood and took a binder from a bookshelf, before opening it on his desk. "I would, perhaps, classify it as conspiracy."

Maria's eyebrows furrowed. "Like I'm making it up?"

He laughed, flipping through the pages. "No, no! An actual conspiring to terrorise, the CO and whoever else you believe is in on the blackmail."

"Trevor McCarthy."

Nicholas nodded slowly. "You're sure?"

"Like I said, I can't prove it without documents from people in the Underground, but he's the one who refuses to put a safer product in production. He's put millions of dollars into our military. Everyone knows that. We're a special client of his, as is the military of many other countries around the world that use AIMs. I can't believe that anyone in his position would be ignorant of what's going on. He's known about these rogue AIMs for years and allowed them to be manufactured, and sold to our country to be used by our soldiers. If there are people within our government and military who support him, then I would have to call that a form of terrorism, yes, and that Trevor McCarthy is ultimately responsible. If you want to add conspiracy to the list, then by all means, do so, but this is so much more than that, Nick."

"And you can't do this alone, not with your CO on your bad side. Does Trevor still believe you're dead?"

She shrugged. "As far as I know, he does. The man who tried to kill me said he succeeded, but I've seen my CO and he may have spoken with Trevor about seeing me. If he does tell Trevor, it won't be any time soon. He'll want to make sure I stay quiet first, before he has to give the bad news. On the other hand, if he doesn't tell him he saw me, it could be his head on the chopping block next."

He snorted. "So, you're saying it could go either way?"

"Pretty much."

"So you need someone who knows how to get to the top."

"Someone I trust."

Nicholas smiled. "I think I can help you. I'm meeting with the General in a few days in Ottawa, actually. I'll bring you along, and you can show him your report to get him on board. We do need to keep this as quiet as possible. This can only be seen by those among the top."

"Trust me, I'm learning that very quickly." Maria glanced out the window into the parking lot where a small group of soldiers were talking. German Shepherds stood next to them, standing at attention as though they were soldiers as well. In a way, she knew they were. AIMs had been an integral part of the military for nearly fifteen years. "Let me know when you'll be leaving. In the meantime, may I take a look around the base, and speak with your AIMOT?"

He froze, and closed the binder. "We actually just sent our AIMOT to another base yesterday to train a new set of AIMs. I can get you his contact information so you can bring him up to speed."

"No, I was just going to see if he's seen any irregularities. I'll show myself around and take a look at the AIMs. That's my job, after all."

Nicholas nodded and opened the door. "Of course. Most of the older soldiers will most likely recognize you, anyway. These are your old stomping grounds, at least they were your father's. You know you're always welcome here at Base Borden."

Maria looked up at him with a smile. "Thank you. I'll talk to you later." She walked back down the hallway and acknowledged the captain as she passed the main desk. She was glad she had chosen to wear her combat uniform again. Her regular uniform made her feel too professional, too…mature. After three years of wearing whatever she wanted to her job, with the exception of her team outfit, she still craved wearing comfortable and casual-style clothing. This was the closest she could get without wearing a dress shirt. She smiled at the soldiers jogging in formation past her, each with an AIM following obediently at their side. When she noticed a soldier kneeling on the ground next to the building with his AIM, she strode over to him.

He looked up when he noticed someone standing before him, and with a quick glance to her shoulder, he stood quickly and saluted.

"At ease," she said and looked down at the AIM. "Is this your unit, Brown?" She was glad for the name tags everyone wore. Using a name always made her feel more comfortable, for some reason. Knowing a name meant knowing your enemy, or ally, that much better.

"Yes, Ma'am." Brown knelt back down to the AIM.

She watched as the man ran his hands over the AIM slowly, the same way a veterinarian would assess an animal for injuries. "Is there something wrong with it?"

"I'm not sure." He glanced up at her briefly; a line of confusion was on his forehead. "I didn't think so, but when I was going through some training exercises, it wasn't responding. I thought maybe the scan was injured somehow and it's not at a level which the AIM regards it as a problem."

"If it can't function properly, it should see a problem. Can I see the AIRC?" She took the offered device and scrolled through the programming. "How long has it been doing this?"

"About a week now, on and off."

Maria looked down at Brown with a stern gaze. "Why haven't you brought it to your AIMOT?"

"I am the AIMOT."

She looked at his sleeve and sure enough, there were three dots in the form of a triangle: the marking of their profession. "I'm sorry, I didn't even look. Malcolm told me you had left the base."

"I was supposed to, am supposed to, but I wanted to check this guy out before I got on the road. I'm about a day late." Brown stood and looked over her shoulder at the AIRC. "I can't find anything wrong with the coding, so I scheduled a maintenance check with the rest of the units for today. I brought the AIRC in to get fixed earlier, but there's nothing wrong with that either. Sorry, it's Kier?"

"Maria Kier, CFB Kingston."

He laughed as he shook her hand. "You're kidding me? Maria Kier?"

She sighed. "Yes, Maria Kier, from Revolution."

"I bet you're glad you're in a thick uniform, not doing any more photo shoots."

Maria's face flushed from both anger and embarrassment. "How many guys have a picture of me?"

"Four."

"Well, it could be worse." She eyed him when she noticed him grinning. She never should have done that photo shoot. Cam never let her hear the end of it, but she had quickly made up for it by doing another photo shoot which involved her entire team, and more clothing. "And you're…?"

"Johnathon Brown, sorry." He laughed lightly before pointing down at his AIM. "So, do you have any ideas?"

"Have you noticed any other AIMs acting like this?"

He shrugged. "Not that anyone has mentioned to me. My last evaluation of the base's units was about a month ago, and nothing came up then. Have you seen anything like this before?"

Maria hesitated. It started now. She handed the device back to him before she began to walk, Johnathon at her side. "I've noticed a few AIMs have begun to disconnect from their AIRC. I saw it when I was deployed, and I've seen it even within the CST."

"Really? What causes it?"

"I have no idea."

"Any idea how to fix it?"

She shook her head. "Nothing that's been approved yet. I know of some work that's been going on, but as far as I know, there's not enough support to bring it into production."

Johnathon stopped as two military vehicles crossed their path. "What kind of support would it need?"

She had him. Maybe this would work after all.

"Honestly, there needs to be a problem, first. It's been so rare that AIMs have been like this that it doesn't seem to be worthwhile for anything to be finalized."

"If it means anything, I think it would definitely be worthwhile. From what I've seen so far, if an AIM can't follow through with military commands, people can die." He nodded to affirm his statement. "I can bring it up with other AIMOTs, if you want. I haven't been in contact with them since the evaluations were circulated, but I can see if any of them have the same concerns. Maybe we could even get some of our own guys working on the upgrade to make sure it will be up to our needs and specifications."

Maria smiled. "That would be great. Don't bring up that there is something in the works. I'm not sure I'm even able to talk about it. Try to see if they can see a need for something, whether it means a new AIRC or a new AIM system completely. In the meantime, keep the problem AIMs in a safe scan, like a cat or a small dog. Treat it like a real animal."

That caught the soldier off-guard. "Why? What happens if the AIM disengages completely?"

"Let's not find out."

Maria was about to get back into her car when she noticed Nicholas leaving the main building. She waved, and he walked towards her. "I'll be staying at a hotel in Barrie until we're ready to go. Here's my cell number," she said, handing him a small piece of paper. "Only a few people know I'm even here in Barrie, and I'm not telling anyone where I'm staying. As you said, we have to be quiet about this, but I want to make sure people know that something is going on. They need to prepare for what's coming."

He leaned forward towards her over the car door she held open. "What do you believe is coming, Maria?"

Maria paused.

"War."

CHAPTER 16

With Maria now in Barrie, and things dealt with at the Ottawa lab the day before, Cam took a moment as he sat in his hotel room to think through what had happened. It had only been two weeks since he had finished training the new AIM. *Has it really only been two weeks since I sat on the bear scan's back as it crossed the river?* Cam leaned back against the backrest of the sofa and closed his eyes. He rubbed his face in an attempt to wipe away everything that had happened.

"I should have stayed a Scanner."

His AIM leapt onto the bed, ignoring all of Cam's previous pleas, and stared at him. "The work you have done has been extremely beneficial to many people. Why would you want to take that away?"

"If I had never joined the Underground, Maria and I would probably still be together. We would have dealt with Lucy together, and neither of us would have left the team. I wouldn't have been caught up in all this rogue AIM crap, and she never would have gone into the military to get involved with it either."

"Maria may have gone anyway. She received a letter from the army with a job opportunity."

He looked at the robot, shedding as a Golden Retriever all over the bed comforter. "What are you talking about?"

"I heard her say she was offered the AIMOT position during the off-season. With her family's military history she would not have stayed a Scanner for long."

Cam sighed and shook his head. "I don't know. I don't think she would have left so soon."

"If that had been the case, and she had left later, you would not be able to help her with her current situation, and you would not have learned how to deal with rogue AIMs. Whether you and Maria are involved in the situation or not, rogue AIMs still exist, and still need to be dealt with."

He was silent for a moment. All of a sudden, he wanted things back the way they were. *But what is that point, exactly? Before Mom died of cancer? Or before Dad left us?* "I hate it when you're right."

"Someone has to be."

He shot his AIM a stern look, before he smiled lightly. "Yeah well, you have an advantage. You have a computer chip for a brain." He grabbed his phone and flipped through the contacts. At least he had not deleted everything from his old life. He dialed a number, and waited for someone to answer. "Hi, I have something you'll want to have on the news tonight…an exclusive with Cam Tylar."

Cam walked into the TV station studio and looked around. He smiled lightly, remembering the interviews he had here in Hamilton. He had created a relationship with the Sports Anchor, and while he had used it in the past to further his career and image, now he actually needed to use it for something so much more worthwhile. He stayed close to the doors as he watched people scramble around, rolling cameras, and various people with clipboards each with an earpiece attached to their head.

"Cam Tylar?"

He turned when his name was called, and he gave his signature grin. "Hey." He reached out and shook the anchor's hand. "It's been a while."

The other man nodded with a laugh, shaking hands. "It has been. I have to say, we were all surprised to hear from you, and even more surprised you chose us as your exclusive. Why didn't you contact the Kitchener station?"

"I always brought the biggest viewership increase here than anywhere else in Ontario. You know that."

He laughed again. "Yes, I guess I do. I'm not complaining you're here. We're just surprised, is all. Susan will take care of you until we're ready for you," he said before walking to his own dressing room. It was still twenty minutes until the sports component of the news began. No need to sit around for that amount of time.

Cam followed the make-up woman and sat in a salon-style chair. He remembered his first interview. He had nearly refused to go on. There was no way he was going to wear make-up. He never felt quite right about it until he saw Maria being prepared for an interview. There was definitely a difference in how they put make-up on a man than a woman, and Cam would take his small amount of powder over what they did to her. Not that Maria really needed the make-up. She had always been stunning, but he figured it was better for the cameras.

"People were starting to think something had happened to you," Susan said as she began to prepare Cam for his interview. "I guess something did. I'm sorry."

"It's fine. I just needed to figure out a time to come back into the public eye. I wanted to get right back into it, you know?" He closed his eyes and winced. It could be worse. "Anyone interesting other than me this year?" Cam grinned.

"A few firefighters."

Cam laughed. "I bet the woman here loved that."

"Somewhat. They kept their clothes on."

"Well, they still needed you to do your job. We can't always get what we want." He paused when he noticed her eyeing him. "My shirt stays on this time."

"You used to be fun." She smiled and backed away. "Beautiful."

"I'd prefer handsome."

"You'll take what you get. Don't mess it up before you go on." Susan smiled again before she left Cam.

He sighed and closed his eyes. It used to come so easily to him, this type of banter. He worked with women so well, or at least he used to. Even when he spoke to Susan, though it was jokingly, a part of him felt as though it had died. He did not want to be like this anymore, whatever *this* was. He wanted to go back to not caring. He wanted to go back to hitting on women, and feeling on top of the world. Personal growth did not feel as good as he thought it would.

"You're on, Cam," a different woman said, pulling him from his thoughts.

He stood and walked to the edge of the stage. He waited there until he was given a signal to join the Sports Anchor on the stage.

"Last season, Canadians were shocked to learn that Scanning Tournament team Revolution was pulling out from the competition. They were even more shocked when star-player Cam Tylar left not only his team, but Scanning completely. Today, we were given the privilege of an exclusive interview with Cam Tylar."

And it begins.

Cam grinned as he walked onto the stage, and shook the man's hand once again before they each took a seat.

"Cam Tylar. It's so great to have you back in the studio."

"Thanks. It's great to be back. I've missed the interviews."

"I have to say, well, it goes without saying that we were all really shocked that you would quit when your team was in the top five. I know a lot happened last season, but can you give us an idea of what was going on at the time?"

He nodded slowly. "I guess it's out of the bag now that Maria and I dated for some time." He shot a sheepish smile to the cameras before he turned his focus back to the interviewer. "Relationships within teams aren't really recommended, but it happened. At the end of the Toronto challenge last season, Maria…we found out she was pregnant, but the baby was stillborn." Cam paused, looking down at his lap for a moment. If this was any other topic, any other time, he would have been playing this up. He had told this story so many times, he thought it would get easier with time.

It didn't.

"After that, I couldn't stay on the team. Maria took time off to recover, and I just needed to get away for a while. It was never my intention to completely leave the team, but I found I couldn't go back. Not with all of that history."

"We're so sorry for your, and Maria's, loss."

"Thank you." Cam nodded, urging himself to continue, but he waited for another question, which he knew would come soon.

"With all of that behind you, or at least while you were still dealing with it, where did you go?"

"I travelled a bit around Ontario, just to pass the time. After a while, it wasn't helping, and I knew I needed to settle down and put my energy in one place. So I focused on AIMs. Scanning has always been a part of my life, and I could never turn my back on that. My strength was always my connection with my AIM, so I wanted to look into upgrades, or anything to improve it." Cam smiled. "It was actually very enlightening. There's so much going on in terms of AIM research that I never even considered while I was competing."

This seemed to pique the anchor's interest. "I haven't heard anything about AIM research."

He nodded. "I hadn't either. It's not something that's really promoted much, but I really think it should be. There are so many upgrade possibilities for AIMs. There was one I had the opportunity to test out, because of my Scanning background. The computer chip connects and responds to the AIRC a lot faster, and the AIRC itself has more storage than the current one. I saw the AIM transform, and it was incredible how quickly it did a full transformation. I really hope the McCarthys continue with their production, because it'll bring Scanning to a whole new level."

"How did you get in contact with McCarthy researchers?"

Cam took in a deep breath. "Not many people know this, but my dad was one of the initial researchers on the AIM project, before they were commercialized. I guess his interest and research genes went down to me, and I wanted to see the kind of work he did."

"You've never mentioned your father before in any interviews. We've all been told he was a banned topic. Is there a reason for that?"

He looked away, and his heart thudded against his ribcage. "I don't talk about him with anyone. He left me and my mom when I was a kid. I never really had much to say about him until now."

"And your focus on AIM upgrades, that was a way for you to get to know who he is?"

"I guess. I mean, he's passed away now, but I wanted to see the kind of man he was. And it did help me, especially with going through the loss of my daughter. Along with that, there are a whole bunch of other things that pushed me in the research direction. But now, learning all of this, and seeing where Scanning can go, I'm ready now more than ever to get back into it, and move forward."

"You say where Scanning *can* go. Do you think it's not going in that direction?"

He shrugged. "I don't think so. As far as I know, the McCarthy company doesn't feel that commercializing this new AIM will do anything for anyone other than Scanners, but from what I've seen, they last longer and are much more durable. I know that plenty of leisure owners would want something like that, especially families with small children. I also know that when I get back into Scanning, that's the kind of AIM I'll want to use, if I can get my hands on one."

"Well, Cam, I am so glad you were willing to come in and talk with us. It really is great to see you again, and see you so well. Are you well?"

Cam thought for a moment. "I'm getting there. I've thought a lot about the kind of man I want to be, and I'm working on it."

"Thank you again, Cam."

The two men smiled and shook hands as the light above the camera went out, and in another section of the studio, a woman sitting behind a desk began to speak about local events.

"Don't hesitate to call us again when you find out more about that AIM you were talking about. Do you know any more about it?"

"Not really." *Hook. Line.* "I just know that the McCarthy company is hesitant. I've tried getting in touch with anyone willing to talk about it, but I'm just an ex-Scanner. They don't really care who I was. It's not like they'll do an interview with me."

The sports anchor nodded thoughtfully. "I'll have to see if I can get any more information on this. I'll try setting up an interview with an executive in the company and see what they can give us."

"If either of us gets more information, how about we let the other know?" Cam suggested.

"Sounds great. I'll talk to you soon."

Sinker.

When Cam reached his hotel room, he sat down on the bed with a grin on his face. He had survived the trip to the hotel, at least, without any problems. That meant either no one saw the interview yet, or they weren't bothering to follow him anymore. He was not sure which worried him more. He pulled his phone from his pocket as it began to ring, but he did so carefully as though it was a bomb waiting to explode. Who knew what Trevor was capable of? Cam smiled lightly when he saw the name of the caller on the I.D display.

"Hey. Is everything okay?"

"Yeah, I'm fine," Maria answered. "I got in contact with an AIMOT in Barrie. He's seen the same signs of an AIM going rogue."

"What did you tell him?"

"Only that there was a potentially new AIM that could be created, but the McCarthys aren't sure it would be worthwhile. The AIMOT is going to contact others and see what they think, and then he's going to send off a request for an upgrade for their AIMs. Of course, that was the other guy's idea completely.

"Of course."

Maria paused for a brief moment. "It's good to see you back on TV. Does Susan still work there?"

"Yes, and no I didn't take my shirt off."

"I wasn't going to say anything." She smiled, although Cam could not see it. She let the silence go on for a few moments before she spoke again. "I can't believe you said all of that on TV."

Cam shrugged as though she was in the same room with him. "We need to make it seem like it's their idea, and we're not the ones pressuring Trevor."

"I meant Lucy. And your dad."

He paused. "I'm tired of pretending the past never happened. Whether I remember it happening or not, it did, and I need to accept it. What my dad did, leaving me and my mom, it's part of who I am. For so long, you know that I've acted like nothing bad has ever happened to me."

"Untouchable."

"Are you okay with me talking about Lucy?"

"I never acted like nothing bad is in my past. It was difficult to hear it, but no, I didn't mind." She paused. "I'm proud of you, for what it's worth."

Cam let himself fall backwards on the bed, and he heard a similar *thump* on the other end of the phone. He smiled as they allowed silence to reign for a few moments. For three years, she had been the one he went to when something was wrong. Even if he could not tell her everything about what he did in the Underground, he went to her with everything else. She had done the same. Sometimes, they would just lay in bed together without saying a word, but somehow they were comforted. Like now.

"I saw Nicholas."

Cam shifted a bit, getting more comfortable on top of the hotel bed comforter. They were never very good. "Oh yeah? How did that go?"

"He's completely behind me. I didn't expect anything less. He was always very supportive, but it's good to know that I have at least one person in the military I can trust. He saved my dad's life, and my dad did the same for him, so I have no reason to think he'd do anything less than that for this. He's setting up an appointment to meet with the Minister of Defense."

"Well, that's definitely on the right track."

Maria turned her head to the side as her AIM leapt onto the bed next to her, and she smiled. "Yeah. I think with my talk with the AIMOT, your interview, and my meeting with the Minister, we actually have a shot at getting Trevor to take the new AIM into production. It'd be nice if we could get some charges on him too, as a bit of an incentive."

"We need to be careful about that, though. If Trevor feels like he's being cornered, he'll snap and attack."

"Hasn't he already done that?"

"Apparently not."

Maria swore. "I would ask if you're staying low, but that interview pretty much advertised your location like a huge neon sign saying 'here I am, Trevor!'"

"No one followed me, and if something was going to happen to me, it would have happened already. It worries me that no one's following me, but I'm going to take advantage of it as long as possible."

"Just stay safe, okay?"

"I will. You too." He paused for a minute. "I'm glad you called." He heard her sigh through the phone.

"Me too."

Cam sat up abruptly in his bed, woken by the sound of his cell phone ringing. With his eyes wide in the dark, he groped around the nightstand. "Hello?" he said, when he finally found his phone.

"Cam, it's Sandra. I got a hold of Henk."

"Finally. Is he okay?"

"He says he's fine, and that he's staying near the border. He doesn't want to go to any labs in case someone's following him. With the way things were left between you two, you must understand why he is hesitant to answer your calls."

"I guess, but with everything that's happened I assumed he would take my calls. But, I understand why he's staying near the border. We both know they will be following him." He swung his legs over the side of the bed and turned the lamp on. He winced as the room was illuminated and he rubbed his face. "Where is he?"

"Windsor. He's trying to collect as much data as he can, backing it up on a secure hard-drive. I'm going to tell everyone to use him as a hub from now on, rather than me. There are fifteen people missing now."

"I don't know why Trevor doesn't just blow up each of our labs. It'd save him a lot of time," he grumbled.

"I don't think he's quite that desperate."

"Or insane."

"What do you mean?" she asked.

"There's a guy in the Ottawa lab who works for Trevor's brother."

"Cohner?"

"Yeah." Cam gently pushed away his AIM, who had nudged him for a catch-up. When the animal let out a whimper, he put Sandra on speaker. "I guess they tried to get Trevor to step down, even before our presentation. Cohner wants enough evidence to prove that Trevor's not a capable leader for the company. I don't even understand how he got the family business if Cohner's older. I don't really care, but this guy in our lab said that Trevor's lost it."

"I hope that's not true. Once lawsuits come in, we don't want him pleading insanity."

"Even if he does, there are enough people working in partner companies to convict them." He swore again. "Even in the military."

"How is she?"

"Dating."

Sandra paused. "I'm sorry."

"Ryan."

"I'm really sorry."

"I'll give her a call tomorrow, or I guess later today, to see how she's doing. She thinks she may have a way to get her report to the Minister of Defense. I guess she has a connection in the military who can get her a meeting with him. If she can do that, we may not even need to approach Trevor. If we get to him before she gets her report in, we can use that threat to support our case to him. She's also spoken to another AIMOT who seems to be pretty into this new AIM upgrade we've sort of been advertising, so Trevor will be getting more pressure from them. I'll fly down to Windsor in the morning. Can you make sure Henk knows?"

"I'll let him know." Sandra paused, and listened to Cam breathe. "I saw the interview."

"Well, it's good to know you watch the news."

"I think a lot of people saw that interview."

"What about it?"

"I think it was good for you."

"We'll see."

* * *

Cam walked through the Windsor airport with a duffle bag slung over his shoulder, thankful for the relatively small size of the terminal, and even more thankful of the small amount of traffic.

"You are sure of this?" His AIM said while in the form of a mouse: its usual form while on an airplane. "Should you be meeting with Henk and risk someone seeing you with him?"

"I have no choice," Cam replied. "He's the only one they'll expect back in Boston, when we get to that point. Maybe they should see me with him, and let them know we're not backing down."

"If Trevor has indeed lost his sanity, it would perhaps be best to approach this with caution. He must not feel threatened."

"It's too late for that."

Soon after, Cam knocked on the door of a motel room across from the airport. He glanced around. Henk should have chosen a more secure area, but it made sense. If he needed to get out of the city fast, this was the best place to be. Or if he wanted to make it look as though Henk was open to the idea of having visitors.

The door opened slowly, and Henk's face came from around the door cautiously. A smile broke across his face and he opened the door wider. "I have to say that I am surprised you showed up. Sandra let me know you would be coming, but I had a hard time believing her after…well, after you quit."

Cam stepped into the room with a clenched jaw. "I was kind of forced back into it. I'm doing what I have to in order to get this fixed."

"L.J., you must understand this: that is all your father and I did. My not telling you about your father was a fulfillment of a promise to him."

He stayed silent, keeping his eyes away from the older man. He looked around the entire room, attempting to find something to keep his eyes busy while the man spoke. He understood now why his father left more than ever. If they had gone through anything similar to this situation, his father would have had no choice. Who knew if Ryan was now in danger because of his association with Maria, even if they thought she was now dead? He turned back to Henk finally.

"Look, I get it. He asked you to make sure I stayed safe. I do get that, but you can't think that it was right," Cam said, meeting Henk's eye.

"It was the safest thing."

Cam sighed. "Close enough."

Henk smiled lightly. "So, you are here to work with me once again."

"Oh, so you're finally saying I work with you, and not for you?"

He laughed. "Yes, well, there is no true hierarchy anymore." His face turned stoic as he motioned to the chairs in the room. Despite the building being a motel, it was still reasonably furnished. "I am glad you came. I cannot do any of this alone."

"I don't think any of us can."

Henk shook his head. The two men sat down across from each other. "I have been approached by an employee of Trevor. He claims to have information about how to get back to Boston and put the new substance into production."

Cam nearly choked on nothing, but thought for a moment. "That doesn't make any sense."

"How so?"

"Did Sandra tell you about Sharar?" He continued when Henk nodded. "He's working for Cohner. From what he said, it sounds like they're still trying to figure how to get Trevor to sign off on it, or step down. Now you've found someone who has a way to get our work into production?"

"Apparently this is someone who works directly for Trevor, not Cohner."

Cam folded his arms across his chest and leaned forward. "And you think we can trust what he says? You know better than I about how long people live when they turn against Trevor. Are there people stupid enough to do that?"

"Stupid is perhaps not the correct word. Instead, I believe the word is 'desperate' or 'converted.' I truly believe that he is sincere. He has discovered that someone he...cares for has been put in jeopardy because of Trevor, and no longer believes in that side of the fight."

"I can't say I blame him."

"He wants to meet with both of us."

Cam cocked his head to the side. "He knew we'd be in touch? That raises a bit more concern."

"Technically, no, but I'm sure he would want you to be there as well, if he knew you were here. L.J., everyone was expecting that we would be in touch. Whether you like it or not, I consider you to have taken your father's role as my second in command." Henk shrugged lightly. "I trust no one more than I do you. You must know that. I am sorry to have wronged you, but it was all I could do to keep my relationship with your father a secret."

Cam nodded and glanced towards his AIM as it sat on the table in front of his arm, its whiskers flickering around as it smelled the table. "Did he give a place and time?"

"Tomorrow afternoon, in a hotel in Detroit."

He laughed. "I guess it fits. I've never felt safe in that city. Very fitting." Cam stood and grabbed his duffle bag, hauling it back onto his shoulder. The attaché case was safely stored inside, but it made the bag rather heavy to carry. "I'll get a room at a different motel and meet you back here. We can drive over. Sunday mornings are always pretty clear to cross the border. I'll send my AIM over to scout it out before we get there. Maybe even tonight to take a look around the city. It's been complaining about never being in a bird form anymore."

Henk grinned. "In the beginning I wanted so badly to destroy it, but your father was convinced you would be able to control it. He was right. You had it under control in only a few days."

Cam looked at the table, and spun around, his eyes trained on the ground. "I wouldn't say I have it under control. It tolerates me." He turned his attention to his AIM to find it missing. "Seriously, where did you go now?" A scratching noise came from a pile of papers on the floor, and a pop can tipped over next to the door. From behind it, a small mouse crawled towards Cam.

"I find the smells this form receives fascinating. There are so many." The small mouse eyes looked up at the human. "Are we leaving already?"

CHAPTER 17

Ryan held a hand up to Rick when his phone rang, telling him to give him a few moments. "Maria, hi."

"Hey, how are you?"

"I'm pretty good. We're about to start a challenge in a few minutes."

"Oh, sorry. I didn't even think to check your schedule first."

"That's okay. I have some time. Are you okay?"

"Yeah, I'm fine, actually. I just...I wanted to hear your voice. There's a lot going on, and I just need that one bit of solid ground."

He smiled, even if she could not see him. "That's good to hear, I guess. You're sure you're okay?"

"Things are going really well, actually. It worries me that things are going so well, but as long as this lasts, I'm not going to complain."

Ryan hesitated, and tried to listen to the background noises over the phone. He closed his eyes, hating himself for even trying.

"What is it?"

"Where's Cam?" he asked softly.

"I don't know. We parted ways after we left you guys in Kingston. He has his job, and I have mine. Ryan, you have to believe me that-"

"I do."

She hesitated. "Do you?"

He copied her hesitation. "I think so. You have to understand how hard it is for me. It was hard when we were all on the team together. It was fine this past year, but now with him back in the picture-"

"Ryan, he's not back in the picture. He's back in our lives, but that's different. And who knows how long he'll be around for. He's…in a completely different place now. We most likely have no place in his life again."

He laughed. "Well, he may not have a place for you. I saw his interview. We all saw his interview. From the way it sounded, he'll probably want to come back into Scanning. We'll have a place in his life."

"If I didn't know you better, I'd think you were trying to make me jealous."

"You wouldn't be jealous if you didn't want something."

"I'm not jealous, and I don't want anything. Not from him."

"Okay." He paused and lowered his voice. "Maria, I watched the interview with the rest of the guys. They said they never knew about Cam's dad. Did you?"

She sighed. "Yeah. He told me. Even before we were dating."

Ryan nodded when he saw Rick waving him over for the start of their challenge. "Rick's calling me. I should get going. Can I call you after the challenge?"

"It would probably be best to let me call you. I'm hoping to have a meeting later today with some government officials."

"Are you allowed to tell me that?"

"I think it's actually safer for me to tell you I'm meeting politicians in Ottawa, just in case."

"In case there's another attack?"

"Just in case of anything. I'll talk to you later."

Maria sighed when Ryan hung up. Maria sat in her vehicle, staring at the dashboard. After her phone conversation with Cam, the foundation she had created for her life without him was left slightly fractured. *Nothing's changed.* When she looked into her rear view mirror she saw Nicholas park his vehicle and walk into the military building. She quickly left her vehicle and headed into the building, and jogged a few steps to catch up with the other soldier. "Nicholas?"

He turned around. His eyes were wide for a moment, as if caught red-handed somehow, but his face quickly adorned a smile. "You got my message then. Good. I finalized a meeting time since I contacted you. He's open to meeting with us at four o'clock."

Maria looked at her watch and looked back at him quickly. "It's ten. There's no way we could drive there in less than six hours."

Nicholas smiled and motioned for her to follow him. "We'll have a chopper bring us in. Do you have everything with you?"

"Yeah. I checked out from the hotel already. When are we heading out?"

"Noon. That will give us some time to get settled in Ottawa. I'm hoping that when the General hears what you have to say, and has a chance to look over your report, we'll be able to speak with the Minister."

She shot a questioning glance up at the man. "Wait, I thought we had a meeting with the Minister?"

"I couldn't get in to see him. Not yet, at least. I thought about it, and this makes the most sense when looking at the proper line of protocol. The General should be the one to approach the Minister with this, along with our support of course."

Maria frowned as she thought. She knew he was right, that this was likely the best route to getting her report to the proper agents, but it only meant one more step to getting to where she needed to be. "How quickly would we be able to see him?"

"I guess it depends if he thinks it's urgent or not."

"Then we need to show him how urgent it is." She looked around the hallway as they finally reached his office. "I think I'm going to take another look around. I found your AIMOT the other day. He has some concerns about the AIMs. I didn't say anything about rogues, but I put a seed in his head at least based on what he's already recognized. I'd like to see some of the AIMs in training before we leave, if that's alright with you. If I notice anything else, it can only help us, and if I don't, it won't hurt us at least."

"Just make sure you're on the tarmac at noon."

She nodded as they turned away from each other, and she headed back out the building. Her mouth scrunched to the side as she thought, wondering where the AIM training facilities were. She had meant to ask the AIMOT when she had seen him, but it had slipped her mind. Maria attempted to picture the base from above, and located each building in her mind. The only problem was that when her father had been here, AIMs were not as integrated into the military, and their training building was shared with the main training building. It was at least somewhere to start.

Maria headed to the south end of the base slowly, making note of each building as she passed. Knowing she would be meeting the Minister, or assuming she was going to be meeting him, she had opted to wear her service dress which looked more formal than her operational dress. She knew she stood out amongst the soldiers who were completing physical training or who were regularly on the base, but maybe that was a good thing. She pushed negative thoughts from her mind; the thoughts which told her that standing out was bad when she was not sure how many people wanted her dead, and where those people were.

She found the training building and she smiled. For once, some things managed to stay the same. With all the changes in the world, it was nice to see even just one thing the same. The world had changed so much even in her own lifetime with the introduction of AIMs, and something like this was desperately needed. At least, that was her stand on it. Maria pulled open the door to the building and looked into the large gymnasium-styled room. Physical training equipment was placed around the open building, and there were various groups at each station. She remembered Nicholas having to deal with new recruits when she first arrived, and judging by the way they attempted to complete their obstacles, these were them. With a grin, she walked over to the closest group. She watched them for a moment, standing next to the drill sergeant.

One recruit stared at the wooden wall before him, and leapt. He desperately clung to the wooden beams as he tried to find his footing. His face twisted in concentration. He moved up two slats before falling backwards onto the cushioning below. Maria looked at the drill sergeant, glancing briefly at his name tag, Brant. "How new are these guys?"

"Fresh out of Basic, apparently."

Maria held back a laugh as she watched another recruit fall. "Did they never have to face the wall before?"

"Only with an AIM."

"I'm pretty fresh out of Basic myself and even I didn't get to use my AIM for the wall." She glanced around. She had not seen an AIM all day, she realized. "Where are the AIMs?"

"They're having their own check-up. Regular maintenance. It's better for these guys to learn how to do it without their AIM in case it becomes compromised in combat. I've heard that happens, so we need them to be prepared for everything."

"It does happen," she said softly as she continued to watch. The sergeant was being kindly silent. The yelling would come later, Maria assumed. "May I?"

Brant grinned. "Please. They need their ego crushed a bit more."

This time, she did laugh. She turned to the new soldiers, and the smile left her face. "Attention, Privates!" When all but a few turned to her and saluted, she stepped forward with a scowl on her face. "Was I not clear enough? Did I say that you could ignore me?" She stopped until she was face to face with a soldier who had continued talking. "Did I, Private?"

"No, Ma'am."

"Oh good. You're not deaf. So you'll just die in combat because of your own stupidity." Maria backed away and eyed the wall. "Are you telling me that every single one of you has failed at this wall?" No one answered. "Someone, please explain how you survived Basic Training. I'd really love to know."

"We worked together with our AIM unit, Ma'am," one answered. "We were taught how to work as a team, not as an individual."

"And what happens if the rest of your team is dead, Private?" she snapped. "What if your AIM has been compromised?" When he remained silent, she stepped in front of him. "Answer me, Private."

"I would be on my own, Ma'am."

"And what would happen if you needed to get over a wall on your own?"

He paused. "I would die, Ma'am."

"Yes, you would." She looked around at the men. "We need to learn how to work together; to feed off each other's strengths and weaknesses, and use each other effectively. I can guarantee you that there will be times when you will be on your own. Whether you were dropped off at the wrong location, you were separated from your group, or the rest of your team was killed in combat, you will be alone at least once during your service. You need to know how to use your own strength, and you need to learn how to use your weaknesses too. In my case," she paused as she untucked her service shirt, "I have extensive background in completing obstacle courses. I will use that to my advantage. On the other hand," she paused again as she stood in front of the wooden wall, "I'm also used to having three other people lend me a hand, plus four AIMs. That's my weakness. I'm not used to working alone. I've only started to be able to rely on myself to get jobs completed. But I still use my teamwork to help me. For example, if my team were here, I would come at this from a running start, and get a boost."

Maria backed up, and ran at the wall. Within a few steps of the wall, she jumped and clutched to the side of the wall, the muscles on her arms and legs taut. She looked up to see how much of the wall she had left to climb. *The one day I wear my service dress, I train. The General will have to forgive me.* "By now, some more of my teammates would be up along with me. One would probably be at the top already. He would lean down and I would need to climb up just a bit more to reach his hand," she called out over her shoulder, as she slowly pulled herself up the slats. Her shoes were too big to fit between the slats, so she had to rely solely on her arm muscles. She managed to find a foothold a few slats from the top.

"Now I have to act as if I'm the one leading; that the success of my team depends on my actions." She pulled herself up the rest of the way. She swung a leg over the side and straddled the top of the wall. "What happens if you're alone, but you notice that refugees are chasing after you, trying to get to safety? Do we help them?"

"Yes," the soldiers answered in unison.

Maria hugged the wall with her thighs and leaned down, using one arm to keep her steady as the other reached down. "Well then, come on."

One by one the soldiers attempted the wall, mimicking her movements up the side until they reached her arm. Some continued their attempt without using her help, and managed to climb up the last part of the wall. When they were all on the ground on the other side, she jumped down and looked at them. "Now do it again."

She walked back to the drill sergeant who still wore a grin on his face. "I haven't done the wall since Basic. I'm glad I could actually do it."

"But you've done walls before, Maria Kier. It's not like you didn't know how to approach it."

Maria returned his smile with a shrug. "I always had rock climbing gear with me. I never took a risk without having the proper equipment with me. Would you be able to tell me where the AIMs are getting their maintenance done?" She waited for his answer as she tucked her shirt back in and readjusted her uniform.

"Through the double doors and in the building across the way. Thank you, Lieutenant."

"No problem." She saluted and headed out in the direction he sent her. Watching the soldiers attempt the wall again made her smile. She did miss the physical part of Scanning. Sure, she kept up with fitness. She needed to. But it was still not the same. There was no rush of the challenge, and for the most part, there is very little teamwork. The thrill of the win was much different from the rush of adrenaline she had felt while she had been deployed. It had not been a good feeling.

She found her way to the AIM training building, and stopped dead in her tracks. There was no one there. Similar to the training facility, this was an open concept with obstacles, but made for animals. There should at least be someone here at all times to watch the AIMs. As she moved further into the building, she noticed that she was not alone. Along the far wall, there was a line of AIMs, sitting at attention as she was sure they had been commanded to do until someone returned. She approached the line, and they stood as though to salute her.

"What is your schedule?" she asked them. Each military AIM was given a schedule, which would include any maintenance needed.

"Maintenance from eleven hundred to fourteen hundred hours, Ma'am," the AIM responded.

Maria glanced around. It was quarter to eleven now. She could wait, but she was not going to wait while doing nothing. "Who is carrying out the maintenance?"

"Officer Markham, Ma'am."

Not that it mattered, really. She did not know the names of anyone on the base, and did not know who was supposed to be doing it.

"Has anyone been in the building today before me?"

"No."

At least no one had tampered with them.

"Is it permissible that I take you through some exercises before Officer Markham comes for your maintenance?"

"Affirmative, AIMOT."

She raised an eyebrow, but realized it had observed the marking on her shoulder. She nodded and took in her surroundings. She wanted to find an obstacle which would hopefully show any lack of communication with the AIM. A table in the corner housed various AIRCs. She went to that first and examined the devices. Maria picked one up and immediately an AIM took a step forward, getting a signal from the device. She nodded. That would do.

"What is your unit number?"

"AIM-2809."

"Good. Follow me then. The remaining AIMs, please follow and observe." She stood in front of a wooden obstacle course. For some reason, no matter the advances in technology, they still used wood for their training exercises. "2809, you will go up the ramp and through the tunnel. I will shift your form so you can climb to the top of the pole. You will find a way to cross to the second pole, come back down, and I will shift you again. After that, you will run a lap around the room and return back to me. Are your instructions clear?"

"Yes, Ma'am."

"Go."

Maria watched as the AIM in the form of a German shepherd ran towards the obstacle. She analyzed every step it took up the ramp, and relied on the AIRC to show its vitals as it ran through the tunnel along the edge of the wall. The AIM stopped when it came out from the other end of the tunnel, and she scrolled through the various scans they used in the military. She found a bear cub scan and smiled. It was not the most popular scan in a soldier's library, but it would be different to use. She chose the scan, and watched as the AIM climbed up the pole, which now that she looked at it closely, it almost resembled a tree. The AIM stopped near the top and looked across to the pole parallel to the one it clung to. It would need to leap for it. Maria waited as the robot analyzed the distance, and then watched as it pushed itself from one pole, and gripped the second pole with the bear claws, slipping down the pole slightly until it got a proper hold of the wood. It made its way down, but stopped just before it got to the bottom.

She watched as the bear seemed to sniff the air and look around itself curiously. It looked over its shoulder at her, and called out as a baby bear would call out for its mother. After a moment, it made its way to the ground and sniffed at the wooden platform it stood on. Maria went to switch it back to a German Shepherd, but the word 'Error' filled the screen of the AIRC. She swore and looked up at the bear again. It called out again and sat down, looking around. It was going rogue before her eyes. She swore again and jabbed the touchscreen of the AIRC as if it would help.

"What do I do? What do I do?" she muttered under her breath as she went into the programming for the bear cub scan on the electronic device. There was something in that file she had never noticed before. Quickly, she pushed the part of the screen that said 'Discharge' and suddenly the bear cub vibrated and shifted into its original form of a whitish gel. Maria stared at the platform while the other AIMs stood next to her.

"Did any AIM unit record that?" Maria asked softly.

"Yes," the AIM which Maria first spoke to answered.

"Please send that to my AIRC, and send it to every other AIM here." She walked up onto the platform and gathered the thick gel. She went back to the table with the AIRCs and grabbed an AIM transportation case from the shelf above it, and placed the gel inside. After securing the case, she turned to leave the building. Her step faltered when her phone rang.

"Lieutenant Kier."

"Maria? It's Sandra."

She stopped briefly, thinking. "Yes, sorry. Hi." Her heart began to pound. *Why would she need to be calling me? Unless...* "Is everything alright?"

"Yes. Well, mostly. I was wondering if you would be able to do me a favour. Cam mentioned you're heading up to Ottawa. We have a lab there which Trevor has infiltrated. We don't know how long this person has been there, but he's not responding to any of our own people."

"You need information from this person?"

"We're hoping we can find at least one person who knows exactly what Trevor is trying to get against us. We know he's been trying to contact Canadian politicians and military officers, but we need to know what lies he's been telling them before we approach them."

Maria stepped out of the building to the near noon sun. It looked like the AIM maintenance was behind schedule. "Why do you need me?"

"We need someone with...advanced interrogation skills."

"I don't know what Cam told you about me, but I'm not an interrogator. I'm an AIMOT. I deal with AIMs, not people."

"But your father was an interrogator."

She stopped. She hated that these people knew so much about her. She hated it more knowing that Cam had been the one who told them. When he had told them, she had no idea, but they knew, and that was a problem for her.

"I'll be heading out for Ottawa in twenty minutes. Give me the location, and it'll be my first stop before my meeting."

"With the Minister?"

"No. That was delayed. I'm meeting with the Chief of Defense first, the General."

"Oh, alright. You'll have full access to the building once you get there," Sandra said, before relaying the location of the Ottawa lab.

As Maria listened to Sandra speak to her as though she was a co-worker, she felt a small part of her die. She realized the person she was only a year ago, the person who spoke confidently against the dangers of the Underground, and the immorality of the institution, it was that person that was finally in her death throes. It should have been a relief, but there were still some things Maria felt the need to cling to. Today would not be the day in which that happened. More than likely, tomorrow would not be that day either.

Maria headed out towards the front parking lot and grabbed her duffle bag from her car. After locking it back up, she looked it over. She would need to leave it here for who knew how long, and leaving it alone for anyone to tamper with. It should be safe on the military base, but then again, she should have been safe as well. Clearly, it had not happened that way. With a sigh, she picked up the AIM case and, followed by her own AIM, she headed for the airstrip. She was glad it was not far away, but she could hear the sound of a helicopter flying in. Looking up, that sound did in fact accompany a chopper landing on the airstrip. She still had ten minutes to get to the airstrip, but even so, she sped up.

Once she got closer she noticed Nicholas just ahead of her, already speaking with the chopper pilot. She fiddled with her AIRC, grabbing it properly, and shifted her AIM from the usual German shepherd to a small field mouse. She bent over to pick it up, and placed it in the front pocket of her shirt. When she had needed to travel on the airplane while in the CST, this was the form she, and many others, had chosen. At least some things never changed.

"Are we ready to go?" she yelled as she stood next to him.

"Yeah." He looked down at her, and noticed the AIM case she carried. "Souvenir?"

"Evidence. I'll tell you in a minute. We should get going. I need to get something done in Ottawa before we meet with the General." She pulled herself onto the military helicopter and fastened herself in. She took a headset from the pilot and ensured everything was functioning.

"Do you need me to go with you?" Nicholas asked as he settled in across from her.

"No. I have to do this alone. No one can know I'm working with you. I have no idea if they already know but I don't want you to get caught in the cross-fire, if it ever comes. But this," she motioned towards the case, "this is an AIM from your base. I was going through some training with one of them, and it began to go rogue as I was using it. I have no idea how I got it under control, but I got it into its default form and shut it down. I want to bring it with me in case we need it."

Nicholas's eyes widened as he stared at her. "You were able to control it?"

"No, not really. I pressed a bunch of things on the AIRC and it reverted back to its gel state." *Was this how it had started for Cam? His AIM was 'special' so maybe he had learned at a very young age to deal with things like this. He knew what to look for.* She made a note to call him after her meeting to tell him about it. Now that she was thinking about it, she would have to tell him that she had run into Jack. Or rather, that he had run into her. So much had happened in such a short amount of time.

"How long will this other work take?"

"I have no idea. It depends how much I remember."

"Remember what?"

Maria looked out from the helicopter as it now began to fly over Barrie towards the nation's capital. "My dad."

CHAPTER 18

Cam tapped his fingers on the car door handle in time with the song on the radio. Sunday mornings typically meant an easy border crossing between Canada and the United States. Today, they were sitting behind only two vehicles, but one seemed to be giving the border patrol a hard time. He looked over his shoulder to the cat in the back seat. He hated the cat form, unlike Maria, but it seemed to be comfortable for his AIM at the moment. He would never understand the feeling of needing to be in a different form. Then again, he always made do with what he had.

"Have you found reports of AIM-related injuries?"

The AIM uncurled its head from beneath the cat paws to look at Cam. "Yes. I have found a significant amount of reports in which people claim they, or a loved one, were attacked by an AIM. I went a step further, knowing you would request it of me, and researched reports of AIMs no longer functioning properly. It seems that the McCarthy Company has replaced AIMs which have been reported as defective, which has been classified as those which do not connect properly with the AIRC system. I have downloaded the appropriate news articles, and will have it ready to send to the media at your request, when the time is right," the AIM added. "As long as I am able to connect with a network."

"Can you make a list of names of the people involved? If there are any military people involved with that, I can send them to Maria."

The AIM shifted in the backseat, preparing to ignore the humans once again. "Cameron, you do not need an excuse to call her."

Cam turned back around in his seat as Henk drove the vehicle forward, now sitting next in line at the border. "I'm not looking for an excuse," he muttered. "Just get me the list, would you?"

"Please tell me that this drive is not going to be a mirror of the past four years?" Henk sighed, glancing over to Cam. When he did not reply, he looked forward. "You need to be prepared for who we are going to see."

He raised an eyebrow and looked at the older man. "What do you mean?"

"You know him. You must remember that what you think you know of him may not be correct. Remember that he has been jilted, and betrayed. While he is seeking revenge, he is also seeking justice, just as we are."

Cam rolled his eyes. "I know this person? Well, that's not saying much about me, or him, I guess." He looked back over his shoulder and poked the robot, earning a low feline growl. "Once we cross the border, we'll need you to scout ahead. That is, unless your majesty wants to continue napping needlessly, since robots don't need to nap. And like it or not, you're still a robot."

"I'm adopting the feline personality," it replied, almost tiredly. "Is that not what I was programmed to do?" It stretched and sat up as Henk pulled up to the border patrol booth. "It will be difficult searching for something unknown."

"Good thing you did that for five years in the CST," Cam said with a grin, passing his passport to Henk.

Henk and Cam remained in the vehicle in the parking lot of the Detroit Convention Centre. Cam's AIM had returned with a report of no suspicious activity. Nothing was happening. That was never a good thing.

"You're sure this is where he wanted to meet?" Cam asked.

Henk looked at him with a stern look. "When was the last time you remember me forgetting something?"

"Two years ago you forgot Sandra's birthday."

He waved a hand with a snort. "That does not count."

"I'd like to be there when you tell her that."

They both jumped in their seats when Henk's phone began to ring. "Hello?"

Cam watched the man's face turn from friendly, to nervous. Henk looked around quickly and nodded.

"Yes, that is fine. I understand." He hung up and started the ignition, speedily pulling out from the parking lot. "He has been delayed. He suggested we find another meeting spot in a few more days."

"Or maybe now he's lying, and it was just to find us," Cam muttered angrily.

"It was not safe for him to come. He is being followed."

"Of course he is."

"You were told that there was no next target by the man who attempted to kill Maria, correct?"

Cam looked at Henk, his eyes wide with surprise. "How did you know that?"

"Because this man knows. He also knows the next target."

"Who is it?"

Henk glanced at Cam. "It is him."

He groaned. "That gets the sympathy vote. Can we make sure he doesn't get killed before we get a chance to talk to him?"

"He is staying in the public eye as much as possible, so no one will make a move." Henk gave a soft smile. "Similar to your move. It is smart. Dangerous, but smart, because however insane Trevor has become, he is not stupid. He will not risk making a scene in public."

"But he'll let people get killed by AIMs."

"I only said he is not stupid."

Maria was grateful for the new advances in technology. Most days, at least. With the new helicopters the Canadian military had bought a few years earlier, they were able to fly to Ottawa in just under an hour at cruising speed. That would give her plenty of time to go to the lab Sandra was sending her to. She hoped so, at least. *Who knows how long it will take for me to interrogate this person? Can I even do it?* She borrowed a military vehicle, and followed the directions Sandra had given her over the phone. As she drove, Maria shifted her AIM back into the form of a German shepherd. It gave her comfort. It was such a strong looking animal, and it always made her feel safe. After close to twenty minutes of driving, she pulled into a parking lot adjacent to a warehouse. It looked similar to the lab she had been to in Niagara Falls. Pulling around the back of the warehouse she found vehicles hidden there as well. She wanted to roll her eyes. Clearly if Trevor wanted to get into the lab, he would not waste time seeing if anyone was there or not. He would get people into the labs before everything happened. Apparently, he had already done that.

She put her hand onto the scanner after she parked the borrowed vehicle and once again cringed as the door unlocked with the gesture. She walked in, and everyone turned to her. Maria looked around cautiously. Sandra had not told her who to speak with. She assumed whoever needed her there would find her, but with the curious and scared looks she was getting from the Underground workers, Maria was beginning to think that no one knew she was going to be there.

After a few awkward moments, a man finally stepped forward.

"Hi, Maria, sorry. Sandra wasn't sure when you'd get here. I tried calling Cam, but he's already been here and-"

"He was?"

"Yeah. He did his own interrogation of someone, but after he left, we found someone else who didn't quite belong," he said as he began to lead her down a corridor. "I'm Walter," he introduced himself and as they left the front entry of the warehouse, people began to continue with their own work. They did not seem to be extremely chaotic, but perhaps it was because of the military presence.

"Why was I called here? I'm not part of the Underground. I'm pretty sure everyone has seen my views on it in interviews when I was Scanning." They stopped in front of a set of double doors and she shrugged. "Why me?"

He sighed. "Because we need someone from the outside. We need someone who can truthfully tell this guy that they don't work for the Underground, and we need someone who has publically shamed the Underground. We also need your ability to ...interrogate."

"I'm not a torturer. Any interrogation skills I have, my dad taught me when I was younger. It's not really my job."

The man laughed. "If Cam can do it, I'm sure you'll have better luck."

She paused. He had a point. "So what kind of information are you trying to get out of him? Sandra didn't go into many details."

"He works for Trevor. We need to know how much he knows, and what they're trying to use to bring us down. We know that he's been approaching people, saying that the Underground is coming up with dangerous products, but we need to know what kind of evidence he has against us. When we find that out, we can use that. You, Cam, and Henk, especially. We know you're meeting with military officials, so this is something you'll need to know as well."

Maria nodded. "Alright. Let's get this over with. I only have an hour, so whether I get my answers or not, I'm leaving." Not quite the truth, but the sooner she left, the better.

"Fair enough," he answered as she stepped into the room. She was surprised to see a man sitting behind a table as she would see in a cop show on TV. There was no one-way mirror, though. Just the man. She looked him over. He seemed to be in his early thirties. She wished she was better at estimating a person's age by looking at them. She knew that looks were not a good indicator, however. With the advances of plastic surgery, any one could look any age they chose. Or on the other hand, some people did not age as quickly as others. She, for one, did not begin to look her age until she hit her twenties.

"I'm Lieutenant Kier," she introduced herself as she sat down across from the man. "I didn't get a chance to get your name before I came in." She waited a moment and she smiled. "I'll call you Henry, if that's okay. I was called in to get information from you, which I'm sure you assumed. They need to know what kind of information you have on them, and I need to know too."

He looked at her, and an eyebrow raised only slightly to show his curiosity.

"They think I'm working with them, but I'm actually conducting my own investigation against them. I'm trying to find as much evidence as I can to bring criminal charges up. If I can get enough information, Henk and his top team will be looking at charges of acts of terrorism. To do that, I need concrete evidence though. You'll remain anonymous, so they don't try going after you or whoever you're working for. They seem to think you're working for Trevor McCarthy, but I have a feeling that's an unfounded assumption. If you have absolutely anything that can help bring down the Underground, it would be a help. But it needs to be concrete. I've already found people who heard something from someone who may have seen it somewhere once. That's not going to be good enough."

The man was silent for a moment, and he looked down at the table, his hands clasped in front of him. He was not bound, which at least meant that he would feel safe. He would not feel threatened. That was important.

"My name actually is Henry," he said quietly.

Maria smiled. "You look like a Henry. Well, no, that's a lie. My first guess was Steven, actually."

"Who are you working under?"

She raised an eyebrow. "I'm conducting my own investigation. Do you think I'd take this to my superiors before I had anything concrete? I'm only a Lieutenant. I have a meeting with the General which depends on the results of this conversation."

Henry nodded slowly and glanced around. When he felt comfortable enough, he looked back to Maria. "They've created an AIM, a new substance and a new chip. They're doing this through illegal imports, and stealing research from the McCarthy Company. We haven't caught them taking it from the mainstream labs, but I have papers, photocopies and second drafts here in this lab that I know were from Boston. Obviously I don't have them in this room with me, but as long as they haven't torn my desk apart, they should still be there locked in my drawer."

"They haven't gone through any of your belongings yet. Will you give me permission to look through it after we talk?"

Henry leaned forward. "As long as you use it to bring this group to the ground, you can do whatever you want with my research."

Maria nodded. "Thank you. Is there anything else? What do you know about this new substance? You said they've also created a new chip too? Who was involved with that?"

"Everyone was involved with the substance, as far as I know. All the scientists at least. They all had some part in it, either in the testing or the production. With the chip, only a select few were part of it." He grinned. "Are you sure you really want to know who was involved with that? You may not like the answer."

"Henry?" Maria leaned forward, mimicking his gesture. "I'm already hating the situation I'm in. Trust me, it can't get any worse than having someone try to kill me."

"Your old boyfriend was the lead chip programmer."

She froze. "Cam?" She leaned back into her chair and stared at him for a few moments. "He's in the Underground?"

"Works pretty close with Henk, actually."

Maria shook her head. "I need concretes. I need proof. I can't go by what I hear from you. I can't…I lived with him for three years, and I never knew any of this."

"Guess he's as good at lying as he is at his job."

She took a deep breath and covered her face. "What exactly is bad about this new AIM? If it's an upgrade, why would Trevor not want to take advantage of the money he can make from it? Is it because of the stigma of the Underground?"

"These new AIMs are dangerous. They say they last longer, but I've seen them attack people. I…I don't have any paperwork for that, but I'm working on it."

"I don't have time to wait for you to figure it out. I'm meeting with the General today. Are there any recordings of these AIMs attacking people that I can get from people working here?"

Henry thought for a moment. "There should be. Ask to see the training exercises. Make them think you're interested in hearing what they have to say."

She looked at her watch and nodded. "Okay. I'll see how much of this I can pass on. Give me something I can tell the guys waiting outside the door. I try not to lie, so I need you to actually say it."

"I know nothing."

She nodded again. "Good enough." Maria stood and headed for the door. "Thank you, Henry, for your cooperation." She walked through the doors and met with the man who had brought her to the interviewing room. "He has evidence in his desk drawers. He claims you guys stole the research from McCarthy labs, but that can be easily cross referenced to show that it originated in your labs. He said that he has evidence of your new AIM attacking people, and he told me to look through the recorded archives of training exercises. You need to be able to prove that the AIMs attacking people in the videos are actually McCarthy AIMs, not your new ones. That's all he has. Oh, and his name's Henry."

The man's forehead lined with thoughtfulness. "I thought his name was Steve."

Maria smiled, and held back a laugh. "If that's all, I'm going to head out."

"Thank you, Maria."

"Don't thank me yet. Wait until all of this is over, and then we'll see who came out on top." She glanced around before leaning in towards him. "That was too easy. I'm not an interrogator. He was too open. I don't doubt anything he says, but something tells me he wants you guys to stick your necks out. Be careful."

Maria headed back into the main part of Ottawa and found her way to a hotel. She took her time, knowing she still had half an hour before she needed to meet Nicholas at the parliament building. Things were moving so quickly, and she needed it to simply slow down, if even for an hour. She supposed she had that the other night, when she had spoken to Cam, and then with Ryan earlier that day. She took in a deep breath and stepped out from her vehicle in front of a hotel. She was diving into the deep end now.

She remembered the challenge last season in Prince Edward Island. They had to jump from a footbridge and swim down to a marker. In that challenge, Rick had been taken away by an undercurrent, his body slammed against the concrete supports of the bridge, and his body had been battered. She had swum down to reach him, but the damage had already been done. Maria pulled him up to safety, but for those moments under the frigid water of the Atlantic Ocean, her body froze, and her lungs burned. And now, jumping into the deep end of her mission to bring down the McCarthy Company, she felt her lungs were about to explode.

CHAPTER 19

"Why are you so nervous?"

Maria shrugged, clutching a datapad tight in her hands. They sat in one of the many waiting rooms in the National Defense Headquarters in Ottawa. "I've only met him once in passing, and I'm nervous that he knows about all of this already, and will do the same as my CO. The General already has a connection with Trevor. It's not that much of a stretch to believe that he's working with him. It's his job to know everything about the technology used by his soldiers."

Nicholas sighed and rubbed her shoulder gently. "He is one of the noblest men I've ever met. I know he will want to help. I wish you had been able to come to me sooner with this, before your life was put in danger." He paused before giving her a small smile. "It could have been better circumstances, but I'm glad for this opportunity to work with you. I've seen you grow up, and I've seen you as a Scanner. Seeing you now as a soldier, I'd like to work more with you, in the future."

She looked up at him with a questioning look. "What do you mean?"

"I'm interested in being more involved with the AIMs, and the AIMOTs. I don't know anyone better suited to help me into that transition."

Maria laughed. "I believe in the saying 'you can't teach an old dog new tricks.' I can work with your AIMOTs, sure, but you'd be a lost cause."

"Thank you for your confidence," he said, returning the laughter.

"You're a soldier, through and through. You're used to relying on yourself and human strength, of course with some weapons, but you know what I mean. If you want to bring an AIM into it, I don't think you'd be able to handle it. There are times, even when I was in the CST, that I would prefer to rely on humans. Now I understand why. AIMs are flawed. Even these new ones that were put together, they're not perfect. Nothing ever is. Humans aren't, but at least you can pull in emotions, and pull in a human's sense of compassion. With a robot, or animal, you can't. That's why it's called 'appealing to one's humanity'."

A woman stepped in front of them in a dress uniform. "The General will see you both now."

Maria followed the woman, leading Nicholas. She could feel her heart pounding in her chest beneath the only dress uniform she owned. It had been Nicholas' idea, wearing their greens. It was an important meeting, and they had to look the part, but she felt more comfortable in the thick uniform which hid most of her figure. After so many years being in the public eye, and being seen in advertisements in revealing clothing as a female Scanner, it was a nice change to be able to hide her body. It was an illogical notion, she knew, to hide who she was, but she needed to be appreciated for her skill, not her looks. She had dealt with that issue when she was first signed to Revolution and was told, in not so many words, that she was there to look at and to let the men do their job. And now, even in her slightly askew uniform – thanks to her decision to climb the wooden wall – now she was included, involved. Probably more than she ever hoped.

She stepped into the office to meet a middle-aged man in full military regalia. It was clear he was prepared for an official meeting, and the look of surprise on his face at seeing Maria there solidified that theory. She hoped he was not shocked at her appearance, but after climbing the wall, and flying in a chopper, she was not sure how she was supposed to look.

"I'm sorry, General Szyzeck," Nicholas said, stepping around Maria to shake the hand of the General of the Canadian Army. "I know you were expecting to speak with me, but there is someone you need to meet. This is Lieutenant Maria Kier, an AIMOT from CFB Kingston."

"I was initially stationed in Camp Julien," Maria interjected, stepping forward as she saluted the General.

The man looked her over. "I've heard of you, Lieutenant. The youngest and lowest ranking AIMOT we sent overseas. You've been raised in ranks pretty quickly," he said off-handedly. He glanced at Nicholas, before nodding. "Well, let's get on with it."

Maria looked at Nicholas, as though to ask permission, before she handed Szyzeck the datapad. "I'll ask you to read this, Sir."

He flipped through the first few pages, and laughed when he saw the amount of data in store for him. "How long do you have?"

"At least read the objective of the report." She fought to keep her voice strong. It was difficult to keep an air of authority around this man. He was a great soldier, and as Nicholas had said, a good man. He had been to every war which had been active during his career, and even those which were unofficial, not that many people knew about those wars. The government had been known for keeping recent wars not quite secret, but downplayed. It was hard to keep confidence around him, especially knowing that he had fought alongside her father. She waited as he read the contents of the first page.

After a moment, his eyes flashed up to meet Maria's. "What is this?"

"I wrote this report nearly three weeks ago, documenting an incident when I was deployed."

"Why didn't you send this to your CO?" he asked, his voice raised in anger. "You are aware of proper protocol, are you not? This is the kind of thing you are to send immediately to your superiors. Instead, you're wasting my time."

"I did send it," she stated simply.

He paused and looked at her. "I never received this report," he said softly, looking back down at the screen. "Can you explain this to me, Lieutenant Kier? I want the rundown."

"The AIMs in production now, and the AIMs we work with on a daily basis, are dangerous. I recorded an AIM killing a Canadian soldier in front of me. And just earlier today at Base Borden, I was working with an AIM and it disengaged from the AIRC as I used it." She placed the AIM case on the desk next to them and motioned towards it. "I can send you the paperwork which goes along with the incident. It was in the form of a bear cub, and had it been any bigger, it would have put me and the other AIMs in danger."

He nodded slowly as he set the datapad down. He removed his beret as he leaned against his desk. "Forgive me for my informality." He sighed as he looked at Maria, and she was startled by how much he looked the way Owen had after his heart attack. It was surprising how quickly one can age with only a small amount of information. "Do you know how AIMs were brought into the military, Lieutenant?" When she was silent, he continued. "It was a way to keep soldiers safe. It was a brand new technology, and for the first time in a very long time, we were able to buy brand new technology from the United States. It was the first time robots were accepted into a government position. With the technology AIMs offered, we were able to do so much more. We no longer needed to put soldiers out into the front lines immediately. We could have safe reconnaissance, and if one of the AIMs was destroyed we were still able to retrieve the information with no human casualties."

"Our training was exceptional," he continued. "We brought in skilled people, mainly athletes like yourself, who knew how to use the AIMs efficiently. We even incorporated McCarthy scientists into our training exercises. We equipped our soldiers each with an AIM which worked as their weapon in some cases. We created programs specifically to be used in combat, hostile situations, and on domestic soil for law enforcement. The Prime Minister had reservations about using these robots in our combat missions, and so he created legislature which enforced the safety of the soldiers before the safety of AIMs. This also meant that while Underground activities were illegal, it also meant that no one other than soldiers and law enforcement personnel could use these combat tactics. Bills were passed in which we were able to alter the programming for AIMs to allow for these programs, but nothing else. Restrictions were made as to which scans could be used in combat, agreed upon eventually by the United Nations."

"Over time, we, along with the McCarthy Company, brought the use of AIMs in the military to other countries, to those who are now our enemies." He laughed lightly. "We've learned nothing from history. How many times have we in North America trained those we would later come to fight? It was something I was never comfortable with doing, especially giving them a technology we were still developing. We created training programs for AIMs, and eventually we created your position, Lieutenant, the role of an AIM Operations Technician. We created those positions even for the enemy, but at least this technology we were giving them couldn't kill our own, not like if we were to give them guns or planes. No matter what training we gave them, nothing could change that."

He held up the datapad. "Now you're telling me that AIMs can kill people."

"Sir, they can't do it on command, nor can they be controlled when they're rogue," Maria spoke. "When they go rogue, they no longer react to the AIRC. If an enemy AIM goes rogue and kills one of our soldiers, it's not because it was trained or commanded to do so. It did so based on animal instincts. The AIM which killed Second Lieutenant Foster was in the form of a tiger, and had been missing for three days. As an animal it would have been starving, and would have attacked the first form of prey it saw, which it did. It was our own AIM which did this. It was not planned."

"What else do you know about rogue AIMs?"

"Very little, Sir, unfortunately. I know that every AIM currently active is susceptible to becoming rogue. I also know that once it goes rogue, it cannot be controlled."

Nicholas turned to Maria with a raised eyebrow. "Did you not tell me that you controlled this rogue AIM? How else did you get it here?"

She shook her head. "I did not control it. I somehow managed to shift it to its default form, but I have no idea what would happen if I attempted to shift it once again into an animal form, if I even could. I don't even remember what I did."

"What is your proposal?" the General asked.

Maria's eyes flashed to Nicholas before continuing. "I have contacts in the Underground. They've informed me that they have created a substance which will not go rogue. They have been working on this since AIMs were first created, and perfected it only a month before the incident overseas. They have brought it to the attention of Mr. Trevor McCarthy in order to bring this new substance into production. They also have…someone who is able to re-connect a rogue AIM to the AIRC."

"I am surprised that they would even listen to a proposal from the Underground, but if they came up with acceptable research, I cannot see the harm in it. Did Mr. McCarthy give a date for this new substance to be available for us? And why would he not report this to people with an AIM contract?"

She cringed inwardly, or tried to at least, and she realized that he noticed the gesture. "He did not accept the substance, and insists there is no problem. That is why I've come to you, not only to show you the report, but to gain your support in bringing in a new form of AIM. I've spoken to another AIMOT about a new substance, although I proposed it as a hypothetical situation, and this person can already see a need for an upgrade in the AIM units."

Szyzeck paused and looked at Nicholas, attempting to read the man's body language. "You are convinced that this new substance will work?"

"General," she started. "During my career as a Scanner, I saw a lot of corruption even within the sport. I saw a lot of backdoor deals, and I saw the consequences of the use of what I thought were products of the Underground. These products, these AIMs, were destructive and dangerous. I learned through my short career so far as an AIMOT that these AIMs I considered to be dangerous were normal, distributed by the McCarthy Company, and had no connection with the Underground. Do I know for sure that this new product is one hundred percent safe and reliable? No. But I am one hundred percent sure that the AIM model we are using now is more dangerous, and needs to be recalled immediately from service."

He nodded and straightened. "May I keep this report?"

"Of course. I have more copies."

"I would suggest meeting with the Minister of Defense. I will forward him a copy of this report so he can be briefed, and I will personally set up the meeting so I know you can see him. In the meantime, refrain from bringing this up with other AIMOTs."

"Sir-

"Do not disclose any of this information. We will deal with this appropriately, and with the right people. Is that understood, Lieutenant?"

Maria bit the inside of her cheek before answering, "Yes, Sir."

"Your contact, the one who can supposedly handle rogue AIMs. I want to speak with him. I'm going to need more information."

Her heart quickened. This wasn't the plan. "I don't think that's a good idea, with all due respect, Sir."

Nicholas leaned down towards her and lowered his voice. "If we want the Minister to understand his role in all of this, he's going to need to know he has someone who can give him answers."

Maria's face remained stoic and she turned her attention back to the General. "He's not able to come for a meeting, but I'll see if I can arrange for some communication."

Szyzeck sighed and tapped the screen of the datapad, going through the report again. "I suppose you weren't promoted to your current rank due to your ability to find or divulge important information." He looked straight at Maria. "Or lack thereof. Dismissed." He waited until Maria saluted, turned on her heel and left before grabbing Nicholas by his elbow. "You find out what else she knows. This is already too much."

"I know her contacts," Nicholas responded hastily. "They won't be an issue."

"I don't care what her last name is. What about your loyalty?"

"That's never been an issue."

"The General will set up the meeting with the Minister," Nicholas said as they drove back to their hotel. "Get in touch with your people and let them know. See if you can get them connected. If we have any luck, we'll have the meeting as soon as tomorrow."

Maria nodded slowly. "He's not what I thought he would be. Szyzeck, I mean."

"It's rare to have someone rise in ranks as quickly as you did with little military experience. He's making sure this is worth his time."

"How he could think I'm wasting his time..." Her voice trailed off as she watched the buildings pass by. "I could have all the authority in the world, and I still wouldn't feel like I'm making a difference."

Nicholas looked Maria with a stern look. "Don't you ever think that what you're doing is not important, that you're not making a difference. Even when you were a Scanner, you made a difference. My little grand-nieces look up to you. You're a role model to them, and still are. You've been through so much, even being in the public eye, and you've survived it all. Never think you're not making a difference. You don't realize how much impact you have on people."

She smiled again. "Thank you."

He returned the gesture and continued to drive. "No need."

Maria unbuttoned the starched blazer and let it fall onto her bed. She kicked off her pants and allowed them to fall to the floor as she allowed her body to fall on top of the blazer. With a glance to the side, she pulled her phone towards her and dialed. She waited as the dial tone blared in her ear, until someone on the other end picked up. She smiled.

"Hey, Cam, it's me."

Cam sat up straighter in the motel chair, and shut off the TV, much to the dismay of his AIM who seemed to find American news fascinating. "Are you okay?" They had spoken only the day before. There should have been no reason to call again unless something was wrong.

She laughed. "Yeah, I'm fine. I'm just calling to catch you up. It's been a pretty eventful day, and I'm about ready to pass out."

He sighed and relaxed. He nudged his AIM away, who clearly did not like not knowing what was being said in a conversation. "What's up?" He would never admit to being so glad to hear her voice. Not out loud, at least.

"I met up with Nicholas again today at the base. While I was waiting to leave for Ottawa, I had the chance to work with an AIM." She paused. "When an AIM goes rogue, how do you get it back under control?"

"Why?"

"The AIM I was working with went rogue. I got it to get back into its gel form, but I have no idea how I did it."

Cam stood and paced the room. "Are you okay? Did it try to attack you?"

"I was far enough away that it was more confused than anything."

He paused and looked at his AIM, which cocked its head questioningly. "For a temporary fix, you go into the scan's DNA programming code, and if you flip a few of the markers, it'll short out and go back to the default gel. But you can't shift it after that. You have to go more in-depth into the coding, but I'm not sure you want to do that right now."

"I think I did something like that. Something popped up and I think it said something about default or discharge. See, I could have your job."

"You really want it?"

"You want mine?"

"Nope."

Cam sat back down in the chair as they remained silent for a few moments. "So, Sandra said you weren't meeting with the Minister today. What happened there?"

"I guess he wasn't available to see us, or at least he didn't think we had anything important enough for us to say, which I understand, but it's frustrating. I just got out of a meeting with General Szyzeck." When he paused, she explained. "He's the Chief of Defense, basically. Head of the army, under the Prime Minister."

That piqued his interest. "How did that go? How did he take your report?"

"I felt like I had just been signed to Revolution. I'm a lowly woman in a man's uniform. But he was hesitant about the report at first, like Nicholas. He's dealt with Trevor from the beginning, so I can understand that he feels betrayed, but he can't do anything without more evidence within the military, and without the approval of the Minister of Defense, and the Prime Minister. He's setting up an appointment with the Minister for tomorrow. He also said he wants to get in touch with you, in case they have more questions. I'm delaying that, of course.

"I don't like that he wanted to know your contacts."

"I don't either. But he made a good point. You and Henk are going to have to meet with them sometime."

Cam sat down on the bed and smiled when his AIM laid its head on his lap. He stroked it absently. "The best way to deal with it is to have that meeting between the Minister and a McCarthy to talk about the new AIM."

"We're going to need to speed things up, then. If we can get the Minister on board, we can look into bringing charges of terrorism on Trevor."

Cam raised an eyebrow, forgetting that Maria could not see it. "Isn't that a bit extreme?"

"It's the only thing we can do. We'd do it quietly, forcing Trevor to step down without ruining the company. We still want AIMs to be produced, so we need to make sure the company itself remains intact." When he agreed with her, Maria paused. "There's something else. I saw Jack just after I left Kingston."

Cam swore. "And you thought you'd wait until now to tell me? Are you okay?"

"Yeah. I'm fine. Actually, he was fine." She paused again. "He blames himself for Lucy."

"Seriously?"

"The fall he caused with his wolf, he thought that was a part of it, and then the stress of attacking us later. I can see where he would get the idea, but I was surprised he would even care."

"Are you?"

She looked around the room. She had stayed in many rooms similar to it while on the road with her team. Gaudy wallpaper and clichéd paintings in all of them. Nothing ever seemed to change. "I'm not blind. He still looks at me the same way. No. I'm not surprised. I think he's in trouble, Cam. He went to see the guy who attacked me. He told him that there is no next target."

"Yeah, the guy told us that too."

"No, he said he gets one target at a time. You don't get it. He told his own co-worker that there was no next target." She waited, hoping it would sink in. "He's in trouble. He didn't even know I had been attacked."

Cam thought for a moment. "There was a guy in the Ottawa lab who wasn't one of us. He works for Trevor's brother."

"Yeah, Walter told me you had done your own interrogation. I bet you're not so upset I dragged you to the conference now, are you?"

He shifted uncomfortably. "How do you know who Walter is?"

She hesitated. "Sandra asked me to go to Ottawa. I guess there was someone else there working for Trevor. They needed information from him, you weren't close enough, and I was on my way to the city. I was the best choice, apparently. Someone told them my dad was a Communications Officer."

Cam cringed. He knew the day he paid for that would come. At least she could not withhold things from him anymore, nothing he cared about at least. "I'm sorry I brought you into this."

"I brought myself into this, remember? I went to the lab looking for you. I could have found you another way, but I chose the Underground route. It did make sense for them to call me, actually. Henry, the guy, he's seen my interviews and knows I'm against the Underground. Or that I was against it."

He smiled. "So, you're not so against it anymore?"

"I'm as against it as you are. So, tell me what this other guy told you, the one who you said works for Trevor's brother? What's going on there?"

Cam told Maria all that Sharar and Henk had told him about Trevor, and Cohner's actions against his brother. He barely believed it, hearing himself say it all over again. When he finished, Maria swore.

"So all of this is just a game to him. It's just a power struggle between two brothers. They're putting lives at risk because they each want power."

"I think Cohner wants what's best for the company, and wants to get his brother help."

"Since when have you given someone the benefit of the doubt?"

"Since I've needed people to do that for me."

Maria was silent for a moment. "Do you think Jack knows about Cohner's plans?"

"I don't know. I'm with Henk right now…don't ask…and he's been contacted by someone who wants to work against Trevor. I'll let you know how it goes on Wednesday. Call me after your meeting, if I don't call you first."

"Sure."

"Take care of yourself, Maria."

She smiled, closing her eyes. "You too, Lucas."

CHAPTER 20

"Eric, go!"

Eric lunged from the starting line. He was the last one to attempt the three-stage obstacle challenge. He was glad he had been chosen to complete the speed leg. Of his team mates, he was the fastest one, with the fastest scans. Well, mostly. Ryan had a faster horse, but his was close behind. He flew into the forest, and sped along the trail. With a quick glance over his shoulder, he saw that the team just behind them had not left from the start yet. They were still waiting for their one team mate and from what Rick had reported, he was having a hard time with the swimming. Those afraid of heights were refusing to jump from the cliff into the shallow lake below. The fears of others only meant that Revolution's strengths were heightened.

Eric continued to run, jumping over roots which grew up and out from the soil. He shielded his face with his arm and kept going forward. A blood hound loped beside him. It was keeping track of a scent that they needed to follow. If they went too slow, they would lose the scent and would need to either wait for the AIM to pick up on it again by hunting around, or wait the ten minutes until the scent was reset. They were ahead by a full ten minutes and they wanted to keep that lead.

"Beginning to lose scent," his AIM chirped through the AIRC's speaker.

He gritted his teeth as he pumped his legs harder. The AIM was not going much faster, but they had to do it. "How much further?"

"No end given."

This was not going to be good. He was going to run out of steam soon. He was fast, but he was a sprinter. If he had to go for a long distance, he was not going to make it and it would give the other teams a chance to catch up. He was not willing to do that. He swung his arm around trees as he rounded them, using the trunks to keep his balance as he followed his AIM. They were going to win. He just needed to keep it up a bit longer.

As he rounded another bend in the trail, he saw a crowd of fans through the thinning trees, and he grinned. "There's the end. Confirm?"

"Confirmed."

He pulled out his AIRC and chose the horse scan they had gotten from Owen's brother's breeding farm. Although it was not the fastest horse scan, it was at least faster than his two legs could take him. He grabbed at the horse's withers as it continued to move and pulled himself awkwardly up onto its back. He had seen many other scanners do this, especially Maria, so why not try it too? He had been on a horse before…a few times, at least. All he had to do was hang on until they crossed the finish line.

"Come on," he muttered, panting as the horse ran beneath him. He held tight to the horse's mane, clutching at the barrel of the horse with his thighs. It was much more difficult than he had thought it would be, but they were so close.

Revolution cheered as Eric crossed the finish line, and they finished first in the third month-end challenge of the season. After all the disasters of last year, they were really pulling it together. They needed this, not just as a team, but as individuals. Eric jumped down from the AIM and raised his fists into the air as his team came around him, his chest heaving from his run. It was their first top finish in a month-end challenge, but each time they had at least been in the top three. Things were looking good for Revolution.

"That was amazing!" Ryan exclaimed, giving Eric a high-five. "It looked like you were about to fall off near the end! And the next team just left the last leg!"

Owen patted him on the shoulder with a grin. "You did good, new kid."

Eric laughed as the two Warners walked ahead of the younger players. He clapped Ryan on the back to get him moving as they strode away to the team vehicles. Typically, they would have stayed at the challenge site to speak with media, but they were on their way to an interview, which was even better. After Cam's stunt at the Hamilton TV station, they were getting request after request for interviews. They chose a popular station here in Alberta, since it would give them the most exposure, and allow them to have similar interviews in sister stations across Canada.

Eric stopped as his phone rang. "Hey, hang on. I'll be right there," he called to his team mates as he turned to take the call. "Hello? ... What? Sir, I really don't think that's a good idea. If he finds out, so will the media...there'd be too many questions with him in the spotlight and we're heading out for an interview...yes, sir, I realize that, but you said yourself you need to play this safe, and quietly...I'll do what I can, but I don't know how long it'll last." He closed his phone with a sigh as he made his way to Ryan, waiting beside a vehicle. "Sorry about that." Eric took the driver's seat of the truck, while Ryan sat in the passenger seat.

Over the past few days, they had been spending more time together. After Ryan had confided in him about his relationship with Maria, he seemed to trust Eric. He smiled as he glanced at the passenger, and he pointed the truck towards their destination.

"So, have you heard anything from Maria lately?" he asked casually. He had been nervous to call Trevor with the news, but he had taken it much better than he had thought, especially after finding out so much about her in a short period of time. That had earned him loyalty points; points which were very hard to come by as of late with that man.

"Nah. Oh, well she called me yesterday morning actually, but we didn't talk for long. She had to go for a meeting I guess," Ryan replied with a bit of a shrug. "I'm worried about her, but she told me I wouldn't hear from her for a while after her meeting. She has a lot of work to do right now, which includes her travelling."

Eric nodded, holding back a grin. "Is she working with Cam?"

"I don't think so. He's not in the army, so I can't see why she would be. She said they had parted ways after they left Kingston, but with her job, I don't know how much of what she says is just to keep me safe or from asking too many questions." Well, that was not necessarily true. They had been working together, but he was sure that part of it would be over with, if it was not already. He hoped so at least, for her sake.

"I was just asking because when I was with them, before you showed up, they seemed really friendly. That's kind of why I asked you so much about her before. I thought they were still together by the way they were acting."

Ryan looked at him from the corner of his eye, trying to hide his interest. "What do you mean?" Cam and Maria both said it was over. That didn't mean that something wouldn't start up again. Last season, there had been times when Ryan was not sure about the status of their relationship. He had once thought Cam would be a fool to not try to put the moves on Maria, and when he learned that they had been in a long-term relationship, their actions and anger towards the other made sense. Despite the anger which had been apparent to everyone on the team, and everyone watching them from the outside, there were moments when Ryan had thought that there was a possibility the two would get back together. Even though it had been a full year, and even though Ryan was now dating Maria, it was still a possibility that the two rekindled whatever feelings they had had for each other despite anything he had said to Cam.

"I don't know, just...goofy, I guess. I don't know them, so what do I know about how they normally act around each other. I mean, I know last season I saw that they were pretty much at each other's throats the entire month you guys were active but from what you said, they didn't have a very clean break. It's understandable that they wouldn't want to be around each other." He turned to Ryan briefly before turning his attention back on the road. "As long as you're sure they're not just using her work as an excuse to hook up, then forget about my opinion. I don't know them, and I don't know what your relationship is like with her. She doesn't seem to be the kind of girl to sneak around, and I doubt she's ever been unfaithful. I wouldn't worry about it." Of course, her sleeping with Jack, as everyone now knew that she had, that was not considered to be cheating, was it? Eric held back a grin as he noticed Ryan go deep in thought.

Ryan was quiet for a few moments as they neared the TV station. Only a few more blocks to go. "They've always been really close. They were never just friends. If they're back in touch with each other, they're just getting used to being friends…friends who had a kid together. Cam knows how much he's hurt her, and I'm trusting that he does the right thing by her when this is over. It's not going to be easy, and I would understand if some feelings were rekindled. But they've broken up so many times, they know that they would never work, especially now. They're just trying to get to know each other. They're completely different people. That's all."

Eric nodded. "Then that's all it is. It'll take some time, I'm sure. If you don't hear from her, I'm sure she's just travelling. Besides, that's a lot of history to get through. A lot of feelings, too."

Ryan looked out the passenger window. "Yeah. It is."

He grinned as he continued to glance at Ryan during the remainder of the drive to the TV station. When Cam and Maria had shown up, it was obvious to everyone that Ryan either had very low self-esteem, or he barely trusted Maria. If it was both, then all of this was going to be that much easier for Eric. With Maria as a soldier, Ryan should be prepared for anything to happen. Soldiers, and even police officers, died in the line of duty all the time.

Eric pulled into the parking lot behind Rick and Owen, and they made their way into the preparation area. He was amazed at how many interviews this team did in a season, and knew there were times they did interviews in the off-season as well. When he had been with his old team, they got perhaps half the amount of interviews, and half the amount of sales from team merchandise and tickets to see their challenge attempts. It was incredible. If he was anything like Cam, he would have been enjoying it more. Normally, Eric would have been excited about the attention the team received, but with the events Trevor had in store for the team, this was not a place he wanted to be. When an atomic bomb is launched, one does not want to stay close to the target city. He realized this was a suicide mission, staying with the team for so long, but there was no way he could say no to the interviews. Not yet.

After nearly twenty minutes of make-up, something Eric refused to receive no matter how bad he looked on the camera, they were sitting with the Alberta News Sports Anchor.

"First, congratulations, Revolution, for coming in first at the June Challenge. I know that none of the challenges are easy, but you guys looked like you had no problem with any of it!"

Owen grinned and looked at the rest of his team. "We've all worked really hard, and trained twice as much as we normally do during the off-season. With the change up in our roster, we knew we needed to do something drastic. Eric and Ryan have both surprised us, and have come a very long way in an extremely short amount of time. As their captain, I couldn't be more pleased with their performance so far this season."

"You mentioned the change in roster. How have you found the change to affect the team's income? You have to admit that Cam brought in a lot of fans, and a lot of interest to the team, and Maria brought in the female fans and a huge change in team dynamics. I wonder how much that's really affected the team?"

Rick shrugged. "To be honest, there was a big drop in viewership and fan attendance for the first month and a bit. I think we proved ourselves to be more than Cam Tylar, and we've won back our fans, and gained a few more. It helped that Eric was coming in with fans from his previous team. And Ryan's gained a few of Cam's old groupies as well," he finished with a laugh.

"Now, I don't make it my job to get into gossip, but Ryan, there has been a bit of a rumour that you and Maria Kier have sparked something up. The fans began to see it last season, but with her being nowhere in sight, it's been a bit difficult to say."

Ryan's heart pounded. They knew this would happen. With her job now, it was better not to say anything. It would put a bigger target on her. After a brief moment, he finally wondered if it would put a target on him as well. "We haven't spoken much since she left the team. She's not around much, trying to keep out of the limelight, so I can't say anything serious is going on."

"But something is going on, then?" he asked.

"We have been spending time together."

Eric swore, making sure the microphone would not pick it up. If Trevor was watching this, he knew now who the connection was on the team. Knowing for sure who it was, now there would be nothing to stop Trevor. It was only Ryan Hampton, after all. He would never leave the team, not the way Cam did. They had nothing to worry about. That was what Eric told himself, anyway.

The ride to the hotel after the interview was silent in the truck. Eric allowed Ryan to beat himself up over his slip-up. It would only bring him down more. But he could not get too down on himself, or his performance would start to be affected.

"You handled that the best you could," he said softly. He would try to be the supportive friend and team mate as long as Trevor had him on the team.

Ryan shrugged, and leaned against the passenger side of the truck. "That could have been really dangerous."

"What's the worst that could happen? So what if the public knows you guys are going out? Who's really going to care?"

"I don't know. That's the problem. I don't know what Maria's dealing with, and I don't know how I could be affected. If something happens to her, it happens to me, and then it moves onto the team." He ran a hand through his brown hair, and mussed it up. "This team can't handle another meltdown like we had last year. We can't handle another break up or the drama we had."

Eric could not help but laugh. "I really doubt it will get that far. Last season was pretty intense, and Cam and Maria left because of tension on the team, not because of outside influences." When Ryan was silent, clearly holding something back, he raised an eyebrow. "What?"

"That tension was because of outside influences. I don't know the full story, but I guess Cam was doing something Maria didn't agree with. He was part of something, from what I gathered. It was because of that they broke up. During the month-end challenge....

we were actually attacked, and sabotaged. Someone pointed a gun at Maria." Ryan looked out the side window once more. "And then the stillbirth. If those aren't considered outside influences, then I don't know what is. I know those things won't happen again, but my fear is that something worse will happen. Maria's in the army now. She has plenty of people who may not appreciate the work she does. She basically tells people who are higher in rank than she is, how to do their job, and works with high security AIMs. She's already been attacked because of her job…" Ryan's voice trailed off, not wanting to think about the situation anymore.

Eric could take a hint. "So, that was a pretty awesome challenge."

Ryan smiled lightly, grateful for the change of topic. "I was surprised, actually. It was a lot easier than challenges have been in the past. Not that I know much, but I found it easier than the other month-end challenges." He laughed. "I wasn't going to say that on live TV, in an Albertan station."

He cringed as his phone rang. "Sorry," he muttered as he answered. "I'm busy. I'll call you later…no, I said later…I really don't care at the moment."

When Eric put his phone back into his pocket, Ryan looked over to him. "You're pretty popular these days."

"Yeah, just some friends. Old team mates, actually. It's strange, moving from one team to another, especially when the new team is in the spotlight more than the old one ever was. I think a few of them are a bit jealous. 'We made you who you are! You should be giving us recognition!' they say. It's a bit immature, I think. Trades happen all the time. I wasn't expecting them to react like this."

"I can understand that. Why you, out of the three other guys you used to work with?"

Eric glanced over to him as they rounded a corner. Nearly to the hotel now. "Why don't you answer that? Give me something to tell them the next time they whine about it."

Ryan thought for a moment. Why had they signed Eric? He had not been around for it, although he was sure they had had a meeting with the board about it. Or had they? With two spots to fill, it had been a very fast turnover. "You know, I have no idea. I know your stats are good, and you've had good scores in challenges, but I don't even remember seeing a list of candidates."

"Maybe I impressed them that much," he laughed.

"Maybe. I doubt it, no offense. They were looking for the next Cam Tylar. I don't even think he exists."

Eric patted Ryan on the shoulder with a chuckle. "Man, *you're* the next Cam Tylar. Don't you get that? You've done all your training on your own. You came into the CST without ever using an AIM. You've been the one to help bring this team back up to the top, not Cam. It took Cam five years to bring it up to last season's rank, and within a single season, it's gone to the top. It wasn't because of him. It was because of you."

He thought for a moment. The same could be said about Eric though, could it not? He had been on this team for only this season, and already they were nearing the top of the CST scoreboard. He smiled lightly. "Well, it's a nice idea."

"I'm serious. You did this on your own. You did this without Cam training you, and you got to this level without Maria on this team either. I doubt you guys train together during your dates. You didn't need her to get where you are now."

Ryan smiled. "But it's nice having her while I'm at the top."

Eric held back a sigh. "I'm just saying, you got where you are because of your skill. Don't let anything else hold you back. If you're having a rough patch in your relationship, and you think it's going to affect your game, just forget about it. Deal with it later. If she says she's not going to be able to call you for a while, then leave it at that and focus on the game."

He nodded. "Yeah. You're right. Worrying is just going to make all of this worse, and we need better right now." But things were never that simple.

CHAPTER 21

Cam sat next to Henk in the rented boardroom. Cam was on edge, and it made him even more nervous that Henk did not seem to mind waiting for this 'contact' of his.

"His being late is not a good sign. You know that, right?" he muttered as he watched his AIM move around the building on his AIRC. It was scanning the area for anyone familiar, and anyone who would possibly be a threat.

"He will be here. Alone." Henk's voice was even, but it did nothing to put Cam at ease.

After a few moments, Cam's AIM reappeared, crawling under the door in the form of the mouse before he switched it into a cougar. Just as the AIM finished its awkward transformation the door handle turned, and the door swung open.

Cam swore and stood quickly, wishing he had kept Maria's gun. "What the hell are you doing here?"

Jack closed the door quickly behind him, and held his hand out to Henk. "It's good to meet you in person, Dr. Baxter, without Trevor over my shoulder." He smiled before turning his attention to Cam, only looking somewhat surprised to see him there. "It's nice to see you too, Cam."

"Again, what the hell are you doing here?"

He looked at Henk with a curious look. "You did tell him you were meeting someone, or is he as stupid as he always was?"

"I did not tell him who you were, no," Henk answered. "I knew this would be his reaction. I had to play the sympathy card."

Cam watched Jack's eyes widen, and his did the same. "Wait, you said this guy cared about someone. Jack doesn't have feelings." He paused, and swore again after a brief moment. "Seriously, Maria? After all this time. You've got to be kidding me."

"Look, we both need each other's help right now, so can we just forget about what I may or may not have said?" Jack said, both flustered and aggravated at the same time.

He smiled as the three sat down. Jack cared about Maria. He knew Jack had been after her for a while, even after they had started dating, but he had always figured it was more of a fight with him rather than actually wanting her. A lot made sense now, but right now they needed to figure out what to do, and forget about Maria for the time being. As though that was possible.

"I guess I can't rely on the sympathy vote, not that it means much to you, Cam," Jack started. "But it does tie in, a bit. I'm assuming Maria's told you I ran into her." When Cam nodded, he continued. "For a while, we've all noticed that Trevor has been…not quite himself. He's more paranoid now, about everything. He takes everything to the extreme. When he had a break down, Cohner suggested he take a leave from his role and take time to get back on his feet. He completely lost it after that, but I still agreed with him, for some reason. I admit that my pride got in the way and I wanted to do everything I could to bring down the Underground. I couldn't do much, not with…not with your connection with Maria. If anything happened to you…" he stopped and grinned in disbelief. "I actually kept you alive."

"Now, with the rogue AIM report Maria wrote, everything's gone chaotic. Trevor's killing off everyone he thinks might get these new AIMs you guys created into his company. I can't…I can't follow him anymore. He's not making logical decisions, and I know I'm next on his list of targets. They've been following me since Kingston, and I was only able to lose them yesterday. If I want to live, if I want to get back into Scanning, Trevor needs to be out of the picture. I need to make a clean start, and I know you need it too, Cam. We'll make sure everything we've done is legal, so we can go back to where we want to be." He paused to examine

Henk and Cam's face. "I'll get you in with Cohner, and I'll help you with the media, whatever you need, as long as you make sure no one knows I'm helping you. To pull this off, we're going to need the help of the government and the military. They're the only ones with an AIM-related death on file. As much as I hate to involve her, she's already in this, so this is where Maria would come in."

"Cam has already found a few cases of AIM-related injuries, and a few claims on deaths, but nothing as formal as the report Maria wrote," Henk spoke as he looked at Cam. "I am not sure how quiet we can be, involving the government, but it must be done. If there is a backlash after the fact, I would much prefer that to anything happening now."

Cam glanced at Henk before he pulled out his AIRC. He handed it to Jack after tapping on the screen a few times. "This is a list we were able to compile. The guy who did it is dead now, so I have no idea what this is a list of."

Jack looked at it for a few moments and he shrugged. "It's a list of potential targets. It's basically a list of everyone who knows about rogue AIMs, has been in contact with one, or is working with Trevor." He laughed shortly. "You want me to go through this list and divide it up by categories, or something?"

"Just tell me who to watch out for. Maria's looking for people on this list too."

He stared at Cam seriously. "If she looks too much into this list, she won't be safe."

Cam shot a glare at him. "Is that a threat?"

Jack laughed. "I'm telling you that this list is a combination of people in danger, and people who are putting them in danger. He looked back down at the list, and pointed to a name. "Like him. This guy's another hit man for Trevor. One of the few Canadians."

Cam looked over at the name, and his eyes widened. He swore profusely and fumbled for his phone.

"Do you have the extra reports?"

Nicholas turned to Maria with a smile. "Of course. I contacted the AIMOT from Borden, and he sent me a portfolio of the AIMs' activity for the past year. He didn't find any abnormalities, but sent it anyway. Were you able to get in touch with anyone last night?"

Maria shrugged, looking at the AIM at her feet. Cam had always liked dog forms best, and she had grown accustomed to the German Shepherd form used in the military. It had given her a small form of comfort, knowing that even though it was not a real dog, it gave her the feeling of that little bit of extra power. Now, the canine form gave her a sense of foreboding. She would need that extra strength her AIM represented. "Not really. I did, but they had nothing to send to me right away."

"Even without that, we have enough to talk to the Minister about. Szyzeck contacted me last night and let me know that he had sent him a copy of your report. He should have reviewed it by now for the meeting."

"I'm surprised he was able to meet with us on such short notice."

Nicholas smiled. "That's what happens when you have the support of the General of the army."

She smiled lightly, and felt her heart begin to pound. Things were coming together. She was shocked that everything was moving forward so quickly. Cam was meeting with someone who could get them close enough to Trevor to let him know they had support, and she already had support from the highest member of the military aside from the leader of their country. It had only been a week, and already things were at the climax. She couldn't help but think of what her CO would think of her now, still sticking her nose where it didn't belong. Suddenly, that sense of foreboding came back as she thought about him. Maria realized she shouldn't have been so open with other AIMOTs. They all communicated together, and if anyone said anything to someone from her base, he would court martial her.

"What do you think the next step would be after this?" she asked, stroking the coarse hair of the dog absently.

He thought for a moment and looked at the AIM. "Why don't we wait to talk to the Minister before we decide anything?" He smiled lightly, forcing it to look friendly. "Your father would be so proud of you right now. He was always proud of you. You're so much like him, you know, fighting for what you feel is right, fighting for this country. It's admirable. I wish more soldiers were like that."

She laughed. "You only think that because you're not my superior. Even if he wasn't working for Trevor, I'm sure he'd prefer me to follow orders rather than go down my own path."

Nicholas nodded. "I'm sure he would. You know, orders are put into place for a reason. Do you know what that reason is?" Before she could answer, he continued, and walked to the door of the boardroom in which they waited for the Minister. "When a commanding officer gives orders to his subordinates, it's so they stay safe. They're a type of shepherd, and everyone below him are sheep. Let to their own devices, sheep will walk straight off a cliff without realizing it. A shepherd is there to lead his sheep to safety. A commanding officer gives his sheep orders which will keep them safe, and keep them from going over a cliff. There are many times when the path the shepherd gives does not look safe, and the sheep fight it, thinking they know best. That's when bad things happen." He looked over his shoulder to Maria with a quick smile. "I'll go see what's taking so long," he said, leaving the room, and he closed the door quickly behind him.

Maria's heart continued to pound. "What was all that about?" She let out a deep breath and took her phone from her uniform pocket. Four missed calls. She was about to take the phone off 'silent' when the screen lit up with another call. "Lieutenant Kier," she answered.

Cam swore at her on the other end. "Why haven't you been picking up? Where are you?"

"I'm waiting to meet with the minister. I had my phone on silent. What's going on?"

"The contact was Jack."

Maria nearly dropped the phone. "What? He's still alive?"

"Yeah. Listen, Maria. I showed him the list of names, and he knows most of them. Where's Nicholas?"

"He went to go get the Minister. Why?" she asked hesitantly.

"You need to get out of there, Maria," Cam said, his voice rose with urgency. "Do you hear me? He's on the list. He works for Trevor as a hit man."

Maria froze as Nicholas walked back into the room, a pistol in his hand.

"Maria? Are you still there?"

She nodded as though he could see her. "Yeah. So is he," she breathed into the phone as a second man stepped into the room beside him. "Tre-"

Cam pulled the phone from his ear quickly. His ear rang from the gunshots through the phone. His hand shook when the shots stopped abruptly. "Maria!" he screamed into the phone. He opened his mouth again to call out to her, but the line went dead.

CHAPTER 22

Cam stared at the phone in his hand, the dial tone droning on in what seemed to be the distance. He barely noticed when Henk took the phone from his hand and hung up for him. After a moment, he felt his heart race and anger surge in his blood. Through blurry eyes, he looked at Jack, who looked the way Cam felt. He watched as Jack breathed in and out deeply, likely attempting to control his anger, or whatever he was feeling. Cam wished he could show as much as him. His cheek tickled and he reached up to scratch it, but his fingers came away wet. After all this time, after all the dangerous challenges? It wasn't fair.

Maria was dead.

Last year, he had saved her life when her rope had snapped while they hung over the side of a cliff. Last year, Jack had pointed a gun at her, and he had stopped him. Now, when he was nowhere near her and had no chance in helping her, she was killed.

"We should have looked at the list better," he said angrily. He stood and shoved his AIRC in front of Jack's rage-filled face. "Who else do we need to look for on this list? Who do we go after?"

Jack looked up slowly, and deliberately. "Trevor. He's in Ottawa right now."

Cam's heart stopped, and he nodded. "She... she started to say his name before...he's there."

He reached behind him and pulled a gun from the back of his belt. "Then we'll meet him in Boston."

Henk stood next to the two men, and put a hand on each man's shoulder. "If we are going to do this right, we need to do this with clear heads. You have even more motivation now, but you cannot go in there with guns blazing. Maria was being methodical, and she would call you both idiots if you did something stupid. Doing something stupid will get you killed."

"Being methodical got her killed!" Cam screamed at Henk, pulling away from his hand. He ran a hand through his hair as he looked around, his eyes wildly taking in his surroundings, attempting to put everything together. "Henk, you said you know a few MPs? Any other politicians?"

"I met with the Ontario Premier last month. I am sure he would not say no to another visit," Henk replied slowly.

Cam nodded. "Okay. Go meet with him. There's an attaché case in my duffle bag. Bring that with you, and show it to him. It has a rogue and a new AIM in it, along with a hard-drive with the research. Show it all to him. Find a way to get to the Minister of Defense. You're going to have to finish what Maria started."

"And what will you two do?"

The two younger men looked at each other with a mutual understanding. "We'll see what Trevor has to say for himself when what he loves is taken away from him," Cam said, Jack nodding in agreement.

Cam took the gun from Jack, and checked the bullets inside. He looked at the man, who had begun to check his own gun, and cleared his throat. "Look, all the stuff that's happened over the years-"

"It's behind us now," Jack interrupted. "What's done is done. We'll just focus on what we have to do." He glanced at him before he continued to gather his possessions in the hotel room in Detroit. "We're not friends or anything now, because of this."

He laughed. "Trust me, I know."

Jack threw his own duffle bag on the bed and paused before he looked at Cam. "I did care about her. I tried to keep her as safe as I could. That's probably why Trevor didn't tell me who the target was. I didn't really think it was a secret."

"I probably just ignored it. I was focusing on getting her for myself."

"Then she started dating Ryan."

They both laughed at that. After a moment, Cam swore. "Ryan."

Jack shot a cautious glance at him. "When are you going to tell him?"

He shrugged. "When this is over, and Trevor's locked up."

Jack nodded as he picked his bag back up and headed for the door. "I'll meet you in Boston. You remember which hotel?" When Cam affirmed the location, he left.

Cam let out a sigh and fell backwards on the bed. Jack would leave for Boston tonight, and Cam would follow in the morning so they wouldn't draw attention to themselves, or show that they're working together. He glanced at his AIM when it jumped up onto the bed next to him in what it considered its 'cute' form of a Golden Retriever.

Both were silent for a few moments, simply staring at the other. The AIM 'spoke' first.

"Would you like to talk?"

"No."

Silence.

"Maria is dead."

Cam said nothing, but his face tensed as he tried to hold back the emotions he felt welling up overwhelmingly inside. He closed his eyes as his AIM laid down next to him. It rested its head on his chest, and he wrapped his arms around it. His body began to shake as he finally allowed himself to sob, and the AIM remained silent and still, knowing its presence was all Cam needed.

Hours later, Jack walked into the McCarthy Company building in downtown Boston. It was an impressive building, showcasing the various research projects the company had funded. Medical research was still the top recipient of their money, with Scanning and AIMs close behind. It was how AIMs came into being, after all. He smiled at the security guard behind the front desk casually.

Glancing around, Jack saw everything as it should be. No one was scurrying around. There was no panic. Yet.

He knocked on Trevor's door, and a soft voice replied, admitting him into the room. He held back a grin when he saw Amanda behind her desk. He never knew what to make of her. Either she was desperate for love and found it in her boss, or she was sleeping with him to get power. Well, he'd find out how Trevor felt soon.

Amanda looked up from her papers, and a slow smile came to her face. “Hey. I wasn't expecting you to be back so soon. How goes things in Canada?”

“Not good,” Jack said, forcing a sense of urgency into his words. “We need to get out of here without making a scene.”

She stood suddenly. “What are you talking about?”

“Trevor told me to get you out of the building and take you somewhere safe. He didn't tell me anything other than that.”

Amanda looked around, taking inventory. “Is something going to happen to the building? Am I supposed to bring anything?”

“What did I just say?” he snapped, and watched as she grabbed a stack of papers along with an AIRC. “Leave the AIM.”

She stopped and eyed him. She put the AIRC back down slowly. “Should we get Cohner?”

“We don’t need to involve him in this,” Jack answered and pulled out a gun. He kept it at his side, but nodded towards her. “Let’s just go quietly, and wait to hear what Trevor has to say for his next move.”

“And what are you expecting him to say?”

“That he’ll step down, but everyone knows the only person he listens to around here, is you.”

Amanda raised an eyebrow. “Why would you want him to step down? When I asked for your help, you were still on the fence.”

He raised the gun finally. “Let’s just get going. I’m done with the questions. Leave the AIRC. It’s no good anyway, remember?” He put the gun back tucked under his shirt, and grabbed her arm gently as she passed. “Don’t think I’m letting you get too far away from me.”

She quirked up the corner of her mouth. "I thought you gave up trying to get close to me."

"I only stopped because Trevor was screwing you."

"I think we should really include Cohner in this," Amanda said in a hushed tone as they stepped out into the hallway.

Jack tightened his grip on her arm, but made it seem as though he was simply leading her down the hall in a friendly manner. "Trevor won't want to hear anything his brother says."

"And he'll want to listen to you? Or me? If you do this, he's not even going to listen to me."

"Let's just hope he'll listen to the military."

She held back a laugh. "The military has been listening to him."

"Not the Canadian Minister of Defense." When he felt her tense, he grinned. "Oh, that's right. The woman who was supposed to be meeting with him was just killed. Good thing someone else is on their way to meet with him."

"Seriously, Jack, you don't want to do this. I don't know what's happened since the last time we spoke, but you don't want to do this. We can still work together."

"How about I catch you up," he snapped as he pulled her around a corner. "Trevor wants to kill me next, and I'd rather live. Then he took something of mine, and now, I don't care if he lives or dies. But to get him close enough to do that, he needs something to come to. That's where you come in, sweetheart. And a bonus, I'd like to come out of this pristine, which is why the Canadian government needs to be involved."

Amanda tried to turn towards him, but he kept her going forward. "Wait, so you do want to work with Cohner? Do you want Trevor dead, or to step down?"

"Yes, I want to-" He paused. "Wait, who said anything about working with Cohner? You said you wanted to get rid of Trevor."

"Do you really think I want Trevor to get hurt? He's not thinking right, and if he keeps going like this, he's going to get himself hurt, or killed. It looks like we're already at that point."

"Maybe you should've thought about getting involved before you actually did," he snapped. He shoved her into a room, and slammed the door behind them. Jack looked around and grinned.

This was too easy, which should have made him unnerved, but for the moment, he was going to go along with it. He walked over to the coil of rope hanging on a hook on the wall and motioned to her. "I don't want to actually hurt you, Amanda. You're a nice woman. You have a problem if you actually have feelings for Trevor, but you're nice. I'd like to make this as easy as possible. If you don't want Trevor to get hurt, you'll go along with this."

Amanda looked at the coil of rope. "You want me to co-operate with you?"

"I am in the mood to kill someone, but I don't necessarily want it to be you."

She thought for a moment. "Can you promise me that you won't hurt him?"

Jack's jaw clenched. "He's hurt, and killed, a lot of people. He killed Maria. I can't promise anything, and you can't expect me to," he said as he took her wrists and began to wrap them with the rope, binding them together tightly. "Can you at least promise me something?"

"What?"

"Forgive me," he said, before he hit her over the back of her head. He caught her before she fell to the ground, and shifted her to lean up against the wall. After looking her over for a moment to make sure he did not do too much damage, he pulled out his phone and dialled. "Hey, it's me. Location's changed. Go to the head office. There's a storage room you can enter from around back. Make sure no one sees you." He hung up before dialling a new number. Jack smiled as the recipient picked up the other end of the line. He never liked the game 'Chicken' but it was all he had now. "Good evening, Mr McCarthy. You'll want to come back to Boston as soon as possible. There's been a new development."

Cam hung up the phone and tossed it across the bed. *Why did I ever agree to work with Jack?* Even if they were on the same page now, even if they had the same motivation and the same goal, Jack was a loose cannon. Everyone knew that. Trevor knew that, which was likely why he had kept him at a distance and did not tell him their plans for Maria. He squeezed his eyes closed once again. His

AIM remained laying its head on his chest. It had not moved the entire night, at least not until the phone rang and Cam had shifted to reach for his phone. But it moved back to stay with Cam. He almost smiled. For nineteen years, his AIM had remained by his side not because it was trained or programmed to do so, but because it had wanted to, and continued to do so. After a moment of thinking, he shifted once again and propped himself up with his elbows.

"Do you have feelings?"

The AIM cocked its head. "Feelings? Emotions? I am not sure. How would I know?"

"Well, I annoy you sometimes, right?"

If it could have shrugged, it would have now. "There is a frustration sometimes, yes."

He nodded, and thought for another moment to word the next question properly. "Do you grieve?"

The AIM paused. There had been many times to grieve since it had been active, and they were all times which Cam had found the need to grieve. When his father had left was the only time there was a difference, because the AIM knew the purpose. But when Cam's mother had died, did it grieve? When Cam's child with Maria was born dead, did it grieve? Finally, it answered.

"I am sad."

Cam sighed and pulled the AIM close to him again. "Me too."

"I have found that anger is a mask for sadness. On you, I mean, and humans in general. I feel your anger has fully transformed into its proper emotion, and now I am free to ask you a question. Are you prepared to follow through with whatever Jack is starting in Boston? I fear he may have more motive than you to do something dangerous."

"He changed the location to the McCarthy main building."

The AIM dog looked at him, and pawed at him with its furry foot as though to claw more information from him. "Who is in the building right now?"

"I have no idea. Probably no one who would actually be doing anything against us currently. His hit men, or whatever, are all out finding AIMOTs or politicians, or whatever else they do. They wouldn't be in Boston. It'd all be support workers, and I guess his scientists would still be working. His brother would definitely be there."

"Perhaps Jack was able to ally with him and gain more support?"

"From what I know of Jack, he wouldn't be so quick to gain allies. I guess that's changed now. He approached Henk, which should have happened after hell froze over."

The AIM let out its version of a chuckle. "Many people have changed this past year. You are not excluded from that statement. Your father would be proud of what you are attempting to accomplish. I did not know him well, or for long, but from what I understand of humans I can assume that correctly." It paused. "I am proud of you, if that means something to you."

He looked at the dog quickly. He stared at it briefly before letting himself fall back onto the bed. "Probably more than it should."

"You should sleep. The next few days are not going to be easy."

"None of this has been easy."

CHAPTER 23

Amanda watched as Jack paced back and forth across the large room. She had only been here once before when it had still been a shipping dock, and now that it was a storage room – or emergency boardroom when Trevor did not feel like putting on airs for guests – it still looked the same.

"What are you hoping to accomplish through this?" she asked him gently. "I find it hard to believe that you want safe AIMs in production like Henk and his co-workers. I know you don't want to save this company from humiliation, because you're not getting anything from it."

"I just want Trevor," he growled.

She hesitated. "Killing him isn't going to bring her back."

"I understand death. Have you ever taken a life, Amanda?" he yelled, stooping down to her level on the ground. "Have you ever watched as the life drained from someone's eyes? I know killing him won't bring her back. After being the one who found her for Trevor to kill, the least I can do is make sure that her mission is accomplished, which is to hold Trevor accountable for everything he's done.

"And then?"

"I'll do whatever I feel like doing." He pulled his gun out quickly as someone banged against the door leading to the outside. He eyed Amanda before going towards it. He opened it slowly, and then swung it wide as Cam stepped in. "You sure took your time."

"People around here recognize me," he muttered. "I was being safe. Why are we meeting here?" Cam stopped suddenly when he saw Amanda sitting on the ground. Her wrists and ankles were bound. He stared incredulously at Jack. "What do you think you're doing?"

"We need leverage," he answered as he slammed the door closed. "Trevor would have blown up the building if she wasn't in it. After his trip to Ottawa, he's feeling pretty comfortable. He thinks he's in the home stretch with Maria not snooping around anymore, so we're going to need another way to get to him."

"And you think taking a hostage is going to get to him?" Cam stepped towards Amanda as Jack watched him carefully. "Are you okay?"

"He knocked me out, but that's it," she answered softly. "I can't blame him for that. I can't promise I would have co-operated." She looked at him for a moment as he looked around the room. "You're working with Jack? You seemed smarter than that in your presentation."

"He's working with me, and Cohner I guess. Neither of us are really in the mood to simply talk things out with Trevor. If you have any suggestions, I'd sure be open to them."

"Once he gets in a rage, he doesn't really care who gets hurt as long as he feels in control. If he does come, try to make him feel like he's in control. Other than that," Amanda said with a sigh, "there's nothing we can do to make sure we all get out of this alive."

Cam swore and ran his hands through his hair as he stood up. "This isn't right, Jack. Do you really think Trevor will actually care? He'd rather kill us all than listen. We were supposed to wait for Henk." He stepped away from Amanda to confront Jack. "He's the one who's going to be able to persuade Trevor with the politicians. They can make the legislature we need to get this cleared up, and can put pressure on his business to bring things to code. Taking a hostage isn't going to do anything other than piss him off."

"I'm done waiting. Henk can bring in whoever he knows, but I'm not going to just sit around," Jack growled, tightening the rope around Amanda's wrists and then moved to her ankles when he noticed they had loosened during the night.

Cam couldn't watch. Instead, he leaned against the wall and slid down until he was sitting on the ground. His eyes were up on the ceiling. "All I ever wanted to do was scan."

Jack finished with Amanda, and glanced at Cam. "What?"

"I'm a Scanner. I'm not a scientist, or programmer. All I ever wanted was to Scan, and win the CST." He smiled lightly. "I even wanted to marry Maria at one point." He shook his head as he closed his eyes. "I never wanted this. I want people to be safe, and I just want to Scan again."

He eyed his old enemy for a moment before he looked at the gun he kept gripped in his hand. "You wanted to marry her?"

Cam laughed. "Stupid, I know. I could barely be her boyfriend."

"If all you wanted to do was Scan, why did you quit? Why not leave the Underground and just keep going with Revolution? You were good." Jack quirked a smile. "Even *I* have to admit that."

He shrugged. "I couldn't be around her, and then we got the presentation date with Trevor. We actually thought he'd listen to us, but it was just to see who was involved, wasn't it?"

Jack nodded. "That and to see if you actually had something worthwhile. Turns out, you did. That's why he's scrambling. I don't think he even cares that this will make him more money."

He sighed and let his head hit the wall softly. "So, what's the plan? Wait until he gets here, and shove a gun in his face until he agrees with us and go on our merry way? I don't think that's going to work out so well."

"If you think Henk can actually get to the people we need, then it'd be a lot easier to stick a gun in Trevor's face until he agrees before I shoot him."

"I know Henk will pull through. Before I caught my flight, Sandra contacted me. I guess the military is already teaming up with the RCMP after…after Maria didn't show up to speak with the Minister."

Jack smiled and looked back to Amanda. "Looks like we won't have too much longer to wait. I already called Trevor to get him back here."

"What about Cohner?" Amanda asked, her heart sinking as she realized the entire situation. "Are you going to involve him?"

"He'll come. They both will."

It had been two days since Henk had gone to Ottawa. Two days since Jack had taken initiative. Two days since yet another person had to die for, what was seeming to be, a meaningless cause. Jack had gone out only once for food, remaining unnoticed. To everyone's surprise, no one seemed to notice that Amanda was gone. She always worked so closely with Trevor that hardly anyone ever saw her outside her office.

Cam held a water bottle up to Amanda's lips as she drank. Her eyes remained on Jack for the time she was awake. "Why is she even tied up?" he asked over his shoulder to the other man. "She's not going anywhere. She wants what we want, and if Trevor thinks we hurt her he's not going to want to listen to us, or Henk, or any soldiers who come."

"And how do you suppose he'll react if he thinks she did this willingly? Hm? That she willingly went against him, and has secretly been working with his brother to depose him from the board?" Jack eyed Amanda. "Which do you think will be worse?"

A sound at the door caused the three to freeze. Cam looked at Jack, and they exchanged glances.

"I hope to God you know what you're doing," Cam breathed.

Jack cocked the gun. "Me too." He moved towards the door and opened it slowly. He forced his best urgent look as he ushered in Trevor and his brother. "It's about time you got here."

"What is this new development?" Trevor snarled. It was bad enough his brother had decided to come along. He never should have said anything, but he had to tell him what happened in Ottawa. Well, the doctors had to tell him. He paused when he noticed two others in the room, and felt a cold metal barrel press against the side of his head. "Isn't this precious. You've grown balls, Tyson."

Jack moved away towards Cam and Amanda, still pointing the gun at the man. "Here's how this is going to work. You're going to let Henk and his people bring in the new AIM."

"Why would I do that? Do you know what that would do to the company? There was a reason why you were next to kill. You're not able to handle this. You didn't understand."

"I don't think people are supposed to understand 'crazy', *Mr. McCarthy,*" Jack snapped. "I wasn't done. You'll bring in the new AIMs, and you'll step down from the board. And if you were smart, you'd take your own life so I don't have to do it for you."

Trevor grinned as he looked at Cam. "You're not like Jack, are you, Cameron? You don't want to do this. This isn't your style."

Cam clenched his jaw as he stared at the man. He was egging him on, he knew. This man killed Maria. He had to keep that locked away if he was going to get anywhere with the madman. But then he noticed Jack handing him something. After a moment, he took the pistol, checked the safety, and cocked it. "No, I'm not like Jack, Mr McCarthy. I wouldn't have taken your girlfriend, and I wouldn't have brought you out here to talk. I would've gone to your house with an entire army, and I would have thrown the grenade in myself."

"This building is my home, Mr. Tylar. This company is mine. So where's your army?" Trevor mocked with an arrogant smile.

The group jumped nearly in unison as a ringtone echoed in the room. Thankfully, Jack and Cam had been smart enough to not tense too much around the trigger. In the future, Cam would likely think it was unfortunate. They watched as Cohner hesitantly answered his phone.

"Hello?" He listened for a moment before he looked quickly to his brother. "Okay…no…yes, he's here…I will." Cohner ended the call and looked around the room in confusion before looking once again at Trevor. "They're here."

"Who's here?"

He motioned with his head towards the other men. "Their army."

Trevor swore. "What are you talking about? How do they even know about this?"

"I guess you didn't do all of your homework," Cam growled. "Maria wasn't the only connection with the army. So killing her was a waste of time, and a way to severely piss us off." He looked at

Cohner, trying to hide his own confusion. *Why would they call Cohner, and what did he mean by 'army'?* "What did they say?" he asked Cohner.

"Boston PD is outside. They just want to talk and make sure no one's hurt."

"You couldn't tell them that yourself over the phone?" Trevor screamed. "They're going to bring too much media to the building. People will ask questions."

"They've made it look like something is wrong with the next building. A gas leak. They've cleared the area so no one will see," Cohner continued. He kept as calm as possible. Everyone needed to in order for Trevor to do the same. "I think Amanda should leave."

Jack moved over to the woman and pulled her into a standing position. He pressed the gun to her head and his eyes narrowed. "No one is going anywhere. Bring in the police, Trevor. Let's see what he has to say."

"They'll say you're a kidnapper," Cam snapped. "Don't think this will make you look any better. Let's bring in the police, and let Amanda go."

"Have you lost your nerve, Tylar? They killed Maria. They killed Mark. You know how they did that?"

Cam bit his cheek. "I was the one who found his body." He looked at Trevor. "We could have done this quietly. We can still do this quietly. Bring in the new AIMs. Pass them off as an upgrade, and after a few months, tell everyone you'll be de-activating the old ones. Everyone will be required to do it, and you'll double your sales in AIM products. Manufacture a few new AIRC models to be sold with it, and triple your increase. We can ignore the fact you knew AIMs go rogue, so you'd face minimal charges that won't even go to the media if you step down. It's about time you did anyway, so it'll bring more interest into the company. Stocks will fluctuate because they'll be unsure of the new CEO, but they always want to take a risk."

"I will *not* be made to look like a failure!" Trevor screamed, pulling out his own gun.

Cam put up his hands. "It doesn't have to come to that. How do you think it's going to look when the cops have to come in by force? They'll see you've lost control of your company, and yourself."

"He's right, Trevor," Cohner said cautiously. "All you have to do is step down as a formality. You'll still have a vote with everything we do, but we need to move forward."

Trevor looked at his brother, and eyed him. "How long have you been planning this? How long have you been plotting to be a usurper?"

"He's trying to help you, Trev," Amanda spoke up. She cringed when Jack pressed the gun harder against her head. "We all are, with the exception of Jack most likely. None of us wants this to go too far. It's gone far enough already, hasn't it?"

Jack gripped Amanda's arm tighter as he stared at the madman. "Enough of this. Step down, Mr McCarthy, or I kill her."

Trevor laughed. "You haven't killed anyone in years."

"That you know about."

"Do you think you've done anything without me knowing?"

"Did you know I met with Henk and Cam? Did you know I took your mistress here to kill her if you didn't co-operate?" His lips curled into a cruel smile. "You're not in control, Trevor. Might as well make it seem like it was your idea."

Trevor's gun fired, and Cam dove to the ground. Jack returned the fire, forgetting about Amanda for the moment. Before he knew what he was doing, Cam fired twice at Trevor, only narrowly missing him. In the background, Cohner ducked behind a desk, and reached for Amanda, who Jack had pushed to the ground. Jack glanced down at the ground. He ducked a shot from Trevor. His face twisted in anger, hearing the shots through Cam's phone once more, and within a second, he sent a bullet into Amanda's head.

Her body went limp just as Cohner gripped her hand. Trevor's eyes narrowed and pointed his gun at Jack, who mirrored the movement. Cam pushed himself up, and before he could aim, Jack's body jolted as two bullets entered his chest.

Jack froze, staring at Trevor. His chest shuddered as he tried to breathe. The gun fell from his hands and clattered onto the ground. Blood began to soak his shirt. He dropped to his knees as he continued to stare blankly ahead. The corner of his mouth quirked up into a smile before he fell sideways, collapsing onto the cement ground next to his gun. The blood poured slower from his chest as his heart ceased to beat.

After a moment, Cam realized that Trevor was staring at him with a grin. He was the only one left against him in the room. Trevor knew now that Cohner was not strong enough to actually stand up to his brother. He was not a threat. Cam was.

Cam shot three times before Trevor could react, hitting the man in the shoulder. His finger tightened around the trigger as the heavy metal door burst open.

"Boston PD!" A man yelled with the proper authority of a police officer. "Put your weapons down!" He held his gun pointed towards the men in the room and he scanned the area. Two dead.

Cam promptly obeyed, but Trevor spun around and aimed for the officer. "Don't you dare come any closer!" Trevor screamed. His eyes were wide in a craze as though he hadn't noticed he had been shot.

While Trevor was busy with the police officer, Cam noticed a stabbing pain in his side. Looking down, he saw his shirt was stained red. He winced and lifted his shirt slightly. He held back a gasp and allowed himself to lean against the wall, trying to slow his breathing. A fast-racing heart meant faster pumping blood. He would bleed out if he didn't try to calm down. He looked back at the police officer as he stood off with Trevor.

The Boston police officer held a hand up, still using the other hand to point a gun at Trevor. "Mr. McCarthy, we just want to talk." He looked around the large room again and saw Cam leaning against a desk along the far wall. "I'm not going to shoot unless you give me a reason to, okay? So, let's just talk."

"What would I have to talk about to you?" Trevor spat, the hand holding the gun shaking as he held it pointed at the cop.

"How about we talk about what happened here?" he suggested calmly, trying to gain his trust.

"They tried to take away my company!" Trevor screamed.

"Trevor, we're trying to help you," Cohner said, pleading to his brother.

Trevor turned to him angrily, waving the gun at him. "Oh, is that what you call this, this ambush? This is what you call helping me? You killed Amanda!"

"No," Cam shouted. "You killed her. Your paranoia killed her. Your pride killed her. Whether you like it or not, you're responsible for that and you can never take it back." He winced as he attempted to stand upright. He pressed his hand against his side where blood continued to drain from the gunshot wound. "People are dead because you won't admit you have a problem, because you won't trust your own brother to take care of the company. You let AIMs kill people because you couldn't admit you were wrong to exclude Henk from the research team. You let the only person who loves you die because of your pride."

Trevor stared at Cam for a moment, his hand still pointing the gun towards his brother. He turned back to the police officer and held his hands up. "How many are out there?" he asked softly, his voice filled with defeat.

"My partner, two other personnel, and two medics. If you come out with me to talk, they'll have their weapons holstered, but you need to leave your weapon here."

He nodded and slowly placed his gun on the ground. He looked at the bullet-riddled body of Amanda before he put his hands behind his head and walked towards the cop. He stopped. "What are the charges?"

"So far? Third degree murder, and assault with a firearm from the looks of it."

Trevor nodded once again, and he allowed him to place handcuffs around his wrists.

"Sir, are you okay to walk?" he called out to Cam.

"Yeah," Cam groaned, and headed out after the two with Cohner close behind, keeping his distance to be safe, but also forced to walk slowly by the pain. He looked at Jack's body as he walked past, and his chest tightened. It was over. *For what?* Three people he knew were dead now because of one man's pride, and because of the Underground's persistence of bringing the new AIMs into production. *Was it worth it?*

He squinted as the sun hit his eyes, and he was immediately grabbed by a medic, who tended to his wound. He winced as they prodded at him, and looking down, he realized the bullet hadn't actually gone in, but had grazed the muscle which caused the bleeding. The medic began stitching the wound when Cam refused to go to the hospital. He looked around to watch the police officer with Trevor. He pushed the medics away when he saw a man in a red coat. RCMP. He grinned, and restrained a laugh when he saw Henk standing next to the Mountie. He began to walk towards them when his eyes landed on someone just behind the Mountie.

Cam's heart stopped. Her face was hardened. Her hair was pulled back into a military bun. A reddened bandage was on her forehead just below her hairline. She stood at attention as the RCMP officer spoke with Trevor, likely reading his charges. He took a few hesitant steps forward.

"...acts of treason against Canada, and Her Majesty the Queen..." was all Cam heard before he met her eyes.

"Maria..." he said softly, his voice trailing off.

She stepped behind the officer and jogged towards Cam who, once she was close enough, grabbed her and held her close to his body. When she cried out, he held her at arm's length and looked her over. "Not so tight." She smiled when he wrapped his arms around her once more.

"Thank God," Cam whispered in her ear, and did nothing to staunch the tears, ignoring the fact he was bloodying her uniform. After a brief moment, he pulled away and held her face in his hands and simply stared at her. "You were shot...I heard you get shot. You were dead. I thought you were dead."

Maria shook her head, tears now streaming down her face. "Nicholas shot at me, but I got some shots at him too, and Trevor. I mean yeah, I got shot. Got a good one in my side, and a graze on my thigh. He's worse, though. He's visiting my other attacker in the ICU right now. Bruised on the chest, because I thought ahead and wore a Kevlar vest. I don't know why, but I did." She looked down finally and noticed the blood. Her eyes widened and she swore. "Are you okay?"

"It's nothing, just a graze." He looked her over again, and nearly said three words he hadn't said in over a year. Instead, he chose different words. "Are you sure you're okay?"

She smiled and nodded. "Yeah. Just glad this is over."

"What happened, then? You got shot, the line went dead..." His thumb stroked her cheekbone. "I thought you were dead. There was nothing from your AIM, either. Where was it?"

"I had my AIM in its default form. I didn't want to be focused on it during the meeting. I'm having a hard time trusting it recently. It wouldn't have helped, anyway. After the first few shots, Trevor ran away like a coward. The Minister ended up finding me in the hallway. He wasn't even supposed to be there that day. It was a fluke. I gave him my report while I was in the hospital. That's where Henk met up with us." Maria smiled again with a small laugh. "We even got the Prime Minister on board. He sent us down here, where Henk said you guys would be, and now we have charges for Trevor from the American government, and Canadian." She watched as the medics came out from the building, pushing a stretcher with a body wrapped in a black body bag. Her eyes went back to Cam, questioning him silently.

He sighed. "Jack killed Trevor's girlfriend." His hesitation earned him another questioning look. "Jack's dead too."

Maria swore and squeezed her eyes closed. "I told him to get out. I told him."

"When we thought...thought you were dead, he made it his goal to make sure Trevor paid for what he did. He wanted to make sure your mission was completed. He wasn't going to quit."

She nodded and was silent for a moment. Her eyes widened, and she looked up at him. "Did you tell Ryan I was dead?" She breathed a sigh of relief when he shook his head. She looked around. It was surprisingly quiet. There was no media, no crowds of people. Trevor was now in an RCMP vehicle, and Cohner was being questioned. She saw the Mountie wave over to her and she looked back at Cam.

"I'll be escorting Trevor back to Canada. The United States will deal with him later, if they even charge him with anything. With a charge of terrorism, first degree and conspiracy to murder charges don't really seem that big of a deal." She gave him a small smile when she noticed him looking at her intently. "The Minister of Defense wants me go around to different bases with the Military Police to help identify and arrest soldiers who may have been working with Trevor. And with the list Sandra gave us, it's all the evidence they really need. For now, at least. I have to go."

Cam grabbed her before she could move away, and pulled her into another embrace. He was careful to not hold her too tight. "I'm so glad you're alive. Maria, I have-"

She stopped him when she pulled his head down, and leaned her forehead against his. "We're both alive, and that's all that matters." She paused for a brief moment. "We have to go forward from here. You know that, right?"

He nodded, looking down into her eyes. He could not deny that absence did something to the heart, but he and Maria both had to look ahead. She was with Ryan now. They were happy together. That was more than Cam could say about how his relationship had been with her. He said nothing as she pulled away and walked back towards the Mountie, and got into the car. He nearly jumped when he noticed Henk standing next to him.

"I am glad you are okay, L.J.," Henk said softly. "I do not need to tell you how foolish this was, coming here like this. Jack paid for it, and I am glad you did not have to."

"I had no idea what Jack was planning. It at least got Trevor's attention."

"And the law enforcement," Henk added. "Cohner is dealing with that on our behalf. Speaking of Cohner…" his voice trailed off as he turned to the younger man. "We have been asked to make a second presentation of our product."

Cam watched as the military and police vehicles drove away, taking Trevor with them. He turned to Henk, finally giving him his full attention. "What do you mean? We just gave them a presentation."

"This one will be in front of the new board, and the new owner of the company." Henk smiled. "Cohner will be taking over, and he is very interested in taking this product to the public."

Cam could not help but smile. He thought for a moment, looking around him. "Where do we go from here?" he asked.

"Home."

CHAPTER 24

"I am pleased to announce that The McCarthy Company has renewed their vision." Cohner smiled as multitudes of cameras recorded his speech. "We have always been advocates of change, and development. We want to continue with this image, and announce decisions and innovations. The first is the new identity of the company. No, no longer are we a sterile company, but a thriving cluster of scientists, entrepeneurs, and so much more. We have rebranded ourselves as The McCarthy Group. To mark this new, forward-thinking image, we have developed something quite extraordinary." He grinned at the people in front of him, and his excitement was quite obvious.

"We have now developed a new AIM. This new upgrade morphs faster, uses less energy, and the substance lasts noticeably longer. These upgrades come with a brand new AIRC device for everyone. Whether your AIM is kept as a pet, or a Scanning partner, there's a new AIRC for it. They come with new features, and improved scanning times, a larger DNA library, and access to more exotic animals. These new AIRCs can connect only with the new AIMs. For the first thousand North American buyers, we'll be including ten exotic scans which have previously been limited to researchers."

Cohner looked to the side at a triad of men, waiting for approval, and continued. "We'll be taking questions at this time.

Yes?" He responded to a reporter with her hand up. A stupid grin was on her face.

"What can you say in regards to the rumours about the product's origins in the Underground?"

He paused and gathered his thoughts. "Over the years, intensive investigations have been completed on the workings of the so-called 'Underground.' We have found that some of our scientists took the initiative to conduct their own research in order to advance the AIMs. Those thought to be conducting illegal activity were in fact conducting McCarthy research. With the approval of the United States government, and the government of Canada, those who were once considered part of the Underground are McCarthy Group employees. Those who actually conducted illegal activity in order to import animals, and export faulty AIMs will be charged. I want to make it clear that those in the Underground are, and have been employees and contractors."

"And what about Scanners who were in the Underground? Wouldn't that be a conflict of interest?" Still with that stupid smile.

"It was necessary to contract athletes, in order to incorporate them into our research, as they are the roughest on the robots and have very specific requirements for their career. Those who have been black-listed in the past have been pardoned, and welcomed back to the AST and CST."

"How will this affect your current employees?" another reporter piped up, drowning out the female reporter, who still smiled.

"There has been a shift in our employees, we do admit that. With the new change in image, Trevor has agreed to allow me to take the reins of the company while he steps into a less public role. It has always been his desire to work from behind the scenes, and support the board rather than lead it. Within our science department, Dr. Henk Baxter will lead our team as we continue to improve the AIMs and develop new uses for the technology. We are still collaborating with the Tel Aviv University and are making exciting new breakthroughs in medical research. We have put several CST athletes onto a contract to assist with programs and AIM training. These athletes have been extremely beneficial to the production of this new upgrade, and we will continue to work closely with these talented individuals. My hope-"

Cohner's voice was interrupted as the TV was switched off.

Rick raised an eyebrow at Cam. "And who said we were finished watching that?"

Cam shrugged. "It's not that interesting."

"Are you kidding? The McCarthys are changing Scanning, they're bringing out new AIMs and AIRCs. How could you not find that interesting?"

Maria smiled lightly. "You should know Cam better. He only likes listening when it's about him." She glanced at Cam briefly, and noticed his cautious look. "Do you believe him? About the pardon?"

He nodded. "Yeah. He had a meeting with all of us about it."

The members of Revolution turned to Cam and Maria as they sat in Rick's living room. They had all gathered there together to watch the special announcement from the newly rebranded McCarthy Group.

Cam looked at his old team mates with a sigh. "I guess I should just come out and say it."

Suddenly, it was last year again.

Ryan stood up quickly, and pointed a threatening finger at him. "If you leave again, I swear to God-"

"I'm not leaving. I'm not dropping off the radar. Actually, I want to come back." He looked at Owen. "If you'll have me."

Rick looked at his father. "With Eric gone to the Raiders now, we need an extra player."

"You should let Cam finish," Maria added. She gave Cam a reassuring look as Ryan sat back down next to her. The stitches on her forehead were healing, and there was barely any sign of the wound on her arm. She had healed quickly in the past month, but Cam was taking a bit longer. Neither had explained their injuries, and no one asked for one.

"Cam?" Owen said, urging him on.

Cam looked around, his eyes resting on Maria before he looked at the floor. "For the past five years I've been working in the Underground." When everyone remained silent, he stole a hesitant glance at his listeners. With the exception of Maria, they looked at him with wide eyes, dumbfounded. "I wasn't even interested at first, and after a year with you guys, I didn't want to risk it. But they…they had answers for me, about AIMs, and a lot more than I even realized at first. They needed me. We found that out quickly, and after that, there was no way I could quit."

Owen's face flushed red with anger. "You put this team in jeopardy, because they needed you? You risked your stats, your reputation, along with ours? For five years?" He looked at Maria and noticed her lack of surprise. "You knew about this?"

She hesitated before she answered, prompted by a slight nod of Cam's head. "Yes."

"You didn't think to tell us? To report him?"

She looked at Cam with a sigh. "I wanted to. Believe me. All of my rants on TV about the dangers of the Underground, how it destroys people, I believed it all, and meant every word. I hated him being in it, but…" Maria paused. "There are few things that are important to Cam, few things he would risk his life for. I wanted to take this one away from him, but I couldn't. It hurt our relationship; it hurt me, so I left when I couldn't handle it anymore." She kept her eyes away from Ryan, but she could see his face turn to understanding. Everyone had wondered why they fought so much, and one of the first things she had mentioned to Ryan was that her ex wasn't able to stop something that hurt her. Now he knew. They all knew.

Owen waited for a moment, collecting his temper, what was left of it. "What exactly did they need you for, pray tell, that we didn't? That Maria didn't?"

Cam shifted his gaze to Rick and Ryan. "You guys remember what happened at the Toronto challenge last year?"

"Jack's ambush?" Rick asked with a glance to Maria.

"After that."

They were silent for a moment before Ryan looked up. "My AIM. It got disconnected from my AIRC. Later that night, you went back and got it for me."

He nodded. "That was my job. Maria didn't even find out what I did until that night. I reprogrammed and trained AIMs that became disconnected from the AIRCs."

Owen shrugged, not fully understanding. "How did they need you so badly if that was all you were doing?"

"Because no one else can do it." Cam sighed in frustration, and wiped his face to start over. "I've been dealing with AIMs like this since I was a kid, without even knowing it. My dad taught me how to do it, how to look at an AIM's programming, how to look at the substance code, and modify it through the AIRC. He taught no one else how to do it, and I haven't taught anyone else either."

"And how was he the only one to know how to do it? In the whole world of AIMs, no one else figured it out?"

"My dad was one of the scientists who created AIMs."

Another moment of silence.

Ryan watched as Maria put a hand over Cam's, and watched as he returned the gesture. He held back a cough and spoke. "Why didn't you teach anyone else? If that was a way to get out of the Underground, and if you knew Maria didn't want you there, why didn't you train anyone to take over for you?"

"I started to. His name was Mark." Cam smiled lightly. "He wasn't bad, actually. No Cam Tylar, though." His smile vanished. "I found him shot in the head in his home." He heard Rick swear, and he continued. "Before you can give me whatever lecture you have about me choosing something dangerous over the sport, over my relationship with you guys, and Maria, I was trying to stop something much more dangerous. I've heard the lecture already from Maria, and honestly, despite everything, I know I made the right decision." He pointed at the blank TV screen. "That speech? That wouldn't have happened without the work of the Underground, my research. The new *upgrades*? I created their programs. They will never disconnect from the AIRC. They will never hurt another person."

Ryan looked at Maria again, and ignored the hands linked between Cam and Maria. "How do you fit into all of this? I know you guys were working together, at least at some point. Was he as valuable as he claims, or is this just the arrogant Cam we always knew?"

"I saw how dangerous AIMs can be when I was deployed," Maria answered. "I mean, yeah, your AIM scared the crap out of us at the challenge last year, but this...what I saw?" She shook her head. "If Cam was trying to make sure that never happened to anyone, there was no way I could be angry with him. There was no way I couldn't be involved. With AIMs so integral to the military, my part in all of this was to find out what's been going on in the military side of things. It's how we were able to find the people responsible and bring them to justice."

Her eyes glanced toward Cam briefly. "The Underground itself wasn't bad. The research they were doing, what Cam was doing, it is for the greater good. Should he have put our team at risk for our stats? Probably not, but if he was going to screw things up, I'm glad it was for this cause. I've already said my apologies. I should have trusted him to know what he was getting himself into. Even if he wasn't sure how far all of this would go, we still came out on top."

Owen stood and paced around the room. "Cam, I'm sure that whatever you did helped, and I'm sure that the world is better for it, but I don't know if I can risk having you back on this team."

"Cohner McCarthy said those in the Underground are pardoned, that they can be part of the CST," Maria said furiously. "This is his life, Owen."

"He should have thought about that before he put it in danger, put us in danger."

"He did it so we wouldn't be in danger!" she said, standing now as she defended him.

"Maria, stop," Cam said softly, and stood as well. "If Owen's not comfortable having me on this team, then it's his decision. Maybe in time he will, but if he's forced to work with me it's not going to be good for the team. We saw that last season when you and I tried to work together. It fell apart. I want to get back on this team, but I don't want to hurt it any more than I already have."

They watched as he headed to the front door and slipped his shoes back on.

"Cam, wait." She followed him to the door, and turned him, making a bit of privacy for them. "Don't you dare walk out on us again. Not after all of this."

He shot a glance at Ryan, who held his gaze with a rare look of anger. He smiled and looked down at her. "I'm not. I'm giving them a chance to digest all of this. It took you a few weeks to think things through. I wasn't expecting them to be okay with what I've done. I'm not even sure I am. People died, Maria. Mark's gone. Jack's gone, now. I'm still trying to work out everything that happened."

Rick picked up on very little, but heard mention of Jack. And gone. "You guys have seen Jack Tyson?"

Cam shut his eyes briefly before looking at the men over his shoulder. "Yeah. He's dead. He was killed. He was trying to help the Underground, because he realized that what we were doing actually mattered. *Jack* realized that. The guy who sabotaged our challenges, pointed a gun at us last season. I think that should say something. He died for it." He looked at Maria and put a hand on her shoulder. "Mostly for you though." When she nodded, he gave her shoulder a squeeze and left the house.

Maria stayed at the door for a few moments before re-joining Ryan on the couch. She was quiet for a moment, and was not interested in breaking the silence. Not yet, at least. She smiled when Ryan put his arm around her shoulders, and she leaned in towards him, resting there.

"I think we should sign him," Ryan said softly.

"Good thing you're not in charge of it, then," Owen snapped.

"Neither are you. Hear him out, dad." Rick nodded towards Ryan, allowing him to continue.

"This wasn't just about Cam. No, I don't know the guy well, but you do. You know what he's like. You know that his main goal is to get attention from the media, and prove he's the best. He could have been advertising his work in the Underground. He could have been making a big deal about being the only one doing what he did. Cam was careful. He was part of it for five years, four of which he was on this team, and for the entire time no one guessed what he was doing. He cares about this team. That's why he didn't quit before, and why he was so careful. He didn't want anything to happen. My guess is that when he couldn't handle both, when he knew he would put the team at risk, he quit in order to finish his work with them." Ryan spoke slowly before turning to Maria. "Is that right?"

Maria nodded, and Owen sat down once more. "I mean, he quit because his work was coming to a close. The last time the

Underground got close to ending a project, people died. It was hard for him to be around me after Lucy, so that gave him more motivation to stay in the Underground, but he wanted to make sure we stayed safe. He cut us off so people wouldn't come looking to us for answers."

"If I knew that I was creating something that would save lives," Rick started slowly. "If I knew that what I was doing was worth my life, I think I would have done it too. I've always been on the side of Scanning officials. I'm not about to stop believing in the system. If the new head of the McCarthy Company, or Group, finds them innocent, I do too. Ryan's right. Cam was careful. He shared it with the only person he felt needed to know at the time, and even though she knew he kept Maria safe."

Owen sighed and looked at the people in the living room. The team had changed so many times over the eleven years of its existence. Two current members sat before him, and then there was Maria. The daughter he never had, and an ex-team mate. She did everything for a reason. She gave her trust slowly, and it was easily taken away. Seeing the desperation on her face, and looking at the faces of Rick and Ryan, he knew something had to be done. Something told him that none of this was ever going to be simple again.

CHAPTER 25

Ryan watched Maria's face as the TV screen flickered in front of them. The scar on her forehead was fresh, but at least it had healed well. Even after two months, she had not told him all of what had happened. She called it 'classified' but he knew it was something more. It was the same reason she did not tell him what had happened when she had been deployed. But he knew she had told *him*. His warning to Cam had not seemed to have made a difference. Knowing now the reasons behind his absence, Ryan had to admit that he could understand it. At least, partially. What the absence had caused, he wasn't sure he would ever forgive that. The words that Eric had said still rang in his mind, and he continued to look her over. She was different. The lines on her face which appeared when she was concentrating were harsher. Her eyes were duller.

"What's this thing you have to go to tomorrow morning?"

She looked at him after a moment, waiting for a lull in the program they were watching together. "What? Oh, the Prime Minister is doing a broadcast. He's asked for military personnel to be there."

"I didn't think you were ranked high enough to go to things like that."

"Guess I'm special," she said with a grin. But the grin was not the same.

He held her tighter, his arm around her shoulders. "Hey, can we talk about what happened?"

She turned her head back to the TV. "You know I can't."

"Then don't tell me what happened. Tell me what happened to you."

Her eyes stayed on the screen for a moment. "I met up with my dad's old military friend. He tried to kill me."

His heart stopped. "What?"

"That's where this came from." She rubbed the scar just below her hairline. "And a few more shots to the chest, but I wore a vest. Still got a good shot to the side." Maria looked at him quickly. "You know I'm okay."

"Why did he try…why?"

"I knew too much, and he was working with people who had tried to get rid of me back in Kingston."

"Where is he now?"

"He got out of the hospital a few days ago. He's been court martialled and going to trial next week. I'll have to go to that as well, I forgot to tell you. I guess the victim has to go and speak. But not everyone will be able to go. Trev-" Maria cut herself short, and looked at Ryan quickly before turning her attention back to the TV. "The person he was working for is going through for his own charges. I have to go to that trial, too. But that's down in the States, so I'll be away for about a week."

Ryan nodded. He hoped she had not been about to say Trevor. He had heard Rick and Owen mention something about Trevor McCarthy, and the circumstances around his stepping down from the board of his own company. There was always something going on in the world of Scanning, it seemed.

"Do you want me to go with you?"

"You can't." She looked up at him and leaned her head against his chest. "I want you to, though. It'd be nice to have that support."

He paused. "Is *he* going?"

"Who?"

"Cam?"

She sat up once again to look him straight in the face. "Where did that come from?"

"You guys were working together, weren't you? I just assumed you guys would be going together."

"We're not going together, but yes, he will be there for the second trial." She looked him over, looking at his facial expression. "Want to talk to me about what happened to you?"

Ryan raised an eyebrow and laughed. "While you were going through all that stuff? I got the best scores I've ever gotten in challenges. Maybe you should be in danger more often. I think it gives me motivation."

"You're upset I was around Cam."

He shrugged. Now it was his turn to look away. "It was just sudden, that's all. I got used to having you all to myself, and now he's back in the picture being...well, being *Cam Tylar*."

She gave him a small smile, and placed a kiss on his cheek. "And I chose you, remember? When I had the chance to be with him again, I chose you."

"He left. You didn't really have him as an option anymore."

"Ryan, do you really think I'm going back to him?"

The TV program turned to a commercial. He watched it for a moment. Another infomercial about the new AIM upgrades. "You guys have so much history, so much between you guys. A lot can happen, especially when you remember how well you guys worked together."

"We have history for a reason. It's in the past, Ryan. We worked well together, but we were destructive as a couple. We're destructive even as partners, we found out." She swung her legs across his lap and scooted closer towards him. "Look at me, would you?" Maria leaned forward dramatically, her face close to his. "You're who I want. At the end of every single crazy day, I want to come back to you. No matter what I go through at work, or if I ever get deployed again, and no matter who I'm going through it with, I want to come back to your sanity. Not Cam's."

Ryan looked down at her, into her pleading eyes. There it was again, that light he thought had died in her. "I don't know, though. I'd like some crazy things to happen between us. Can't just be all sanity."

She grinned. "Well, I'll see what I can do."

He hugged her for a moment before remembering something. "Am I at least able to come to the press thing tomorrow, or is it closed to the media?"

Her mouth twisted to the side. "Um…I think it's okay for you to come. You probably won't be able to sit, but it's a public announcement so I can't see it being a problem. Cam…he'll be there too. But that wasn't my decision. Where did all of this stuff about Cam come from? I know you've been dealing with it the past year, and that's fine, but this is new. Tell me the truth. Who was talking to you?"

"Who said anyone was talking to me about you guys?"

"You've already dealt with this, so someone had to bring it up again for you to start questioning."

He shrugged. "I was talking to Eric about you, and he was just asking questions."

"What kind of questions?"

"Your history with Cam, and what you do now."

Maria swore, and moved away from him. "I told you not to talk to anyone about me."

"He's my team mate. I didn't think that would be a big deal."

"He was your team mate. Do you know why he left the team for the Raiders?"

He shook his head. "Better pay? More exposure?"

"Over Revolution? Are you crazy? He left the team because he was working with people trying to kill me and Cam, and when that went down the drain, he had to make distance between himself and the team. He was trying to figure out my next move by asking you questions, and to put doubt in your mind about our relationship."

"Wait, if he was working with them why hasn't he been arrested?"

"There wasn't any evidence. He never even really came out and said it to me, but he didn't need to." She sat properly on the couch again before she stood. "I can't believe you talked to him about me."

"I didn't think it was a big deal. I thought you meant if any officials or whatever ask questions," Ryan replied in an attempt to defend himself.

"But it was a big deal, Ryan." Maria slipped her coat on and grabbed her purse.

"Don't leave. I'm sorry. Maria," he said, and took her arm gently.

"Ryan, with the job I have, there are always going to be people out to get me. I'm a soldier. I have a unique job, and there are few people to take the fall if someone isn't happy with AIMOTs. When I ask you to do something, it will always be a big deal. When someone asks about me, even if you know them, don't tell them anything. If they ask 'hey, what's Maria doing this week?' you can't tell them." She sighed and looked up at him. "I know I'm asking a lot of you, and I know that it's not fair. I hated it when Cam made me do it, and I swore I'd never do it to anyone else." Maria closed her eyes for a moment before she opened them. Her face was stoic, prepared. "If you don't think you can handle this, or if this is too much for you, I will understand. I don't want to make you do anything you're uncomfortable with, and I don't want you to be unhappy."

He thought for a moment. It was going to be hard, she was right. It was going to be much harder than he had thought. She would never be able to tell him about her day at work aside from basic details, and she would never be able to bring him into her life. *Can I handle that? Is this how I really want my life to play out?* After another brief moment, he leaned down and kissed her. When he pulled away, he smiled. "I think I can handle it. You'll have to be patient with me, because I'm not going to know what I can and cannot say. I'll try to play it safe and not say anything at all, but you'll still have to be patient with me. If you can do that, be patient, I'll stick around and put up with you."

"You have to be absolutely sure."

He took her arm again and slid the sleeve up. "I was there for you during this part of your life. I want to be there for the other parts."

Cam looked around the crowded room. For the first time in a year, he was comfortable around a plethora of reporters and cameras. Moderately. He kept looking around cautiously. There were some things that he would never get over. Even if Trevor was now contained, or his anger was at least contained, there was never any assurance that people would be safe. Until the people working for Trevor were either found and dealt with, or realized that Trevor was insane and not worth following, no one would be safe. At least Trevor had been mostly smart about it. He had never done anything in public. But with this kind of gathering, Cam had no idea what kind of people he was mixing with.

He watched as the Minister of National Defense took the stage in his ceremonial uniform. He looked around, and could not find Maria, but assumed he would be able to see her at some point in that uniform rather than her fatigues.

"Mesdames et messieurs, ladies and gentlemen. Thank you for coming. It is my honour and privilege to introduce to you today the Right Honourable Prime Minister of Canada." He stepped away from the microphone as the crowd erupted into polite applause. He smiled and shook the hand of the man who approached him. He wore a distinguished suit, but even that paled in comparison to the decoration of the military attire.

He waved a hand with a grin, and waited for the claps to die down. "Thank you, Minister, and thank you, Kathryn, for arranging this announcement today." He straightened himself, and Cam thought, for a brief moment, that this man looked the part of a man who could lead this country. For a moment. "Mesdames et messieurs, ladies and gentlemen, thank you for your welcome. Twenty years ago, Artificial Intelligence Morphers became a part of our culture. They have been welcomed into our homes. We have utilized them in law enforcement, and in our military. Recently, a shift has been made. Recently, our military has made extreme advances in the usage of AIMs in combat. This will affect National Security, and I am honoured to say that our great nation continues to be guarded by courageous men and women, working in partnership with their AIMs. There was a threat of terrorism on our country, which was quickly interrupted by a member of our Canadian Forces, and we can continue to live securely." He paused for the applause of the media, and other dignitaries present.

Maria looked out into the crowd as the Prime Minister spoke. She stood to the side of the stage, in between the Minister of National Defense and the newly appointed General. After Szyzeck had been found out as an employee of Trevor McCarthy, he was quickly detained and another soldier had been promoted to take his place. When Maria had arrived to the building, she was surprised to learn that she was the only junior officer. It worried her at first, and now she was anxious.

Standing there in front of a room of strangers should not have been such a big deal for her. She was used to it after being in the CST, and giving interviews and signings, but this was different. Her dress uniform was pristine, as it should be, and she nearly smiled at the thought of how she looked in it. This was probably her favourite part about growing up around the military, seeing her father dress up for ceremonies.

"This is something that is normally done in private, but in light of recent events, I feel this deserves special circumstances. I would like to introduce, and call to the stage, Lieutenant Maria Kier, AIM Operations Technician."

She continued to stand as she was, until his words registered in her mind. Her eyes widened, and she finally found Cam in the crowd. His head was motioning for her to move, and she finally felt her legs move. Maria turned and walked up the steps as a small applause came once more from the audience. She stood at attention, giving the Prime Minister a proper salute until he dismissed it.

The Prime Minister turned to the General who had followed her onto the stage, and took something from a small box presented to him. "Lieutenant Kier, it is my honour to present to you the medal for Meritorious Service, for your work defending this country on foreign, and domestic soil."

As he pinned the decoration to her uniform, her heart was pounding. When he moved away, she gave him another salute, but none of it felt real. A decoration. She had been in the Canadian Forces for less than a year. This did not happen. Then again, rogue AIMs were not supposed to happen.

"Thank you, Sir." She began to turn to the audience for their photo opportunity, but turned back to the Prime Minister. "May I ask for something, Sir?"

He gave her a questioning look before he agreed.

"This...incident...it was quelled not only by me, but also a very talented programmer I trust with my life. I don't feel right accepting this on my own. He's a civilian, but has done as much for this country as any soldier. He has sacrificed his life as many times as I have. Maybe more. I just want to make sure he gets the recognition he deserves, whether it's in public or private."

He nodded after a moment. "That can be arranged."

She saluted once more before she was escorted from the stage. Arriving back to her original position beside the platform, she finally eyed Ryan and the rest of her team. She was surprised they had all been allowed entrance to the room, but then again, if they had planned on giving her this decoration, they would be more open to having people there to support her. Dr. Baxter and Sandra were both there, as well, she noticed. That was no surprise.

As the Prime Minister continued his eloquent speech about the near-threat, and the advances in National Security, Maria forced herself not to look down at the decoration now pinned to her chest. It usually took years to earn any medal, decoration, or honour. There was nothing usual about this situation, she noted. Rogue AIMs, and an unintentional terrorist threat. At least, she hoped it was unintentional. If Trevor was as insane as he seemed, then it was likely not his plan to commit an act of terrorism, not that it mattered in a criminal court.

"As our first action against the growing global threat, we will be phasing out the now outdated AIMs, and we have signed a contract with the McCarthy Group to purchase two upgraded AIMs for every unit we have now. We have high expectations for these new models, and are looking forward to using them to further protect this country. Thank you, and I wish you all a good evening."

Maria and the other military members saluted as the Prime Minister passed them on his way off the stage. The Minister of Defense turned to her with a smile.

"Congratulations, Lieutenant."

She returned his smile. "Thank you, Sir."

"How many bases have you visited so far?"

"Three, Sir. Many people who were working with Trevor have gone into hiding, but all of their locations so far have been uncovered using the new AIMs." She had needed to act quickly after Trevor was arrested. Maria had been happy to see that very few were members of the military, although they were all troubled when she discovered a surprising amount of politicians on it.

"Good." He nodded happily, as much as a soldier could, of course. "Are you in need of anything, now that you've begun and have experienced particular requirements?"

Maria thought for a moment. "Nothing as of yet, and I don't think I will need anything material. I will ask for one thing, however. I'll ask for your permission to bring in a civilian to assist me in interrogations if I ever find the need."

He raised an eyebrow with consideration. "Would this be the person you feel deserves the same decoration you received?"

"It is, yes."

The Minister nodded and handed her a thin, square box. "Do what you need to do, Lieutenant. It's needless to express how much the Prime Minister trusts your judgement, so I have no qualms with any of it either."

"Thank you." She turned as she noticed her old team mates approach, minus Cam. "For everything." She greeted the other men with a smile as the Minister left her. "I'm glad you guys were able to come."

"I thought I saw Cam earlier," Ryan said, wrapping an arm around her waist as he stood next to her. "But he left already."

"I wonder why," Maria muttered. "You guys aren't exactly welcoming. What you guys are doing, shutting him out, it's not fair and I think it's wrong that you guys are even doing it. He put his life on the line for this team, and because he did some things which could have ended up badly, but didn't, you're ostracizing him," she said emphatically.

"I was afraid of seeing you guys again because I had a miscarriage, something out of my control. Now, Cam comes to you, the only family he has, admits his transgressions, and gets kicked to the street. I should be the one most hurt by what he did and none of you seem to get that what he did was right." Maria shook her head, keeping her composure as well as she could. "And if you think you guys can keep going without Cam on the team, you're idiots." She caught her breath when she realized Rick and Owen were smiling. "What?"

"We've agreed with the board that we want him back on the team," Owen announced. "You were right. You both were. No, he should not have put this team at risk. When he first joined the Underground, he did it with selfish motivations. He continued with them because he knew it would help people, and that's what we should focus on. No one counts the men a soldier kills, but the number of lives she saves."

Maria nodded and felt herself shaking free tears from her eyelashes. Ryan pulled her against his chest and she grinned into his shirt. "Can I tell him?" Her question was muffled by the fabric.

"We assumed you would."

Rick nudged his father. "Well, tell her."

Maria looked out at her old captain with a questioning look. "Tell me what?"

"In the next few years, I'll be looking to retire. It's time, and we all knew it would be coming," Owen started. "When I do, depending where you are in the military, we, and the board of course, want to re-sign you as well. Before you say anything now, wait until the time comes to make a decision. This is just something for you to keep in the back of your mind. Ryan mentioned your service will be up in four years, so wait until then to decide if you stay with the military or come back to us."

She looked down at herself and back at Owen. "I don't know what to say. I mean, this uniform looks so much nicer than our team outfits." She grinned when the others laughed. "But thank you. Let's not tell Cam, though."

"Exactly what we were thinking."

"You should not have left so early," Cam's AIM spoke through the AIRC. "Were you not comfortable in the room?"

Cam shrugged. He was glad he went to the public address. They had all been surprised to see Maria awarded a medal, but he knew better than his teammates that she deserved it. A small part of him was hurt, as usual. He knew his work had been important too. He made sacrifices, and risked everything, but because of his association with the Underground no one could ever know. Sure,

Cohner had mentioned a particular person who helped create the AIMs, and knew it was him, but it still was not the same. He tried to tell himself that he did not need recognition, but an acknowledgement would be nice. He had felt this way the entire time he was in the Underground. *What do I have to show for five years of work? Four walls, and a desk.* At least maybe now he had the knowledge that an AIM he programmed and trained was in production. Not that he would actually buy or own one. He was fine with his.

"They have not spoken to you since you approached them?"

"Nope," Cam said with a sigh as he fell onto his couch. He looked around his apartment at the boxes he had begun to fill. "Maybe it's better, though. I can finally move on, and away from all of this. I can clear my head, and maybe start coaching. Might as well do that as soon as possible, or people will forget who I am again."

The AIM hopped onto the couch next to Cam, and laid the golden retriever head across his lap. "Will you be able to handle living in your old home?"

He thought for a moment. His mother had moved them away from the farmhouse after his father had left because of the memories. It had been too hard to look in every room, and expect to see him there. Now that he was older, and now that he knew what had happened to his father, the ghosts did not seem to be so scary, and the anger was slowly being replaced by happy memories.

"I think it'll be good. Everything comes around full circle. The house is pretty run down now, so that will give me something to work on. Maybe I'll even rope Rick..." his voice trailed off. No. Rick would not help. He would barely speak with him. "Okay, well, maybe Ryan could help, and probably only because of Maria."

"Oh, yes, that would be wonderful to have a man help you who is sleeping with the woman you once slept with."

Cam shot a glance down at the robot. "It's fine." He paused. "They may not even be sleeping together."

"If that thought makes you feel better, I agree."

He grumbled under his breath as there was a knock at the door. "Always have to ruin things, don't you?"

"Let us face it, Cameron. Your slippers had it coming."

He rolled his eyes as he opened the door. He stepped back when he saw Maria standing there and he looked past her down the hallway. “Hey. I thought you’d be busy for the rest of the night.”

“I am.” She looked into the apartment behind him. “Can I come in?” She entered when Cam stepped out of the way, and she smiled when Cam's AIM trotted over to her. She knelt down and patted it on its head. “It's nice, thinking of you as an animal rather than a robot.”

“Would you mind sharing that with Cameron? He still seems to treat me as a servant.”

“I'll try. No promises,” she said with a smile.

“Is everything okay?” Cam asked in an attempt to bring her attention back to him.

She stood once again and nodded. “Yeah. I'm a bit surprised, but it's been a pretty good day.”

“Then you must not have listened to the same guy,” he joked. Their Prime Minister was not known for being a wonderful orator, by any means.

“I have something for you,” she said finally. She pulled out a box from her satchel and handed it gently to him. “It's not really from me.”

“Do I have a secret admirer?” Cam grinned as he opened it. Inside, was a duplicate of the decoration on Maria's chest. He looked at her quickly. “What the hell is this?”

“It's a medal of Meritorious Service. I'm presenting this to you on behalf of our Monarch, the Right Honourable Prime Minister, the Minister of National Defense, and the Chief Defense of Staff in recognition of your work in the Underground as a contribution to our nation.”

He simply stared at her for a minute before he looked back down at the box. He took a step back and leaned against the wall in his front entryway. “Is this for real? How did they know?”

“I didn't use your name, but I couldn't accept this on my own.” Maria stepped towards him and put her hands on his arms. “Lucas, you've done amazing work, and you risked so much over the last five years. You deserve this, and even if you can't have public recognition, you at least have something to show for what you've done.”

Four walls and a desk. "I bet four years ago, you never thought you'd admit that," he whispered.

"I thought a lot of things four years ago." They shared a glance before she looked away. A guitar case sat down the hall, propped up against the wall. She motioned towards it with her head. "When did you start playing?"

"What?" He followed her gaze before he smiled. "Oh. I haven't." He retrieved it and opened it up, showing a Martin guitar. "It's for you."

She reached out and took it gently, looking it over. She shook her head before placing it back in its case. "Cam-"

"To replace the other one. You better treat this one like it deserves. Don't go hitting people with this one." Cam grinned. "It's a *Martin* after all. Ryan should be happy."

"Thank you," Maria said gently. She paused before looking at him again. "There's something else."

"They want me to be Prime Minister? I'm flattered, but I don't think Canada's ready for me."

Maria laughed. "No, although I don't think most of Canada would notice. I talked to Rick and Owen." She paused when Cam looked at her, sobering quickly. "The board made a decision about your proposal. It looks like you're in a bit of a situation. You're going to need to rehire your agent if you want as many interviews as you got before."

"They're taking me back?"

"I told them they'd be idiots if they didn't."

He let out a short cheer before he grabbed Maria, hugging her. He held onto her, and smiled into her neck as she returned the embrace. "How much influence did you actually have?" he asked quietly, not wanting to scream into her ear.

"Oh you know, they do whatever I ask of them. They're pretty much bound to my will."

"Which means they decided to let me back on the team before you yelled at them with a lecture."

"Naturally."

Cam backed away and looked down at her with a thoughtful look. "I should be happier about this, but I'm going to have to work some things out. I was planning on fixing up a house."

She raised an eyebrow. "A house? How much are you being paid to do manual labour?"

He laughed and led her into his living room. He watched as she looked around at the boxes. "I bought a house."

She was sure her jaw hit the floor. When she felt nothing below her chin, she shook her head and looked around the room once more. "You bought a house?"

"It was my house growing up."

Maria thought for a moment. "You lived on a farm as a kid. You bought a farmhouse?"

"We never really did anything with the property." He pulled a photo album from one of the open boxes and flipped through the pages. He stopped and showed Maria a page of pictures. "We kept it as a forest, and when I went to see it last month, the owners hadn't re-designated it as crop use, so it's still there. The house needs a lot of work though, so that's how I was going to spend my time."

"Oh, well in that case, I'll just tell the others you'd rather work on your house." She ran her hand over the photographs and smiled when she saw the image of a man who looked like a slightly older version of Cam. "I think we'd all want to help you, unless it's something you need to do on your own."

He looked down at her with a smile. "I'd love for you guys to help. I'm done hiding my past, and what's going on with me. It never really worked out well for anyone." He sighed and ignored his AIM, pawing at his leg. It would hate what he was going to say next. "I shouldn't have let you break up with me. I didn't fight for you, and I should have. I mean, it worked out for the best, but I didn't do enough. I didn't share enough. I'm sorry."

Maria put a hand over his. She reached up and placed a kiss on his cheek. "Who are you, and what have you done with Cam?"

"His name's Lucas."

She smiled and leaned against the stack of boxes gently. "Yes it is." She looked down at the picture once more. "Are you going to continue your research? On your AIM?"

"I do not give consent to experiments, Lucas."

Cam rolled his eyes while Maria grinned. "Eventually. But for now, I think I'm good with how things are. For once."

"Do you think all of this is over? Rogues? The Underground?"

Cam shrugged and knelt down as his AIM happily wagged its tail. "I don't know. It'll take years to clean up Trevor's mess. I handed Henk all of my research, and soon all the old AIMs will be deactivated. I'm not sure how I feel about this, but I think my part in it, it's done."

Maria glanced briefly at the decoration on her chest and wondered if it really was, if it ever really would be over.

ACKNOWLEDGMENTS

Above all, I thank God for the strength and motivation to continue to use the gifts and talents He gave me. To Him be the glory.

To my friends and family, thank you for all of your support. 'Revealing the Revolution' would not have been as successful without you or your extra copies laying around when guests come over for them to buy. It helped convince me that this second novel needed to be finished, and finished fast. Thank you for believing in me.

I want to give a special thank you to the members of Authonomy.com who read 'Chasing the Underground' in its very early stages. Your comments and suggestions are invaluable.

Thank you to my beta-readers for your time and comments.

A big thank you to my readers. That means you! It brings me joy to know that I've created something other people can enjoy. Thank you for sticking with me, and following the lives of these crazy characters.

And of course to Ben, my partner and best friend. You've given me this world to write about, and for that I'm so grateful. Thank you for your support, your dialogue about this concept, and of course for your unwavering love.

ABOUT THE AUTHOR

Nichole Sotzek has a B.A Honours in Near Eastern Archaeology and Medieval Studies. Her husband developed the idea for the novel as a child, and in 2010 the two began collaborating on 'Revealing the Revolution' until he gave her full control of the novel and concept a few months later. Nichole is currently working on the third book of the series and is busy reviewing books written by other indie authors. When she's not writing or reading, she spends most of her time outside with her husband, scanning.

'Chasing the Underground' is her second novel.

If you enjoyed reading 'Chasing the Underground' why not let people know? Leave a review on Goodreads and Amazon. Authors always love to hear what their readers think.

56048317R00158

Made in the USA
Charleston, SC
13 May 2016